T0304865

The American No

The American No

RUPERT EVERETT

abacus
books

ABACUS

First published in Great Britain in 2024 by Abacus

1 3 5 7 9 10 8 6 4 2

A CIP catalogue record for this book
is available from the British Library.

Hardback ISBN 978-1-4087-1419-5
Trade Paperback ISBN 978-1-4087-1418-8

Typeset in Caslon by M Rules
Printed and bound in Great Britain by
Clays Ltd, Elcograf S.p.A.

Papers used by Abacus are from well-managed forests
and other responsible sources.

MIX
Paper | Supporting
responsible forestry
FSC
www.fsc.org
FSC® C104740

Abacus
An imprint of
Little, Brown Book Group
Carmelite House
50 Victoria Embankment
London EC4Y 0DZ

An Hachette UK Company
www.hachette.co.uk

www.littlebrown.co.uk

For Henrique

Contents

THE AMERICAN NO.

A phrase originally coined by a producer friend with a gallows sensibility. In showbusiness, particularly in the world of 'pitching', here's what happens. We achieve a meeting – no mean feat in itself – then, if we're an actor, we 'appear' in a room of executives to pitch our story. If we're surfing in on the wave made by a successful movie, we can behave any way we like, possibly even passing out during the pitch. It will be written off as a part of our star quality – our raw talent finding its way. However, if we aren't riding in on a hit – my lot, except for once – don't be late. Have fun. But not too much. Be thankful. But don't go down on all fours. Make it vivid. Be prepared for questions and qualms. Normally the meetings go well, but don't be fooled by everyone's casual manners or dazzling smiles. Particularly in America. There are codes of behaviour in Hollywood more complex and nuanced than attempting to do business as a geisha.

'Let's do this. I'm psyched. We love you here at Bottomy Bay Productions,' they say, walking you out, arms slung casually over your shoulder. You leave the meeting walking on air. It's in the bag. Then you never hear another word.

It's called the American no.

HARE HARE

I was sitting outside Bar Italia on Frith Street one afternoon last November. That ship of fools has been my home from home from home since I first moved to Soho in 1988. Sitting there, drifting, wrapped up against the drizzle like a pot in a tea cosy, was a singular experience verging on bliss. Surveying the street from this old bird's eye view, the straight Georgian lines of its brick flanks merging on Soho Square, was like looking at a negative, or a double exposure because the black faces of ghosts seemed to stare through the walls, memories hidden in doorways lit suddenly by the long-forgotten flare of a match. With a wink of the mind's eye, the focus was pulled to the distant past while the present moment bent and blurred in the patter of rain.

In the old days I had breakfast every day at Bar Italia, lunched next door at Little Italy, conducted my business meetings, my promotional endeavours and my love affairs on the strip of pavement between the two establishments. Most of my friends lived within walking distance – Alan, Julia, Baillie and John. Occasionally I acted in a play and tottered back and forth to the theatre. I rarely left Soho, perhaps to meet the old Chelsea crowd from before the war, but I always ran back as soon as I could. Once you had lived in that strange corner, nothing else would ever do.

On an ordinary evening I would leave my room at the hotel, ring the bell of Alan's flat, collect him, pass by Princess Julia's and then go on to Baillie and John's on Charing Cross Road. This was all thirty years ago now. All gone, like tears in the rain. Alan killed himself. Julia moved east. John lives in Italy. Only Baillie remains. Apart from him, Soho is another country.

Briefly we queens achieved supremacy, but we were moved on with the hookers and the homeless at around about the time of Paul Raymond's death. I too had some kind of ascendancy. Traffic stopped when I crossed Old Compton Street. Well not exactly, but you know what I mean. Today I am just another old oddity with scowling lips, haunting the streets, walked through, another ghost, as I cross the road at Cambridge Circus. Occasionally some medium from the old days sees one and screams. Sometimes, greetings are exchanged. Sometimes not. Often things are better left behind.

The only group to survive, rain or shine, it seems are the Hare Krishnas and here they come now in the headlights and the spitting rain, turning the corner out of Soho Square, quite a big group today, clashing their cymbals and singing their songs, transcendental Morris dancers weaving around to the beat of their little drum, fully made up, pink and apricot, saris and dhotis, sandals and trainers. Some had backpacks crammed with their day drag. I used to find them annoying but today, looming through the gathering dusk, they were enchanting, strange, a caravan of wonderful freaks crossing the asphalt desert. They arrived from a fairy kingdom with their cymbals, their drums. Someone had a portable sound system and his voice rang out, amplified and bounced across the street, urging the others on. 'Hare, hare,' they sang back. Unlike myself, they still stopped the traffic. People still looked out of windows or stood and gaped.

In the old days there were always a few familiar faces in that conga line to nirvana. Club world crashes often found their way to the Krishna headquarters on the north side of Soho Square, where you could at least get a good meal if and when you reached rock bottom. They gave you a new focus and an opportunity to swap methamphetamine for cucumber raita. Today I didn't recognise anyone until, at the end of the line, swathed in beads and shells, weaved a well-known producer I had last seen a few years ago at the London offices of a Hollywood studio.

'Rupert!' he shouted as he danced past. 'Hare, hare, hare!'

'Hare to you. My goodness. When did all this happen?'

He broke off from the group and stood before me panting, tambourine in hand.

'Didn't you know? Steerforth left to go to work at Wildcat and didn't take me with him. So I got fired. Dumped actually, from a great height.'

'Didn't you want to go somewhere else?'

'Nobody wanted me. I was dead meat. Too old. Not enough flair. Not gay. Or black. Or a lesbian. Just a big old white straight blob on the verge of a nervous breakdown.'

'I know how you feel.'

'But I don't. I don't feel anything. It was all a storm in a teacup. Just because some group says you're worthless doesn't mean you are. Right?'

'I suppose so. Although I seem to have been sent to the knacker's yard with the old white straights. I keep screaming "I'm gay" but no one listens.'

'Well, keep going,' said the producer. Alistair was his name and he looked anxiously towards his disappearing band of brothers. (Not many girls in the Krishnas, by the way. Just saying.) 'You definitely have something. I don't know what, but it *is* something. Never forget it. That story you pitched us last year. It was brilliant. Original. Funny too.'

'But you didn't buy it.'

'I know. Sorry. I really tried. Steerforth thought it was too gay. Ha!'

Someone shouted to him from the group, something like, 'Come on, Shashi Pur.'

'Coming,' he trilled back. He looked at me. I'd never noticed what lovely eyes he had before. Filled with affection. His lashes had raindrops on them. 'Hare Krishna, Rupert. All the very best. Call me. I still have a phone.' And off he ran, backpack bouncing, tiny ankles in large trainers galumphing along the street under the fluttering skirts and the winter sky. He merged with the group and soon they were just an orange swaying smudge as they crossed Shaftesbury Avenue and disappeared into Chinatown.

I sat there for a long time, wondering. Perhaps I too should retire to a monastery. Certainly, if the reception engendered by my latest script was anything to go by, I was spent. Hardly anyone had bothered to read it and those who had were not biting. Showbusiness is not for those who bleed easily. Kean said that. Up and down. In and out. One moment they are hanging on your every word. The next, they're looking right through you.

The project Alistair was talking about was the latest in a long line of ideas that I had pitched over the last twenty years. A couple of these ideas had been commissioned. Only one made it to the first night. The rest are nothing more than jugs of dust in the underground vault in which my meagre talent will – at this rate – remain forever buried.

And that's when I had a rare brainwave. I would write up these ideas into a book of short stories.

The rain began to pour down. People scattered. High heels clicked and cantered down the street. Georgian London – what remained of it – shone majestically in the dusk, dripping brick pediments, shining windowpanes, doors, bricks, all those harsh unbreakable facts, blurred by the rain, converging on the black and white beamed hunting lodge, that wicked witch's cottage in the middle of Soho Square. Underneath it all, buried somewhere in the bricks and mortar, were the echoes of a lifetime in the West End, the scattered applause of a midweek matinee, the standing ovation of a first night under the heavens spangled with a billion forgotten ideas.

THE WRONG BOX

John Schlesinger opened his script. It was bound in leather and embossed with his initials. The names of the dead – his films, more hits than misses – were carved down the spine in tiny gold letters and it looked like one of those Bibles you find in hotel bedrooms, care of the Jehovah's Witnesses or the Mormons. He opened it religiously with chubby pink fingers at a certain page that seemed to offend. His face momentarily clouded.

'Ah yes. The bloody funeral scene. Well. I love what we've got.'

He looked sheepishly over his reading glasses at me and Mel on the other side of the table. It was a sore point.

'But John,' wailed Mel, 'it's just dull. Nothing happens.' Mel was my writing partner. She called herself my pet scribe, but she was hardly a pet. To start with there was nothing domesticated about Mel. She was wonderful and feral and looked a bit like the movie star Frances Farmer. (After the car crash but before the electric shock treatment.)

Mel had hooded blue eyes and now they stared at John beseechingly.

'It tells the story,' reasoned our director.

'But nothing remarkable happens.' It was my turn.

'Yes, dear. In your Tennessee Williams world it probably is nothing. But we're dealing with Middle America here. Not to mention that cunt Sherry Lansing over at Paramount.' He covered his face with his hands.

Yesterday we'd had a bit of a set-to. It had started off as a bit

of fun. I suggested that John play a leather queen in the funeral
scene.

'You could wheel a gigantic wreath up the hill to the cemetery.' John was quite small, and I imagined the wreath and him
being the same size. 'It could give the funeral a new dimension,
a comedy element.' The funeral – incidentally – was for a man
in the story who had died from AIDS just before the movie
starts in the summer of 1986. In the scene, we are all standing
round the grave. Me. Madonna. The friends and relations of the
deceased (including Gavin Lambert as a bridge-playing fairy).
And suddenly John arrives, in a biker's cap and aviator shades,
a kind of leather Grumpy, pushing the huge wreath sent from
all the boys at the Tom of Finland Foundation. Had our dear
friend been a secret leather queen? This would be the question
crossing the mourners' minds. It might have given the scene
an impish spark to neutralise the dreary emotional candy floss
conjured up by the writers of the original material.

'Too late, dear,' was John's only response. 'My last acting job
was in 1952. What we need is a surprise. You and Madonna could
arrive late.'

'Fascinating,' snipped Mel.

'Wait a minute.' I suddenly remembered: 'I have rather a good
story about being late for a funeral.'

'Well? What is it?' sighed John. 'Bearing in mind we have a
lot to get through this morning.'

At that moment I think I'm living the American dream. John,
me and Mel free-associating in a pagoda at a rented house in
the Hollywood Hills during the spring of '99, about *my* film for
Paramount. John seemed to me to be the last tenuous link to
the Movieland of my dreams, the place I could have belonged,
where the scent of orange blossom wafting up from the Valley
was so strong in spring that people in the hills would pack up
and move down to Hollywood because they couldn't sleep at

night. Now those orange groves were buried in asphalt and the Garden of Allah was a parking lot but there was still something holding on.

John. He didn't wear breeches and riding boots, but he still moved like a great director, dressed for safari, pristine and pint-sized, his snow-white beard as manicured as a putting green, his foreign-ness as clearly marked against the casual blur of modern California as those extraordinary exiles from Germany must have been among the cowboys and Mexicans between the wars. He held all that history in his every gesture, in his working manner, in his behaviour at dinner, in the recollections of his love life. 'There are some things that went on in a certain hotel room during *Cowboy*,' he sang, 'that I still haven't got to the bottom of.' I was in heaven.

On the subject of poppers, both of our favourite drug, he was very clear. 'Oh yes, dear. That stuff in the bottle was nothing. The vials were the thing. There was a chemist on 34th Street back in the day. He'd see me walk in and he would shout "Have you come for your heart medicine, Mr Schlesinger?" Those were the days. Now, come on, dear. We digress.'

The Valley and the San Bernadino Mountains winked in the background. They'd heard the story before. The Santa Ana wind rustled through the eucalyptus trees by the pool. The low burp of an earth tremor shook the pagoda with a little jangle. Faraway phones. Hoovering inside the house. The hum of distant traffic, like a hive of bees, each one in production of something. Charades really. A play, a film, a TV, a script.

The story. Cue accordion and subtitle over establishing shots – Paris 1986.

There was a strange queen on the scene that summer, who always made us laugh. Me and Lychee and her band of gypsies, tramps and thieves. Every Sunday morning, he danced alone at the Kit Kat Club, spinning like a whirling dervish in slow motion, his head lolled back, eyes closed, large lips poised in a frozen kiss beneath a Hitler moustache. Round and round he went until there was no one left on the dance floor – just him – bathed in shards of light from the glitterball. The rest of us watched, stacked up against each other in the fever of the seventh ecstasy – that new (ish) drug on the scene. Occasionally the door upstairs to the street would open and a bright summer day would be revealed like a parallel universe and the real world beckoned. It was time to choose your chill-out partners and adjourn to someone's apartment, close the shutters and wind down until night fell at least, maybe longer. In those days the party could go on for days. Slumped around some flat, the doorbell ringing, the dealer arriving, more guests, but never him.

Until one Sunday we went to a Brazilian restaurant called Chez Guy in the Latin quarter. Down some narrow stairs into a cellar off the Boulevard Saint-Germain.

Inside, an ageless sea goddess named Clea sang sambas with a band, while the clientele, jammed into tables under thick stone arches, drank caipirinhas and ate feijoada. And smoked.

Everyone smoked in those days. Clea rode through the haze like the figurehead of a galleon, with long black hair, a flower tucked behind one ear, her voluptuous body thrusting against the waves. She sang with tremendous feeling and was artfully accompanied by a small group of pirates, all squeezed onto a kind of poop deck behind.

This was the year the dictatorship finally collapsed in Brazil and the exiled crowd was highly excitable. They roared at the start of each new anthem and sometimes stood up as one and sang along in floods of tears. At just such a moment we came in.

There were six of us. With glassy eyes and crazed smiles – nobody had been to bed – we held on to each other as we were led in a kind of stumbling conga line through the crowded restaurant to a long table where another party was already en-joying lunch at one end – and there he was, head lolled back as usual, transported by the music. He opened his eyes as we squeezed by.

'There you are,' he drawled, as if he expected us. 'You're late! She's almost finished.' A new song started and he leapt to his feet. Round and round as usual, eyes shut, tears glistening on the edge of each lid as he sang along.

In such a way we crossed the line, from the dance floor into the real world, and became friends.

His name was Napoleon Fernandes de Souza. He was unremarkable-looking, ageless and sensibly dressed, of mixed race and not at first glance a queen. In fact, he looked rather severe, like somebody's uncle. But he had surprised eyes and an extraordinary scar reaching from one ear to the other under a thinning Afro. All enquiries exacted the same response. 'War wounds,' he would giggle, fingers crawling protectively to the formidable slash. Off a confused face he would occasionally extend the explanation. 'Dr Pitanguy. Fils.' Looking at you sideways. 'A new method. At the time.'

'When was that?'

'A while ago.' About his age, he was evasive. Somewhere along the line – 'Fire Island in the seventies with my uncle' – he learnt to speak good English and was very funny with it. He seemed to have a lot of uncles.

Napo had the infectious smile of a naughty beaver, or a Looney Tunes chipmunk. It suddenly burst out. The Hitler moustache lifted to reveal a mouth of feral teeth stained by the smoke of thirty Gitanes a day. He used those famous blue packets to great effect as pretend powder compacts, opening them as if they contained a mirror, appraising himself like a lady, moving his face from left to right, swishing an imaginary head of hair. He would perform this trick to strangers in the middle of a serious conversation. In short, he baffled everyone, including his family. According to him, his father had been a powerful general in the dictatorship. From an early age it was clear that Napo was never going to fit in. By the time he was sixteen the terrible truth was painfully apparent. To his father, his clawing mother and their other children, two older boys and two fat sisters. 'Sissy. This is the English word, Rupert, non?' We were sitting in the Tuileries Garden on a hot summer afternoon, waiting for a dealer.

'It all happened very fast. I was too young to understand. I used to sit on my father's knee in his uniform and feel terribly thrilled. He was an important man, you see. I felt the power.'

'Between his legs?'

'You are, as usual, very perceptive, Rupert.' He giggled nervously, fingers like spider's legs climbing across his face. 'We were mad about each other. Then one day he saw who I really was. And his love snapped off like an electric light, so I left.'

'Do you still hear from them?'

'Do I hear from them? Every minute of every day. They're all here. Now that the dictatorship has collapsed, they had to get out quick. And where did they come? To Mummy. I was French by then. You see, I could hardly refuse.'

'Darling,' said Corinne, the model agent, later. 'His mother was a cleaning lady from Fort-de-France. Napoleon was born in Châteauroux. His name was Noury.'

'I don't think you'll find that's true,' I replied tartly. I wanted Napo to be Napo.

One Sunday morning we found ourselves together at the Kit Kat Club as usual. It was about nine o'clock. Napoleon was sitting bolt upright and staring.

'What are you up to later?' he asked as I slid into the banquette. I glanced at the dance floor, where the number I had been tracking all weekend was dancing in a group of friends, juddering in the strobe lights like a cartoon in a flip book. His head turned. Our eyes locked. Was he up for it? A look of sheer hatred was often indistinguishable from a queen's idea of come-and-get-me. Reading the difference was the life and death talent that made for a successful player on the circuit.

'Nothing much,' I replied finally. 'Why? What are you doing?' He looked at me with revolving eyes.

'My mother is having her funeral at half past eleven. I wondered if you might join me.'

'I'm a bit high.'

'And I'm a bit higher.'

The street shimmered as we made our way to the taxi rank on the Boulevard de Sébastopol. Ripped from the brain-numbing cocoon of the thumping club into the open air, we could barely put one foot in front of the other. We moved with difficulty through the crowds, suddenly in sharp focus, pores, noses, clothes, voices close. The sun flickered through the plane trees and the driver looked suspicious as Napoleon opened the rear door of a taxi, his black face grey, slack and empty, leaning in with mad wide eyes staring out like a blind marquise arriving at the guillotine. He lowered himself in slow motion towards the back seat, one hand gripping the roof of the car, the other groping shakily inside.

Finally in, we both lay back as Paris rolled past the windows towards Napoleon's flat in the Rue Saint-Martin. Not a word was spoken. Instead, the strange flatulent shuffling of rubber tyres rolling over cobbles, a sound peculiar to Paris, reminded me suddenly that I was actually there, living there. I had escaped my past. This feeling of release crashed in often, a mainline injection of sheer joy, like falling through space, as I crossed the Champs-Élysées, or arrived in a taxi at the Place Blanche and saw the Moulin Rouge through the rain, its red-lit sails creaking slowly across time, or sat, as now, on the way to Napoleon's mother's funeral, Paris shaking and tipping, upside down through the rear window. These views took in all of my dreams. Pebbledash England, dripping and soot-stained, had not yet taken root as the romantic memory it was shortly to become. There's a tipping point in the life of an exile and I had not reached it. London simply represented the me I wanted to lose. In Paris that year a new character had emerged – mute, since I still couldn't speak the language, watchful, intent. None of these qualities could have been attributed to the old me. The old me was a live wire, hissing and flaring across the floor towards an explosion that never came.

A funeral.

'I don't think I can make it,' I said finally. Or was it someone else? My voice seemed far away.

'Nonsense. We'll have a pick-me-up when we get home.'

Napoleon's flat was five floors up. With the tenacity of a mountain goat he trudged ahead while I collapsed at the second-floor landing. I could hear his keys turning in a lock far above. A door opened and slammed. He had probably forgotten I was there. So much the better. I sat on the stairs, my head in my hands, and the silence screamed. Through my fingers the ratty stair carpet, amber whorls on downtrodden red, spiralled round and round, down and down. Hours or minutes or a second later – the pills bent time – a cockroach began to make its way across this colourful terrain, stopping every so often to wave its antennae and look around.

The perfume of every Parisian stairwell had its own particular allure. In the competition between polish and cabbage for the top note, in this case the vegetable was the victor. Its cooked breath hung over the waxy parquet. A door opened somewhere and the voice of the concierge blared out, coarse, Auvernois, trilling abuse at some footsteps tumbling down the stairs. The buzz and click of the big front door, followed by an earth-shaking crash as it slammed shut, then silence again. I was about to go downstairs and return home when another door opened high above and a voice called out.

'Hurry up. We're going to be late.'

Inside the small flat Napoleon had rustled up a party atmosphere. He had opened the windows and drawn the curtains. Thin and red, they blew into the room, drenching it in a flapping pink glow. He had cranked up the stereo and a couple of long white powder rails of coke were stretched out across a mirror on the kitchen table. The window in that room was wide open too and the breeze moved through the flat like a poltergeist, flapping the pages of magazines, suddenly slamming the loo door, and drifting the coke on the mirror. The kitchen looked onto a well of peeling walls and windows, a kind of megaphone that amplified snatches of conversation, the clatter of plates and washing-up, all the noises of a Parisian Sunday morning.

'Look what Mummy found,' said Napo, wielding a tiny piece of paper the size of a postage stamp, and a pair of scissors.

'What's that?' I didn't have my glasses on.

'A little trip, querido. Essential for funerals.'

'You must be mad. Your mother might suddenly rise up from her coffin.'

'Good. There are several things I forgot to mention on the deathbed. Just a nibble. To give things a bit of colour.'

He neatly cut the tiny piece of paper into quarters.

'Open wide, and I'll put the rest in my wallet for later. Come on. We're late.'

Napoleon had a Mini. 'Shouldn't we take a cab?' I wondered nervously. He was bending down, trying to grasp the door handle, dressed in a dark suit. I was wearing a borrowed overcoat, my dancing gear – cargo pants and work boots – underneath.

'We must go first to the funeral home and then to the cemetery,' he said, like an explorer. 'We will never find a taxi. And I'm not going with my brothers. No. We must go in my car. Relax. I can drive.'

And he could. He produced a joint from his breast pocket, long and wiggly in his mouth, bouncing up and down as he spoke, billowing thick smoke as he lit it, while simultaneously screeching headlong into the traffic. The Mini quickly clouded over but Napo drove on regardless.

I opened the window. It was a lovely day. Paris at its best, alive. Often it looks grey and dead. But today the boulevard was honeycomb and the red geraniums, blotches in the windows, superimposed almost, were like the flowers in the postcards of one's youth.

'Will they all be there? The brothers and the sisters and your father?'

'All.'

'Won't they wonder what I am doing?'
'Of course. That's the whole point.'

The funeral home was in Neuilly, on the other side of the Arc de Triomphe. We arrived at a low white building on the edge of the Bois and parked round the back in a kind of service area. Ten hearses and a Mini. It was a death factory. Inside, the vestibule was light and airy. Crisp, friendly air hostesses presided. Pall-bearers were dressed like bouncers. The names of the dead were listed and numbered on a large board like the specialities in a restaurant, and we set off down a long, wide corridor, accompanied by our own air hostess, past identical chapels, one after another. For some reason they made Napoleon giggle. 'Another. And another. Tomorrow and tomorrow and tomorrow.' These chapels were actually called lying-in rooms, according to the young lady, each with its own lurid stained-glass window – 'individually designed by some of the greatest artists of the day'. These backlit fruit salads threw spangled lights on all the ghoulish drapery of death, the altar, the lectern, the coffin swamped in flowers, and managed to make everything look somewhat magical. (A *Shrek* aesthetic before its time.) There were no crosses. Jesus wasn't looking down. Nor was the Virgin Mary looking up in this industrialised deathworks. The coffins were deposited through a hatch and were squeezed back out, like calcified loaves, straight into the open mouths of the hearses backed up against the drab concrete cliff of the service area where we had parked. From there they set off to the church or the crematorium or the cemetery, depending on the order of the day. In one chapel two men hoovered. There was a smell of dead flowers. From a closed door the muffled sound of a hymn. Two rooms were empty. 'Resting,' said Napoleon, whose mood seemed to be improving by the minute. More bouncers observed, faintly threatening.

From a chapel ahead came the sound of screams, like a torture chamber. 'Don't worry. It's the acid,' said Napoleon knowingly.

But it wasn't. As we passed, we both stopped dead in our tracks. A group of Vietnamese women were hurling themselves at a tiny child's coffin. Their faces were purple with grief, but the men too were howling as they tried to pull their women off the casket. A monk stood above the fray, expressionless in a shaft of orange light. His acolyte banged a gold bowl on the altar and a beautiful sound rang out, sharp but soothing, and the congregation was suddenly becalmed. The monk sang through the silence, a lilting guttural stream of ancient prayer, and time briefly stood still.

'I can see the words coming out of his mouth,' said Napoleon and I had to push him on.

Nothing could have been more of a contrast than the de Souza chapel next door. Three large men in black sat in a row, staring ahead. They had thick necks and dyed hair. Two matronly women sat on the other side of the aisle, also with thick necks and dye from the same bottle. There was no music, no flowers, just the coffin, short and wide, dividing the family group.

As we came in, they turned as one. Napoleon visibly shrank. As if on cue the screaming started again next door, stranger and more frightening, muffled now by the wall between us. Greetings seemed to catch in everyone's throat – and for a second we all looked at one another, frozen, as if by a power cut from which, after a moment, we juddered back into action.

We gingerly sat down behind the men as they shook Napoleon's hand and stared at me suspiciously. Napo didn't bother with introductions. With nothing better to do I stared back. The necks seemed to be pulsing, pink, throbbing. I could see their younger selves buried alive in the mounds of blubber; their blunt child's eyes imprisoned inside the folds of flesh. Too much rice, I thought. The acid had kicked in. A little bell tinkled and we all stood. A tiny Brazilian priest swished through a side door and the show began.

Once a Catholic, you can follow the Mass in any language and still thrill to all your favourite bits. Once I had I learnt French, I adored the translation of the Hail Mary. 'The fruit of thy womb' turned into 'les fruits de vos entrailles'. Mary's entrails gave the prayer a whole new dimension and she lost the dreary virginal quality. Portuguese sounds rather like a game of ping pong – tudo bem, tudo bom – and the Mass had a strange clockwork feeling. Soon it was time for communion and Napoleon rose like a zombie and lurched towards the altar, where he collapsed dramatically to his knees. His eyes were on stalks watching the host going into his mouth. Perhaps the transubstantiation was finally happening. He definitely looked as if he was sucking Jesus' toe on the way back. The acid was surging. Billowing with visible ideas. I could already hear Napo's mother scratching the coffin from inside. I clutched the pew. The screams intensified next door. The flowers were taking over the chapel, growing and bending, new buds unfolding, lilies everywhere, it was like Jack and the beanstalk. The priest seemed to be laughing. Then everyone was laughing. Roaring. Then the coffin started to move. Was it moving? It was. The family filed out of the chapel but we remained in our pew – clutching the handrail for dear life. 'Two more minutes,' Napo suggested.

'Phew,' he said finally. 'That was intense.'

Outside, the family were climbing into a limousine waiting at the bottom of the steps. They acknowledged us briefly. Funeral pleasantries were exchanged but no one suggested giving us a lift to the cemetery. So we galloped off to find the Mini, just as Napoleon's mother was being slid into her hearse from the hatch in the wall. We waited while the bouncers secured the coffin to the brass rails and fastened the flowers on top before climbing inside. Then we followed the hearse out of the compound.

On the way to the cemetery Napoleon was in a reflective mood. He lit another long waggly joint, extracted a bottle of cachaça from under his seat and told stories of his childhood. I closed my eyes and drifted with the story.

'The day martial law was declared there was tremendous excitement in the streets. We knew that our father was involved. He had hardly been home in the last weeks. Nothing much changed for us but of course the military tightened their grip and the people began to wake up. I didn't really know what politics was until one of my friends had been taken by the police at a demonstration and with wires from a telephone, one attached to his you-know-what and another to his mouth, had endured three hours of electric shocks. He told them everything, although there was nothing much to tell. Another friend – a girl – asked me to intercede for him with my father. With the heart in the mouth – isn't that the expression? – I did. My father listened. Said nothing, thanked me and left. We never saw my friend again, by the way.

'When my father came back – much later that night – I was summoned to his study. He said it was dangerous for me to remain in Brazil, that I was a threat to the survival of the family, that my unnatural way of life was not going to smear their chances. I just watched him – and I watched my mother, who had been summoned to witness my dismissal. She was in her nightdress and carefully kept her head down but did not offer a word of support. By then I didn't care. But even I was surprised when my father produced an air ticket. I was being banished. I was to leave in two days. I was to have a room near the Brazilian embassy in Paris for a few months while I found my feet. And that was that.

'"When am I coming back?" I asked. He just looked at me and left the room. Waking up the next morning the first thing I thought was that I must have been dreaming. But then reality crashed into place. The house was empty. A shell of whispering memories. My mother had taken the others to our place in the mountains by Petrópolis. Only the old maid stayed behind. Magali. She helped me pack. At the end we sat on the bed and held hands. She gave me a medal of the Virgin Mary. I still have it. And that was it. The next day my father's driver took me to the airport. I was tremendously excited. Travel in those days . . . well, no one really went anywhere – and there was I on my way to the future. A door was closing and I ran through it, you see. So, you can imagine twenty years later, there I was living happily in Paris, naturalised, a French citizen, and suddenly they needed me. How could I refuse to help? I ended up being their lifeline.'

We arrived at the gates of the cemetery and time and space were beginning to bend. A second was taking an hour and an inch turned into a mile. The hearse ahead stopped and we parked the car. Charnel houses lined the avenue. They looked like skyscrapers, the Fifth Avenue of death, stretching for miles.

'Ai meu deus. Mama's coffin seems to have shrunk,' said Napoleon as the glittering box slid from the hearse.

'So it does.' I looked at him. He was all mouth and moustache.

'What are you laughing about?'

'You look like a Picasso.'

'Well, you look like *The Scream* by Munch.'

'Yes. And the coffin is the size of a skateboard.'

'It's tiny.'

'It is.'

'Is it?'

Other cars appeared and we braced ourselves. The funeral limousines seemed like tanks suddenly, or the people had shrunk. Either way, the family seemed to be jumping from them.

'I don't think that's them.'

'It's them, all right,' said Napoleon firmly.

We made our way to the grave. The mourners recoiled in

horror, but we took it in our stride. Then one of them started to shout.

'Let's talk about this later, Papa,' reasoned Napo.

'Are you sure that's your father?' I asked.

'Claro. She has a terrible temper. This is a most amusing trip. The whole family have shrunk.'

'And there are so many of them.'

'They must have arrived from somewhere else.'

'But where?'

Only when we arrived at the grave – a mere three feet long – did reality dawn.

We had followed the wrong box. Napoleon's family snapped suddenly into the Vietnamese party from the next-door chapel, and they were not in the mood for apologies.

Napoleon scoured the horizon for his mother's funeral party and started running up the tomb-lined avenue, looking wildly from right to left. He slowed down at the brow of a hill and stopped, a strange silhouette with flat feet and billowing breath. He was still panting when I caught up with him, tears streaming down his face. And then we saw them, far off, leaving the grave-yard. Napoleon waved and shouted, and they turned, a strange herd in the valley of death, and then disappeared through the cemetery gate.

By the time we got to the grave the diggers were already getting to work. I hung back and Napoleon stood at the edge as the black dirt thlunked on to the coffin of his mother and suddenly he began to howl like a wounded beast. I took hold of his arm, afraid for a moment that he was going to throw himself in. He didn't. Instead we went for a coffee in a Moroccan restaurant nearby and it started to rain.

'You see,' explained Napoleon, 'I do have emotions. Shall we order a couscous?'

*

'Well dear, that's all very well,' sniffed John Schlesinger. 'But do you seriously imagine Madonna is going to take acid? Your idea of what "goes" in commercial American cinema is way off the mark, I'm afraid.' Smoke was coming out of his ears.

'It's just for the idea,' I snapped. 'No one has to take any drugs. Nor do they have to be starting off from a nightclub. They just get stuck talking and then they follow the wrong box. It was you who wanted them to arrive late. I'm providing you with context.'

'Well I prefer it as is.' And he slammed the script shut. I wondered if our film's title would ever make it on to the spine of his bible.

The end of the story.

Eventually, Paris became too familiar and I moved on. To New York. Los Angeles. Florida. I lost contact with Napoleon. Occasionally, I would hear about him. Napo was still dancing. Napo was arrested in Rio. Napo lived with a fireman. (But not like that.) He continually lost his phone, so little by little everyone slipped away in the virtual age. I bumped into him – years later – near the Gare du Nord. He hadn't changed. Still breathless. Still the surprised eyes. We arranged to meet, but he never showed up. And then a strange thing happened. A few weeks ago, I was in Paris and came across an old friend from the disco days. 'Whatever happened to Napoleon?' he asked. Good question. I told him all I knew. 'Sad,' we agreed. 'She was a lot of fun.'

The next day the same disco friend called me. 'You won't believe it,' he gasped. 'You know we were talking about Napoleon de Souza? Well, he's dead. Last week. He had a heart attack at some Caribbean nightclub in the suburbs. He got up to dance and collapsed. The perfect death, non? For once.' The disco friend went on and on.

I couldn't help wondering just how perfect death in a strobe light could be. Did they turn the music off, or did he drift away to 'Hey! Macarena'. Not very restful, nor a very promising arrival at the pearly necklace. Quite possibly St Peter would say, 'Back to square one, Napoleon.' Or perhaps they would take pity. If it exists up there. Maybe he is dancing for eternity. Round and round. Bathed in shards of angelic light.

SEBASTIAN MELMOTH

The Morning After and the Night Before

I conceived the idea for a movie about the last days of Oscar Wilde at lunch one day with the director – now dead – Roger Michell. We had worked together in the theatre back at the end of the century and had kept in touch.

He liked my idea of setting the story inside the frame of a fatal night out.

I have always been fascinated by death. One never knows when the last moment is. The last goodbye. The last drink. In my version of the story, drifting Oscar of the boulevards scores some cash, some drugs, goes out on the town and dies.

'Perfect,' agreed Roger. 'With flashbacks. Go and write it.'

I did. We had a reading. Everyone loved it. Roger would direct. Scott Rudin and Robert Fox agreed to produce. Things were all set. Next stop, the Oscars.

Then Roger dropped out and the whole card house slowly collapsed.

Ten years later I finally made the film myself. It became a life-or-death challenge to create my own portrait of Wilde. I felt the other movies about him – each with their own strengths – had not fully captured the weird magical destructive whole of that extraordinary character. They seemed reverential. Oscar was a god, but also a wonderfully flawed fairy. I think that's what it means to be Christ. With his death the road to liberty was born. It had found a face.

Paris, autumn 1900.

Eyes closed, spinning with drink, slumped in a chair, life re-
duces – or expands – to a green-drenched darkness of swaying
sunlight and faraway sounds dimly perceived through purple lids
and one deaf ear. Motionless he sits, a crumbling sphinx in the
blur of movement, only a fat cigarette-stained finger tapping on
a hand spread wide, up and down, conducting some new thought
into an interior symphony – a slow movement, on a slow day
where business is thin.

In this way he has passed the long, hot summer, day in, day
out – at the same table on the boulevard – in last year's suit,
darned and stained, with an old felt hat worn low to conceal.
His face, a marbled slab of raw meat, was once – not that long
ago – at the very centre of fashion. Those famous features are
a memory now, submerged in folds of livid flesh. The muscles
on his cheek have snapped or frozen or simply given up, so that
one eye hangs and the left side of his mouth is gloomily set
while the other still searches for the old jokes. Today the weak
October sun is the right light for this ruin and later the gaslight
will be kinder still and there may even be one last chance for
romance and tragedy in this shell, this chrysalis, from which the
shade of a long-dead butterfly may yet spread patchwork wings
and flit through the beams of light up and down the boulevard,
maybe even sucking some cock on a side street before the night
is over.

He dreams and drowns slowly, his whole life parading before

him for review. Memory is the last thing that holds him to life, the clutched straw, and now an image suggests itself – an attic window on a long-forgotten street – and he swims towards it.

It is that magic moment of a June dusk when the sky is almost white over the rooftops and stars begin to glitter like dice thrown across space. Pigeons flap in the black trees and smoke winds dreamily from chimney stacks over waves of slate towards the river and the Albert Bridge. A voice calls from the street, a cheeky cockney selling the evening paper, and a horse and cart clatters through the deepening silence.

Inside the darkened room tucked beneath the eaves he is reading to his two children. His darling boys. The same dream. The same story. The same fading light. The boys lie together in the same bed (a rare truce), and he sits at the end with a book in his hands – although he doesn't read from it. He knows it by heart. He leans back now, transported by the magic of his own words.

'Swallow, swallow, little swallow, you tell me of marvellous things,' he whispers.

Is it really him? So young, so thin, so many teeth and such skin. What clothes! He wears a long fur coat (never retrieved from Willis's) over evening dress. Peeking from starched cuffs, his hands are plump and wilting, heavy with agate and emerald rings curled around his fingers. The drama of the scene is not lost on his little sons. They watch in awe, eyes glittering, as their father incants the bedtime story.

And the voice. Sweeping the registers, seductive and fantastic, coming and going in great crashing waves.

'But more marvellous than this is the suffering of men and women. There is no mystery so great as suffering.'

'Papa, I don't understand,' says Cyril, the elder boy.

'One day you will, my dearest. One day you will. All will be revealed.'

(An easy answer. He too does not yet understand. He wrote this when he knew nothing of life. Now that he knows it – there is nothing left to write.)

'Fly over my city, little bird and tell me what you see there. So the swallow flew over the great city and saw the rich making merry in their beautiful houses, while the white faces of starving children looked out listlessly at the black streets.'

Now he too seems to be flying. Right to the top of the half-built church on the hill. Perched on the milk-white shell of its unfinished dome he can see the whole city humming with life. He jumps from it and plummets like a comet towards the black streets, the overflowing gutters, the dim courtyards, the stinking alleys, the snatched faces of the rich and the poor, the salons, the sewers, the success, the sex – a whole life tumbles past, his stomach turned upside down in the fall.

With a gasp he awakens. Just as his head lolls dangerously into the glass in front of him, an emerald puddle of absinthe. Reflected in it, a hanging mouth which now grins as the familiar noises return, the boulevard, the complaining waiters, the footsteps on the street, the emptiness.

'It's a dream,' he says to no one in particular, draining the glass. He rummages for change and rises with difficulty. It is not easy to squeeze blood from a broken heart.

Hands press down on the table. Veins and capillaries strain across his neck. His sphincter distends with the effort (sometimes to disastrous effect. But not this time.) With a groan he is on his feet and the momentum sets him off, weaving through the tables and stumbling down the busy street.

The whole world is out in this warm October dusk. The glaring electric light spills from the café onto the crowded terrace. In the shadows couples walk under the plane trees, men in silk hats, women in furs, urchins selling violets. Over the rooftops a pink moon hangs and the stars bleed in the mist.

He shuffles along the busy street like a crab – diagonally – this way and that, his hat pulled forward, his face buried inside the patchy fur collar of his old coat.

A beautiful woman flanked by two men in evening dress tumbles laughing into the street. They are a high-spirited trio, arms linked, talking loudly in English and they plough – oblivious – into the flow. He hears the familiar Mayfair slang too late and crashes into them, eye to eye with the woman, before ducking sideways while they saunter on.

'That old tramp looked familiar,' sniggers one man to the other, chatting over the woman's head as they amble through the trees. The Jockey Club and the Dreyfus case are discussed and dismissed. A poor joke is cracked, and they throw back their heads laughing.

'Surely you agree with your husband, Mrs Arbuthnot? It couldn't be more of a scandal. A typical whining Jew if ever there was one.'

'Oh yes, indeed,' she agrees half-heartedly. That old tramp did look familiar.

'You look worried, my dear. Is anything the matter?'

Suddenly the woman stops. 'I think I left my fan.'

Without waiting for an answer, she turns around and heads back through the crowd.

'What the devil is she doing?' asks one man of the other.

'No idea, old chum. She's your wife.'

Her body shudders with adrenalin at this act of rebellion. There is a price to be paid by an unreliable woman who runs off in the middle of a strange city. 'I shall be smothered with ether and abducted to China, and they'll say I asked for it.' However, she fixes her eye and her resolve on the bobbing hat floating over the crowd – far away now – and she follows, swimming against the current – all looming towards her – the monde and the demi-monde, taking their time, blocking her way. Further and further she follows, from one boulevard to another, never getting any closer, and suddenly he's gone. She runs on – stops – turns around, colliding with an old woman who appears from a crack between two houses – and there he is – a lumbering silhouette at the other end of a thin, dark alley. She hesitates for a moment – then follows, diving into the darkness, adjusting her senses as the roar of the boulevard suddenly contracts to subtler sounds: dripping water, a window closing high above, a snatch of conversation and the drum of her own heartbeat. The passage, just wide enough to walk through, leads to an old lane of derelict cottages built into the flanks of the streets on either side. An open drain flows through it, silver in the moonlight, and she carefully crosses it, lifting her dress, grasping at the dank wall for balance. A street lamp glows in the distance. He is walking towards it and his shadow grows with every step.

'Mr Wilde,' she shouts, unwilling to go any further. 'Oscar Wilde?'

He stops for a moment, then turns, his face hidden under the rim of his hat.

Suddenly she is unsure. 'Mr Wilde?' she repeats, moving closer – further into the shadows. 'Surely you remember me? I came to all your first nights. I'm Mrs Arbuthnot.' For some reason her throat tightens and her eyes begin to sting. He comes towards her, takes off his hat and bows. She can't suppress a gasp at the toothless smile, the thin greasy hair, the ghost of a face, and tears pour suddenly from her eyes.

'Of course I remember you,' he says gently. 'One never forgets such a face. How kind of you to speak to me. You are well, I see.'

'I am well. But how are you?'

Before he can answer, the two men tumble around the corner.

'Lydia. Come here at once,' shouts her husband.

'I shall have to go.'

No one moves.

Oscar has an idea. 'You couldn't lend me five pounds, could you? Things are a little tight at present. I feel ghastly asking like this but . . . ' He trails off.

'Lydia,' shouts her husband again, striding into the alley.

She rummages in her bag, sobbing now. She thrusts all the money she has into his hand. 'I'm coming!' she calls. 'Goodbye, Mr Wilde. I wish—'

'Never wish, Madam. It may come true. But thank you for a moment's harmony in a discordant fugue.' He neatly pockets the cash as the man arrives.

'Lydia. Go to Ronnie. Now!' her husband commands. She obeys. With a last glance she retreats, her elegant silhouette bowed and shrinking towards the crack of light. Mr Arbuthnot comes very close now, seething with rage. Will he strike me? Oscar wonders, empty, waiting.

'Never speak to my wife again, do you hear? Or I'll kill you.' He spits out the words.

Staying still is the best thing to do in these situations. The man waits for a response but none comes so he turns with military precision and marches back to his wife and their friend. Oscar watches them – still not moving – until they have disappeared around the corner, dissolving into the movement of the street. He feels for the cash in his pocket, chuckles and walks on.

The Alsace is one in a string of run-down hotels on a dirty white street that runs between the boulevard and the river. There is gaslight and running water and cheap rates for permanent guests. There is no sign of the concierge so he strains over the small desk, takes his key from its box and moves on point as fast as he can through the hall. In the gloomy stairwell there's a smell of cabbage and drains and the sound of a piano. He hauls himself up the stairs, clutching the banister with both hands.

Thank God he is on the first floor and not in the attic where he was cooped up for months last year. (That was before he had charmed the proprietor. He can still charm.) He stops for a moment to catch his breath – large hands on large hips – and is suddenly frozen by a searing pain cutting through his ear. He sways slightly, nearly losing his balance, catching the banister just in time. With a gasp the pain dissolves. He gathers his strength and climbs on. A door opens on a higher floor – the sound of the wretched piano is louder for a moment – and footsteps announce the proprietor, a pleasant-looking man of fifty wearing an apron holding a tray of food.

'Ah, Monsieur Melmoth,' he says. 'How are you this evening?'

'Medium, Monsieur Dupoirier. Fairly medium.'

'Any sign of your bank draft?' M. Dupoirier has not been paid for the last month.

'Alas, no!' counters Oscar with as much flair as he can muster. 'But fear not. Monsieur Ross arrives tomorrow with contracts, royalties and cash.'

It's a lie and the other man knows it, but he has developed a soft spot for this strange vagrant who migrates with the season from hotel to hotel, sometimes in the dead of night. No one quite knows who he is, a poet, a spy or even a murderer. One thing is certain: Sebastian Melmoth is not his name.

But to me, thinks M. Dupoirier, he has always been charming.

'Très bien, Monsieur Melmoth. Très bien,' he says now, and the two men continue their journeys.

Oscar's room is at the end of a dismal corridor next to a communal water closet. (Thanks to this contraption his long 'at home' days are accompanied by the intriguing sounds of ablution – footsteps and farts, trickles, gushes and groans.)

He closes the door and leans against it for a moment, breathing deeply. The familiar smell of old clothes and cigarettes calms him. It is dark except for the vague shape of the window and the remains of this afternoon's fire glowing in the grate. He lights a match and with shaking fingers applies it to the gaslight on the wall. With a little explosion the flame leaps around the glass lamp into a quivering tongue that draws the room slowly in from the dark. It is certainly not the Savoy, he thinks ruefully for the thousandth time. The small window looks over a grim courtyard of hard earth with a solitary tree like a dead spider – its legs in the air – climbing the sheer wall of another building, another cheap hotel. In the corner of the room a matronly bed overflows from its frame next to the fireplace – with a blotchy old looking glass on its mantel. Beyond that a small table, a chair and a cupboard are all wrapped up for Christmas in wallpaper seething with tightly packed bunches of flowers.

'I have only been here a month and I am already on nodding terms with these snowdrops,' he mutters to the looking glass as he inspects his face – a breathless grimace with bulging eyes.

'Oh dear, what's this?' Blood oozes from his eardrum. He touches it with a finger, cautiously, watching himself, horrified. 'Goodness.' He examines the finger, sniffs it, then smears it across the glass with a drunken grunt.

'See, see, where Christ's blood streams across the firmament,' he whispers and then a strange thing happens. The room suddenly lurches behind him like a capsizing boat – or so it seems – and his legs buckle. He grabs the mantelpiece to stop himself from falling. His sight blurs and the sharp pain returns for a second, stabbing through his head, and he can hardly breathe. He squeezes his eyes closed, willing the malaise to pass. It does. When he opens them, the room has righted itself and is sailing on.

'What is happening to me?' The mirror provides the answer. He looks like death. 'I should stop drinking, but then what?'

Undaunted – he has five pounds in his pocket, after all – he applies rouge to his cheeks and an evil tincture from a jar to his hair. He sprays scent into a mouth of green teeth, extinguishes the gas and leaves the room.

He takes a cab to Place Blanche. A greasy mist hangs, thick and wet, on the sails of the Moulin Rouge, a blur of coloured lights creaking slowly round. A group of young women cross the boulevard, arms linked, laughing and trying to cancan. Their screams bounce back at them in the thick fog. There is only noise, just footsteps and the sound of water gushing from the drains on the side of the street as Oscar heads blindly up the hill towards Montmartre, exhilarated and alert, the gloom and apathy – the years, even – falling off as he heads deeper into the Parisian interior. A little way ahead the light spills in thick beams from the Calyasa Bar. On the terrace a couple argue, comic silhouettes wagging their fingers against the large windows of the café – an aquarium crammed with odd fish. A fat man presides at the bar, bottles and glasses glimmering behind, and a fierce crowd pressed against it shouting and laughing under a cloud of smoke. They are a different set, wilder, dirtier, and Oscar feels the familiar creeping in his groin as he squeezes through the door into the blast of noise and heat. Thank God for pickpockets and street boys, he thinks, waving at several old friends as he ploughs through the crowd. He is weightless now, no past and certainly no future. 'I am lost from my own life.' At the back of the bar a young man and a cadaverous child sit at a table. The child is crying. The young man, with a flat nose and cauliflower ears under his cap, sees Oscar and whistles.

Oscar's face – built for comedy – looking this way and that, lights up and the weight of ruin falls from his shoulders.

'Johnny, darling boy. I have news.'

The little one sees Oscar and cries with renewed vigour.

'But what is wrong with our little sparkler? Dear Leon, weep no more. Dear boy.' He squeezes himself into the banquette, kissing the little boy on the forehead as he slides down, then looks to Johnny for an explanation.

'The sisters from the orphanage came for him and all his matches got nicked.'

The little boy grabs his older brother by his coat.

'Don't let them take me back there, Jo. I'll be more careful. I promise.' Fresh tears pour down his face and then he starts to cough, a deep wrenching sound turning his wan cheeks the colour of blood oranges.

Johnny rubs his back. 'All I'm saying, Leo, is it could be better for everyone. You'll be safe and I won't always be worrying. It's getting too fucking dangerous around here.'

'But we're brothers. We're meant to be together.' The little boy buries his head in in his arms and wails.

'Well this is too frightful,' says Oscar. 'But I too have news. A sudden windfall enables me to offer you both at least absinthe and cocaine on the eve of departure – and a purple moment for me, if, Leon, you will lend me your relation for the usual consideration.' He produces a coin from his pocket. The boy looks up, tear-stained and greedy. 'Well, all right then. Twenty minutes. And then you have to finish that story.' He grabs the coin. His brother whacks him over the head. More tears.

A little later Oscar has gone to heaven on a dirty mattress with his trousers down in the knocking shop over the Calyasa, while Johnny squats by the window washing his arse over a bucket of water. The rhythmic squeak of bedsprings through the ceiling, the wild shrieks from the room next door, and the poor cockroach halfway up the wall isn't sure which way to go. Oscar lies dreamily watching its long antennae wave around and strokes it with a fat finger. Horrified, it scurries up the wall and hides behind a flap in the peeling wallpaper. Thank God the room is dark, just the street lamp outside cutting through it in a ghostly strip of orange light slicing the young man in half. Oscar watches him for a long moment.

'You know,' he says finally, 'I don't think I've ever been happier in my life.'

'Oh, yes?'

'In this room. At this moment. The light from the street!'

'What light?' The young god has finished his ablutions, dries his hands on his trousers and sets to work tipping granules of cocaine from a small envelope into two wads of cotton wool.

'What light? It carves you in marble, dear boy. We are lost in our own world. Shrouded in a symphony of adjacent copulation.'

He sits up with a sigh and reaches for the pocketbook inside his coat, and extracts money.

'I know you love me, Johnny. Even though our purple moments are sullied by green notes.' He hands them over. Johnny stuffs the cash in his trousers, comes over and opens Oscar's mouth with one hand and wedges the cotton wool between his cheek and his gums with the other. Oscar – thrilled – sucks at the fingers with the wide eyes of a submissive.

'Oi! Enough. That should sort you out,' says Johnny, putting the other ball in his own mouth.

'I wonder if Antinous addressed Hadrian thus on the eve of deification?' mutters Oscar, getting off the bed. 'But what can one do? One must catch the shooting star when and where it falls.' He walks over to the door and opens it. Little Leon falls into the room. 'That was nearly an hour,' the boy shrieks. 'Story time.' He drags Oscar back to the bed and they jump aboard, to a screech of protesting bedsprings. 'Everyone downstairs will be getting the wrong idea. Now. Where was I?' laughs the poet.

'Under the bridge.'

'Ah yes. Under the bridge.'

Johnny comes over to the bed, settles down carefully next to his little brother, stroking his hair, looking out the window.

Oscar is about to begin when someone falls with a crash in the
room above. A woman laughs. Dust falls from the ceiling. The
little boy coughs. Oscar breathes in. His mouth begins to feel
deliciously numb. (Numbness is the great aim.) In a low, melodious voice he begins.

'Under the bridge two little boys were lying in one another's
arms trying to keep themselves warm. How hungry we are, they
said. You must not lie here, shouted the night watchman and
they wandered out into the rain ... '

Later this odd trio are walking down an empty street through
the mist. Leon takes Oscar's hand. The poet shakes dark
thoughts from his racing mind – another child lost in the mist –
somewhere – who knows where, searching perhaps. Perhaps not.

Don't think. Keep going. Just keep going. The cocaine is
playing tricks.

'Where was I?' he asks hoarsely. 'Oh yes. The swallow flew
back and told the Prince what he had seen. I am covered in fine
gold, said the Prince. Take it off leaf by leaf and give it to the
poor. The living always think that gold can make them happy.'

'It can,' observes the little boy.

They have arrived at the Café Concert on the Rue de Clichy.
A witch in black stands at the door, conjuring up a small crowd
from the mist.

'Make way for the fucking poet,' she says, seeing Oscar.

'Boudicca, dear, may I bring my young friends?'

'No children, Sebastian.'

'He's a dwarf, dear. Look closely.' Without waiting for an
answer Oscar pushes the boys in to the theatre.

A stringy woman sings to a rowdy audience, harshly lit by
footlights and dressed for a beggar's ball. She is accompanied
from below – in a sort of orchestra pit – by an ancient man on a
squeezebox, a skeleton with a double bass, and a lady violinist.
They smile out crazily as they play and stand up as she reaches

the final chorus and the whole place erupts in song. The dance floor sways as one. Men in top hats, with girls on their knees, bellow along with the music from tables underneath the rickety circle. Smoke curls from a galaxy of cigars towards the stage, wrapping the singer in strange tendrils. Waiters in aprons balance trays of drinks above their heads. They weave through the crowd with blank faces. The place smells of sweat and sawdust and all the usual things too – piss and shit if you're upwind of the chiottes. At the end of the song the applause is rapturous. Oscar surges towards the stage. 'Sing to me, Lottie,' he screams. 'Sing to me!'

The lady raises her hand to shield her eyes from the glare of the spotlight, recognises the great whale and blows a kiss. 'Sebastian,' she mouths.

'Lottie,' he screams back. 'Crack my calcified heart with your warbles.'

The band takes off with another song and Oscar, led by the witch Boudicca, is shown to a table at the back of the hall.

'What's the little dwarf having, then?' she asks when they have finally sat down.

'Absinthe. Three,' replies Oscar evenly, and then suddenly, 'Look. There's Maurice.'

On the other side of the room a handsome young soldier – in uniform – is talking earnestly to another man.

The boys nudge one another and giggle as if to say wait for it. Here we go.

'Maurice, mon colonel,' shrieks Oscar, but the young man doesn't hear.

'Maurice! Come here immediately and ravish me.' The soldier turns and smiles, excuses himself and prowls through the crowd towards a mesmerised Oscar, finally standing before him at the table. Oscar reaches out, eyes bulging with lust.

'Kiss me, mon colonel, before the battle begins.'

'What battle?'

'The battle for your soul, dear. I already have your body.'
Maurice sits on Oscar's knee, takes the poet's head in his (big)
hands and kisses him deeply. The embrace lasts for nearly a
minute, although it seems like hours. The boys are now laughing
helplessly.

Not so a man at the next table with a garishly made-up
woman on his knee.

'Revolting pig,' he sneers. 'He's like a dog returning to its
own vomit.'

Maurice looks up. Without moving from Oscar's lap he grabs
the man by the lapel. The woman screams. Oscar, delirious, face
covered in slobber, his mouth wide open, is oblivious.

'You insult my friend, Monsieur,' spits Maurice, pulling the
man towards him. 'Apologise immediately or I will kill you.'

'Get your hands off me. Stupid fucking fairy.'

Maurice lunges, knocking over tables and chairs, landing his
forehead hard against the other man's nose. Glasses crash to the
floor. The woman screams again. An overturned wine bottle
glugs from the table. Everyone looks round.

'How could I resist?' asks Oscar to no one – anyone – in
particular. 'The profile of Napoleon, without any of the more
disappointing features.'

Maurice shakes the other man like a rat. The woman is
screaming blue murder. The man is sprawled on the floor, his
nose bleeding, Maurice on top of him, slapping him hard.

'Don't speak to my friend like that, understand? Cunt.'

Standstill. The music comes to a halt. Waiters merge on the
table, followed by Boudicca and her bouncers.

'Him. Out. Take your fucking tart with you.' The bouncers
heave the man from the floor. He begins to complain. 'Shut it,'
commands Boudicca. 'You – soldier. Sit down.' Maurice obeys.
Oscar rises.

'Oh, très chère Boudicca. Milles excuses. A few ruffled plumes. No more.'

'You – shut your fucking face. Look at the damage. Who's paying for all this?'

'I shall,' says Oscar. 'I shall sing for you.'

'Sing?'

'Be quiet, Oscar. Sit down,' says Johnny.

'Yes, I shall sing for you,' he repeats. Boudicca laughs. This man is insane. Oscar puts his hand up to his heart. 'May I?'

She looks at him for a second, affection and irritation in equal measure. Finally, to the crowd, 'What do you say? Sing or pay?'

'SING,' answers the crowd as one.

'What the fuck's going on?' shouts Lottie from the stage.

'Don't ask.'

The boys pick up the table and haul Oscar onto it. He whispers instructions, which are relayed to the band. 'Do you know it?' he mouths. The accordionist nods. A shaky follow spot moves from the stage across the hall, past all the glassy eyes and open mouths, finally settling on Oscar, panting and livid. Maurice starts a round of applause. It is taken up uncertainly. A few whistles and cheers as the music begins.

'The boy I love is up in the gallery,' warbles Oscar to a ripple of laughter.

'The boy I love is looking down at me.

'There he is, can't you see?' He points to Maurice, waggling his finger.

'As merry as a cricket that sings on the lee.'

Boudicca watches with a wry smile, shrugs her shoulders and returns to the door.

The audience sings along with the chorus, to Oscar's delight, and the applause is high-spirited as the song ends. His face is exultant, luminous, streaked with sweat. His eyes are on stalks.

He swoops down into an elaborate bow, loses his balance and crashes from the table to the floor.

Blackout. Brain cells flicker and freeze as his head cracks hard against the ground. Still bowing inside, he flails and mutters as the boys try to move him. They drag him to the pissoir and lean him against the wall. They hold his head and call his name, but he can't hear because inside the applause is deafening, frightening. He must get up or he'll drown in it.

'They are calling for the author,' he says to no one in particular and passes out.

From the darkness, Oscar rises from a deep bow, throwing a villainous shadow against a blood-red curtain encrusted in brocade – bloated, squeezed into evening clothes, a green carnation exploding from his buttonhole, hair neatly curled and oiled over a ringed pouting face, white as a ghost in the limelights. Applause crashes over him and he bows again. His long, thin legs buckle under the weight of his gut as he hauls himself up, hands on knees for support. He surveys his glittering audience complacently. Smoke coils from a gold-tipped cigarette in his gloved hand. It is taking his prayers up to the gods via the dress circle and the balcony, a gilt and cream chest of drawers, open and bursting with puppets in fancy dress, the cream of London society. This moment is the pinnacle of an extraordinary career – a fairground ride that has reached the top of a thin, dipping track on stilts and is now poised for an ecstatic moment before the stomach-turning descent. Does he know, has he an inkling of what is to come as he winks tonight at the Prince of Wales in the royal box and puffs insolently on his cigarette? (Probably not, and yet somewhere inside a bell always rings.) Green carnations are spattered across the audience, faces laughing with the rest – but somehow apart, coiled, watchful, their every gesture scratching the atmosphere with a secret vibration.

They are his disciples, secret practitioners of illegal acts – the love that dare not speak its name – and Oscar is their saint. This play, his latest – *The Importance* – is his capolavoro. He knows it. He holds out his arms for hush – Jesus walking on water – and the audience is silent.

'The actors have given us a charming rendering of a delightful play.' His voice is conversational, high-pitched, lazy, and the audience is mesmerised. Constance, his wife, watches nervously, her hands clenched on her knee. When will the spell end? Who will break it?

'And your appreciation has been most intelligent.' A roar of approval. Glistening teeth, whispering lips, surprised eyes. Mrs Arbuthnot sits between her husband and their friend, all laughing and clapping.

'I congratulate *you* on the success of your performance,' continues Oscar blithely, pointing at the Prince of Wales.

A deafening round of applause. Oscar bathes in it before raising a little finger. 'Which persuades me you think almost as highly of the play as I do myself . . . '

He waits for the next laugh. It doesn't come. Something is happening. The dream is bending. The light flickers and the theatre shrinks, collapses, folds in on itself.

'Wake up, Oscar. Wake up,' pleads a familiar voice. They're all looking down at him or he's looking down at them. It's unclear which.

He opens his eyes and gasps. Now he's somewhere else. But where? A hundred men with dead eyes are watching him. Not a woman in the sight. His heart bangs against his ribs, his neck, under his eyes.

'Order. OR-DER.'

This is it. If only he can remember where he is. He is poised on some edge, ready to drop, high above a hostile crowd, all looking up.

'Guilty!' someone says. Now he knows where he is. The floor falls away and the courtroom erupts.

'Order. OR-DER.' The noise cuts out. He watches the waving arms, the jeering faces, swaying and shouting. At another time this could have been rather exciting, he thinks. But now it's not.

'Wake up. Wake up, Oscar. Lift him.'

For a moment he's conscious. 'Boys,' he whispers.

But then a hammer knocks three times, crashing through his head, dragging him back out. He turns slowly through air as thick as liquid towards the judge sitting on his throne. He could be three yards away or three light years. Oscar thinks, This world is no longer mine. The judge regards him with unconcealed disgust.

'Oscar Wilde.' He spits out the name. 'The crime for which you have been convicted is so bad' – Oscar is powerless to break the gaze. He begins to shake – 'that one has to put a stern restraint upon oneself from describing the sentiments which must rise to the breast of every man of honour who has heard the details of these two terrible trials.'

The judge looks towards the Marquess of Queensberry sitting at the front of the court. The two men nod to each other. Job done. The marquess turns to Oscar with a razor-toothed smile of victory.

'It is no use to address you,' the judge sneers. 'People who can do these things must be dead to all sense of shame. I shall under the circumstances be expected to pass the severest sentence that the law allows. It is in my mind totally inadequate for a case such as this.' He starts to collect his things. Almost casually – as an afterthought – he concludes: 'The sentence of the court is that you shall be imprisoned and kept to hard labour' – he smiles slightly – 'for two years.'

Mayhem in court.

'May I say nothing, my lord?' The judge waves him away.

'May I say nothing?' Two policemen appear beside him, grip him under his arms and shove him down the steps into the bowels of the Old Bailey.

'There's quite a crowd out there,' a policeman says to one of the drivers of the Black Maria. 'Watch your horses.' He whistles and two huge oak doors swing open, and a mob seethes into the yard.

Terror. Oscar can just glimpse the world disappearing through the small grate in the back of the van.

On the steps of the Old Bailey, Lord Queensberry clasps his hands above his head – a victorious boxer on the shoulders of an exultant crowd. He is shrieking something about the fathers of England. Loose women dance around on the street. Newsboys wave papers. 'Oscar Wilde guilty'. Fists bang on the sides of the carriage as finally it breaks free of the crowd.

'It is no use to address you.' The judge's voice rings in his head.

'People who can do these things must be dead to all sense of shame.'

Yes, I am dead. But the shame is yours, he thinks as he is stripped of his clothes by two prison warders in a white-tiled room smelling of ammonia. 'Stand over there against the wall.' They give him a bar of evil-smelling soap.

They begin to unwind two obscene hoses attached to huge taps, which they turn, and the flaccid canvas tubes start to bulge. They take aim. The jets of ice-cold water wind him, pinning him to the wall.

'Well, wash yourself, you great pansy,' one of them says and the other laughs.

'And inside your pussy.' More laughter. 'Right inside.' They aim the jet into his arse. It seems to go on for ever but at last it stops and now he is standing naked, shivering uncontrollably, while the men write their reports. Finally, one of them gives him a towel and clothes – prison overalls. There's no time to think, otherwise he would be crying. He dries himself and dresses. The clothes feel rough against his skin.

'Sit,' one of them orders. 'Don't blub, for God's sake.'

The other cuts his hair. It falls in clumps on the concrete floor. When it has been cut short the other man attacks his head with a pair of shears.

He is escorted to his cell, the colour of custard with a wooden board and a blanket – no pillow – just a bucket in the corner and a barred window high above.

The door booms shut. Locks turn. One. Two. Three. He sits on the board, head in his hands. 'Oh Christ. What have I done?'

A small peephole opens in the thick metal door and an eye peers through it and watches for some time as Oscar sits motionless.

'Monsieur Melmoth.' A voice comes through thick darkness, throbbing and grainy. 'Monsieur Melmoth.' He opens his eyes.

Three men are leaning over him, blurred faces, shining eyes. If only he could concentrate, he would see them. He strains, forcing blood to the optic nerve and a room appears through the mist. His room. 'Dupoirier? Is that you?' He recognises the owner of the Alsace hotel – far away – and he makes for him with a superhuman effort, swimming up from the bottom of the bad dream. 'I was in prison again,' he says now as the familiar things return – his bed, his books on the table. Tears of relief pour from his eyes. He looks from one man to the other. 'Dr Tucker! What's going on? I thought I was . . . ' He trails off.

'You had a bad fall, Mr Melmoth. We have bandaged your ear.'

He feels for his head. Where is it? His hands wave in the air and the third face smiles.

'Can't you find your own head, Oscar?'

'Robbie? I can't see you. Come closer.'

Robbie Ross kisses Oscar on the cheek.

'My lonely rider of the apocalypse. You took me into exile, dear boy. Where will you take me now?' He struggles to get up.

'I really don't . . . '

'Ireland, you say?' Oscar gasps, still on the high seas. 'What ship?'

Robbie strokes his hair.

'No ships, Oscar. I have brought your allowance.' Money focuses the mind wonderfully and now Oscar climbs aboard the real world and the dream recedes.

'Good. I have been dinnerless.' He turns his head to the wall. The flowers on it shimmer and coil.

'Do you have a cigarette for me, dear?'

Obediently Robbie produces one, puts it in Oscar's mouth and lights it. Oscar draws deeply.

'I am in mortal combat with this wallpaper, Robbie. One of us has to go.'

'Apparently you made a pretty good scene last night.'

Oscar regards his friend for a long moment before continuing, a shadow of irritation clouding his face.

'It is more or less impossible to make good scenes in circumstances as reduced as mine. But I believe I did my best. Ah Robbie, charity, please. My brain is a furnace, my throat a lime kiln, my mind a coil of angry adders. Last night I dreamt I was supping with the dead.'

'You must have been the life and soul of the party.' Robbie is not cowed by Oscar. Not any more. Neither is Dr Tucker from the embassy. He is an old man who knows the score. He knows who Oscar is but addresses him as Mr Melmoth. Now he prepares an injection – a huge syringe with a thick needle produced from a black travelling bag lying open on the bed. He rolls up the sleeve of Oscar's nightshirt and searches the chubby arm for a submerged vein.

'What is that?' asks Oscar sharply.

'Morphine,' replies the doctor.

'Morphine is mere seltzer to me now,' he snaps – shouts almost – but the doctor is unruffled, tapping Oscar's vein into life, inserting the needle into it, looking through half-lensed spectacles.

'But good Dr Tucker will only give me ether, or chloral on holidays of obligation. I have had a very bad time lately, and for two days not a penny in my pocket, so had to wander about, filled with wild longings, trapped in the circle of the boulevards, one of the worst in the inferno.'

Dr Tucker pumps the clear liquid from the syringe, slowly, like a lover almost, and Oscar watches him with a strange mixture of feelings as his eyes – on stalks with indignation and longing – grow heavy-lidded and his face is suddenly slack. He looks back to Robbie – now surrounded in radiance. 'Why does one run towards ruin? Why does it hold such a fascination?'

A SHORT FILM

'Sort Me Out Before We Go~Go'

The son of a friend was studying at the London Film School to become a director. He asked me if I could think of an idea for a ten-minute short. One set. Three actors. A few extras.

Someone had told me this story. I thought it would be ideal. 'Too racy,' he said, instead making a film about an old man waiting for an ambulance to arrive. At least he offered me the part.

'Fucking schlemiel,' she hissed, crashing into the ladies' lavatory at the Perkins Tea Room. 'Geez, does life turn on a dime, or what?' She rummaged in her bag and then, with a sudden strangled scream, tipped the contents into the sink.

'One moment you are young. The next you are . . . ' She found an elusive lipstick and applied it with shaking hands to quivering lips. 'NOT.' Hot tears teetered inside her eyelids. 'NO,' she commanded the mirror as she brushed her hair. 'No. No. No.' She leant in closer, scrutinising her face in the glass. 'No deeper wrinkles yet.' And yet. There was nothing gradual about ageing. It all happened in a second. One moment you were a tree covered in beautiful foliage. The next moment a tornado passed and bang – you were a tangle of naked branches with one leaf fluttering on. Death in a tea room.

This is what happened.

When anyone expressed surprise that Renata Goodman Orlov was a Russian countess she told them that it was actually a step down since she had been a Jewish princess for a long time previously. Born in Westchester, New York, her father was that legendary divorce lawyer Mort Goodman, a name that threw dread into the hearts of the unfaithful husbandry of Yonkers. From the Bronx all the way to Far Hills he was a renowned killer. Mort had your ass if you had the cash. No expense was spared in Renata's education and, keenly intelligent, she studied law at

Harvard and came away with a first-class degree. She had been a large baby, a tubby girl, and now in her gown and mortar board at graduation she was a wonderful shape and size. While she hated the word fat – 'no glamour' – she loved to be called buxom or – 'my favourite' – pulpeuse. She was thrilled when a friend called her the Mama Cass of Westchester. In short, she was full of confidence and while not a beauty she had tremendous allure and knew it. She had that trick of giving attention at a hundred per cent and the scrutiny of her intelligent, nut-brown eyes made you feel that you alone existed. She had lush, kissable lips that quivered with humour and a substantial bosom displayed in a provocative and gravity-defying décolleté, rain or shine. She adored being looked at. Long, thick honey-coloured hair fell about her neck and shoulders, coming to rest in snakes on the white marble shelf of her perfumed breast. She adored men and was adored by them. She challenged them in a way that was not threatening, with her eyes, her conversation, her independence. Equally, she was a girl's girl.

She moved to England after college, aged twenty-three, and fell in love with the declining world of the British upper classes, their country houses and particularly their shooting weekends. She was an excellent shot and loved going out with the men, dressed in a tweed cape and a kind of Robin Hood hat. She acquired a pair of Purdey guns and was soon to be seen at all the best houses, from Bowhill to Badminton, holding forth on a shooting stick. She dressed well and sensibly, although as time went on she became a slight parody of herself. Who doesn't? Somebody gave her a monocle and she developed a taste for cigars. She wore wonderful jewellery, knots of pearls and bracelets of jingling charms. She knew about art, wine, books and horses. In short, she was a proud American Jewess with a penchant for posh totty. Her voice was melodious, soothing, amused. She called herself 'Renaada'. English additions had

been discreetly welded to her lazily delivered American brogue.
Everyone thought she would make a stunning match, but she
finally settled on the rather exhausted remains of White Russia,
a bony man with receding blond hair called Mike Orlov. Why?
Nobody knew. He was nice, intelligent, older, moneyed up to
a point, but it was generally felt that she was throwing herself
away when she could have had anyone.

'Only as lovers,' she corrected friends who voiced this view.
'None of them would have married me. Renaada Devonshire?
Renaada Westminster? Please.' She was realistic.

The Russian prince did marry her. In great tumbledown style
at the Russian church in Chiswick. A strange, pickled crowd of
shabby Russian nobles, their slightly less shabby English coun-
terparts and le tout Westchester made for a singular experience.
A choir sang dirges, wonky crowns were held over the couple's
heads and the priest's voice echoed across time. For a moment
she was in imperial Russia but as she stepped out of the church
she was back under the flyover. They had one child and divorced
six years later.

This was all long ago, she reflected, sitting at a small table in
the Perkins Tea Room at four thirty, one winter afternoon in the
leafy market town of Rothman, against which leaned a leading
public school, where at this moment her son was playing rugby.
She had long ago stopped feigning interest in sport. 'You don't
mind, sweetie, do you? I just hate standing around in the mud.
It's not very Renaada.' Now they had reached an arrangement.
She happily had tea while he played. She would take him out
for dinner later, after a rest at the hotel on the high street and
maybe a visit to the hairdressers for a manicure.

Today, she was a glossy forty-three, in autumn colours, still majestic, still low-cut, still turning heads. She had been faithful to her
husband until the day of her divorce and after that she started to
play the field. 'Then they all started looking like the same person

and I got tired of the person,' she said to herself as she poured the tea. Sex was for the young, and while she still loved to turn a head, she could no longer be bothered to give it, even though she had been a mistress of the art. 'Keep breathing. That's the secret,' she told the younger girls. Nowadays she adored sleeping.

Along with the pot of tea in front of her lay her hands, stretched over the cloth, manicured, moisturised and ringed. She was observing them, stretching her fingers out like a cat and scratching at the starched linen with her nails, when she became aware that she was being watched. She looked up and, standing across the room, was a tall, rugged man in jeans and a sheepskin jacket. He had thick black hair, a single black eyebrow and large black eyes. His ivory skin was stippled – he hadn't shaved – and when he smiled a gold tooth flashed in the light.

The Heathcliff of Wiltshire, thought Renata to herself, and she modestly smiled back. She was used to attention and shifted slightly, arranging her various drapes and shapes while putting the tea things in order. Her hair fell sweetly over her face as she poured and the man laughed. This time she shot him her Lady Diana, a swooping look from under her brow over a sphinx-like smile.

It worked a treat. The man walked across the room and sat down at the next table, looking at her all the time. Impertinent, she thought, but very attractive if one was in the market for a country farmer. She ordered a boiled egg from the waitress and pulled a magazine from her bag. *The Economist.* She put on her glasses and began to read. She could feel him undressing her with his eyes and she swam in the attention, glancing up occasionally as she turned a page or pretended to look towards heaven for the answer to some economic problem posed by the magazine. Her egg arrived and the man beckoned to the waitress, who seemed to know but not necessarily like him.

'I'll have what she's having,' said the man in a West Country accent that thrilled Renata into a faint flush of colour across her cheeks. All four of them.

'There should be a law against it,' was all the waitress replied.

'A law against having an egg? What a cruel world that would be.' He laughed. Renata looked up and he winked. 'Enjoying it?'

'Very much,' she replied.

The waitress looked aghast and stomped off.

'You seem to have upset our waitress,' remarked Renata with a twinkle.

'Don't worry about her. She's just jealous. We had a thing a while back. Didn't work out.'

Renata smiled graciously and went back to her magazine. The man kept watch, black eyes boring like drills. Finally, more amused than aghast, she looked up. 'Are you all right?'

'I'm more than all right,' the man replied. 'I've got a massive hard-on just from looking at your tits.'

Well. This was slightly more than she had bargained for. But then again, she was very much accustomed to weathering the storms of male lust relating to her darlings. So, in the electric pause engendered by this unusual declaration, she ran through a selection of reactions, deciding on an enigmatic smile (*Mona Lisa*), and her chest heaved slightly as she infused it with an extra blush. She had discovered she could manufacture these changes, like a chameleon, and she knew it drove men wild. Sure enough: 'Oh, my sweet lord.' The man's eyes were rolling. 'Can I just say something?'

'Of course.'

'I really want to fuck you.'

'How wonderful. But look. One thing you should know about me. Right off the bat. I hate all those words.'

'Words?'

'Yeah. Dirty words. Fuck. Tits. Hard-on. They mean nothing to me. They leave nothing to the imagination.'

'Oh, I really don't agree. I think they are the pepper and salt on the meat and two veg,' parried the young buck. 'Is that better? My meat and two veg are coming to the boil.'

'Let me put them in the microwave. What manners. We haven't even been introduced and we're already talking menus! Perhaps you should come and have your boiled egg over here and we can discuss it.' She had a couple of hours to spare and there was nothing she enjoyed more than watching from above the magnetic pull of her darlings. They had been creamed and powdered, buffed and perfumed back at the hotel and were really looking their best.

'I can't get up,' the man said.

'Why ever not? I never heard such nonsense.'

He stood, and sure enough his cock was straining against his jeans.

Renata put on her monocle. Not bad. 'Can't you fold it up and get over here?' Her breath quickened. Her monocle misted up. She checked her watch while he limped over, covering his groin with his hands. They both giggled.

No sooner had he sat down than the waitress appeared and slammed a plate down in front of him. 'One boiled egg,' she snarled.

'Put it on my bill,' breezed Renata, with an elegant and dismissive wave that made her charms jangle.

'Don't worry, I will,' replied the young lady.

'What a very unpleasant person,' said Renata, looking at the departing rear of the angry waitress.

'Don't mind her. Let's talk about us.'

'Very well. Where shall we start?'

'In bed.'

'Slow down, soldier. I don't even know your name.'

'What's in a name?' he sniggered and reached for her hand under the table.

She removed it. This was getting fun. She wriggled a little in her seat and felt that familiar surge run through her body. 'Well? What do they call you? Down on the farm.'

'Ridian.'

'Ritalin?'

'No. Ridian.'

'I'm kidding. I love that name. I'm Renaada. What brings you to the Perkins Tea Room?'

'I saw you in the window. What are *you* doing in the Perkins Tea Room?'

'I am visiting my son.'

'You have a son?'

'Come on.'

'OK.'

They were looking into one another's eyes. The chemistry was electric. An old couple tottered across the room on sticks and frames. 'Young love,' the man said to his wife, and she sighed.

'Not so young,' laughed Renata. She had no hang-ups about her age. His, on the other hand ...

'How old are you?'

'Twenty-three.'

'And what do you do?'

'I like to fuck.'

'Those words again,' warned Renata.

'I like to make love. That better?'

'Much. Apart from that?'

'I'm a farmer.'

'Arable?'

'Pigs.'

'Do you live nearby?' she asked.

'Yeah.' A pregnant silence.

'Nice.'

'How? Nice?'

'It's a nice town. Rothman is a nice town.'

'For a pig. Let's go back to my place and—'

'What kind of girl do you think I am, exactly?' she asked, knowing he knew the answer.

'I think you are *exactly* my kind of girl.'

And so it went on. They finished their eggs. Ate some toast. The temperature kept rising. The air got close. Renata fanned her darlings with the menu. Bad move. It was a heavy laminated thing of many pages and didn't have quite the desired effect, flapping over the hills like an old vulture, making a faintly obscene noise. She asked for the bill. Luckily another waitress arrived with it.

'How nearby is nearby?' she asked in as casual a voice as was possible.

'Two minutes. In five minutes, I could be inside you.'

'Rush, rush, rush. There are many stops before penetration.' She ran her hands down the sides of her body, squeezing the darlings into a deeper and more mouth-watering valley.

Ridian went pale and swallowed hard. He had a sexy Adam's apple. 'Oh yeah,' was all he could say. He got up and edged past her. The fly of his jeans was within inches of her face. She could almost feel herself sucking him off. Behind her now, the room spinning, he pulled her chair back and she got up.

'Quite the gentleman,' she said, tottering slightly, clawing at his taut body with her long beige fingernails. 'Let's go.'

'One thing,' he said with a dazzling smile. 'Could you sort me out before we go?'

She turned, suddenly aware of her heartbeat. 'Sort you out?'

'Yeah. It's a hundred and fifty.'

'A hundred and fifty what?'

'Quid.' He looked at her, still the dazzling smile. She looked back. God knows what look she had on her face. Midnight. Then dawn. Cold and grey. Old age.

'You mean I have to pay you?' Now she went red all over. Beetroot.

'If you don't mind.'

'I do mind. I mind very much.' Was all she could think of to say. She looked at her watch. Another silence. She wanted to scream, suddenly. No point. The nasty waitress was spying on them through the hatch from the kitchen.

He had no shame, just that shit-eating grin.

'I'm going to the restroom. I'll say goodbye here. Goodbye.' She moved off before he had a chance to reply.

In front of the mirror, she calmed herself. Carefully re-lined her eyes, glossed her lips and brushed her hair. She sprayed Evian on her face, Mitsouko on her darlings and stood back to admire the effect. 'Creamy. If I say so myself.' She was beginning to feel a little better about life. 'Don't forget you are a very intriguing woman after all.' She wagged a finger at her reflection and sallied forth from the loo. Life did indeed turn on a dime. From one side to another and back again.

He was still standing where she had left him, by the entrance of the tea room. Set in stone, the Wessex farmer, puffed up for action. It pleased her.

'You still here?' she laughed carefully, hands on hips, hair falling over her eyes, Marilyn lips. He didn't reply. Just looked. Deep, sultry, intimate. She giggled again. He smiled knowingly and winked. Nobody moved a muscle. A Rothman stand-off.

'Is there a cash machine nearby?'

They left the Perkins Tea Room arm in arm, observed by the angry waitress, herself observed by her colleague. 'Don't let him get to you,' the colleague suggested.

'Get to me!' snarled the angry waitress, wheeling on her friend. 'Whose idea was it to scout the school for clients? I told him: there's a lot of money in those rich bitches. With my brains and your cock we could make a killing. And look. Not even a fucking tip.'

CUDDLES AND ASSOCIATES

The chimes ring out across the floor. A thousand hungry faces look up at another ticker tape dusk on Wall Street. A strange group clusters round the bell tonight, next to the mayor and some other dignitary – the head of the stock exchange, maybe. A princess from somewhere, in impenetrable shades and immaculate hijab, tall and severe; a faded movie star, rugged and pockmarked by scandal, but still turning heads; an ageless lawyer, small and perfectly preserved with a whirl of white hair; and a strange English couple, the worse for wear, the better for the day's news. This unlikely quintet has just floated their company on the stock exchange and the share price is going through the roof. This evening, as the bell tolls again, another American fortune has appeared in the sky. A new cluster of stars, whipped up from nothing, blink shyly in the firmament. It's called Cuddles and Associates – a company that deals in fertilisation. In sperm, eggs and wombs. In buying and selling. Cuddles has offices around the world, from Hong Kong to Hollywood. Tonight, they have fertilised a cool six hundred million dollars. Everything has paid off spectacularly, beyond their wildest dreams. A film is about to be made about their story, their struggle, the scandal. Once they were pariahs. Now they have taken their place at the apex of the American power structure. The tables have turned. Twenty-four years ago, on the other hand . . .

*

Harry Dent arrived in Hollywood on a prayer and a whisper in the spring of 1983. The whisper was a small part in a British miniseries, perhaps not enough for him to make a sufficient impact, a big enough splash for the prayer to be answered. True, he was good-looking, in that floppy, collapsed way the English endlessly spawned in those days. But he was shy and uncertain – a fatal combination in Hollywood. On the other hand, he was born with a silver spoon in his mouth and fully assumed that he would grow up to acquire a whole canteen of cutlery. (His mouth was certainly big enough.) Unsurprisingly, his dream of being discovered and catapulted to stardom had so far not been realised. But he had achieved a pint-sized manager called Sadie White, who had an office off La Cienega, and she had perhaps landed him a job. A B-movie in which he might play the hero. For the villain, 'they wanted Laurence Olivier,' explained Sadie.

'Oh wonderful!'

'Don't jump the gun. I said they *wanted* Laurence Olivier. They would have *accepted* Christopher Plummer. But they got Roddy McDowall. You've got an STV situation.'

'STV? Is that a disease?' He was shy but he could be funny.

'Yeah. It's a killer. Straight To Video, babe.' Sadie only liked it when she was telling the jokes.

The role was a young man in love with a robot. The film was called *Terry Two Million*. One audition had led to another and then to a screen test and then to another. Now it was between him and another young hopeful. In short, he was living the dream. Competitive juices drooled from his lips. He made friends with the other young actor in acting class and neatly disembowelled him to everyone as soon as his back was turned. For a shy boy, Harry also had a vicious streak.

He lived on the first-floor landing of a ramshackle house at the west end of Hollywood Boulevard, just before Laurel Canyon, where that formidable artery pumped the diseased blood from the old 'silent' worlds of Silver Lake, Echo Park and Los Feliz towards Beverly Hills, the Palisades and the sea. (The names are romantic, the places less so.)

At the block on which the house was situated, the boulevard turned from a four-lane concrete highway into a weaving capillary clinging to the crumbling cliffs above Sunset.

The house was a colonial clapboard galleon that creaked and shivered as the traffic rolled by or the front door slammed. Big and ramshackle, with paper-thin walls and a linoleum roof, it was – according to a young actress who lived in an apartment at the back of the house – haunted by a bitchy actress from the silent days.

The place was filled with young aspirants, actors and directors, none of them silent. Couples wrote scripts in the garage. Actresses rehearsed scenes for class with their partners. Everyone banged down the stairs in the morning while Harry lay on his landing bed like the family dog. The front door slammed and slammed again as they all made for the 8.30 meeting of the West Hollywood chapter of Alcoholics Anonymous. Hollywood was still living in the collective hangover of the heady seventies and, apart from anything else, it was the most efficient way to meet directors. Whether or not everyone in the house actually *was* an alcoholic or a drug addict was something Harry often wondered about. They certainly didn't look like the junkies back home. On top of that, a good description of a person's latest antics at a crack den could earn them anything from a job at a studio to a role in a pilot. Such was the air of camaraderie in AA. It was the only place in that cruel town where somebody might offer you a straw to clutch at.

Harry's friend in the house was in fact its owner, a young director called Tristan Hodge. Tristan was born in the business – he was the son of the legendary producer Harry

Hodge – and he had money. He came out of the womb and said 'Action!' He had long dark hair and looked at you from somewhere inside its fringe. He was funny and generous and paid for everyone. He had made friends with Harry at a strange crammer for public school dropouts in South Kensington. In Hollywood, the two friends drank on resolutely while the rest of the household ground through their twelve steps, chain smoking and breaking down, in meetings and acting classes, in the kitchen and on the loo. It was a world with all the dials turned up. To escape this whirlpool of raw emotion Tristan and Harry went out to dinner every night at a small restaurant on the corner of Sunset and Havenhurst called Oscar's, next to a parking lot that used to be the Garden of Allah, that famous apartment building between the wars where – among others – Scott Fitzgerald famously failed, another Christ nailed to a palm tree. Oscar's was owned by an English eccentric called Arnold Pickford, a marooned hippy who had arrived in LA during the late sixties. By the eighties he had largely grown over himself and had turned the colour and shape of a beetroot. He cooked and served shepherd's pie and toad in the hole to a perplexed local clientele and the restaurant was largely fre- quented by down-and-outs from the old country peppered with a few showbusiness freaks who were charmed by Arni's running commentary through the hatch from the kitchen, where he presided like the devil in a haze of bubbling pots. The clientele was encouraged to join in, and the repartee could be lively. Once, a lady of a certain age, the wife of a famous producer from the fifties, sent a lobster back to the kitchen, only to be attacked by Arnold waving the offending crustacean – 'Your husband hasn't had a hit since *A Tiger in Spring* and you can put this lobster up your fucking cunt.' The lady gave as good as she got: 'Why thank you, Arnold. Those claws will make more of an impression than my husband's dick. Huh, Marty?'

The husband, deaf to the world, politely agreed and the whole restaurant applauded.

Tristan and Harry sat at their usual table in the corner. Arni watched them fondly as they plotted and planned. It felt romantic and important to sit there night after night, comfortably sloshed, and feel that the future could still happen. They were both young. They both had fabulous ideas. Tristan had serious money. Harry meanwhile had been left ten thousand pounds by a great-aunt, but that was beginning to run dry when his friend Dorinda cut to the chase and suggested he apply for a job in the mail room at the William Morris Agency. Dorinda was an actress, a recovering junkie, and the daughter of an English lord, who had come over to LA to clean up. In terms of addiction she was the real thing. One night she relapsed and nearly burnt the house down with a blowtorch, freebasing in her room.

'They need someone.' She was a professional best friend and busybody. One of her nearest and dearest was a reptilian publicist called Clive Rich, who fed her the news from the stables and studs of Hollywood. 'You might make it and become an agent,' she drawled.

'But I'm an actor. I don't want to be an agent.'

'Can I tell you something, Harry?' She was very pretty, by the way, with slightly vacant eyes because of the drugs. She combined this with a patronising manner which had earned her the name Mother Superior.

'Of course, Dorinda. What is it?'

'Well, I've been watching you in class and you act like you've got a candlestick stuck up your arse.' She cocked her head to one side and took a thoughtful drag on her cigarette.

'Hang on a minute. That's not very nice.'

'Well, someone's got to tell you the truth, darling. Otherwise, you could waste your life never being discovered, which would be hell.'

'Thanks. But look here: I'm up for a film called *Terry Two Million*. I'm down to the last two. Plus, I got wonderful reviews in *Princess Polly*. It was called a breakout performance.'

'Breakout of what? Chicken pox? Jail? All I'm saying is – think about it. Clive's rully amazing. He likes you.'

'But I'm not gay.'

'Rully?' She wasn't convinced. She stubbed out her cigarette and surveyed Harry through the smoke. 'It's a job. Not a blow job. In the mail room. You don't have to go down on all fours.'

'But why Clive?'

'Clive is rully plugged in. He knows everyone.'

'In the mail room at William Morris?'

'Darling, it's the usual thing. He knows someone who knows someone who knows someone who danced with the Prince of Wales. How the fuck should I know? I just do. Is that the time? I'm meeting my sponsor in Santa Monica.'

Dorinda's sponsor was the director Dick Dupré.

'Can't you get me an interview with *him*? Now that would help.'

'I'm already trying to get myself a meeting with him, darling. He's casting the new *Superman* film.'

'But you *are* meeting him. In Santa Monica.'

'Yes, but as an addict. I can't just suddenly put on my actress hat.'

'Yes. The shock may be too much.'

Harry spent all that morning in bed, looking gloomily from under a filthy duvet at the pairs of legs running past his bed from various directions in the house. All roads converged on his landing nook. Some tiptoed by, their breathless girly voices whispering 'hey', then running, tumbling down the stairs with shrieks and giggles followed by the slamming of the front door and the shaking of the whole termite-ridden matchstick construction.

That night the Garden of Allah seemed far away, and Harry felt that he too was buried in concrete.

'Dorinda said I should go and work in the mail room at William Morris.'

'I think you should do it,' Tristan said. 'You don't even have a decent agent. You've been here for six months. What are you going to do?'

'Wait a minute. Isn't that Matt Dean?' A glossy-looking stud 'appeared' at the door of the restaurant. A thin girl in a miniskirt clung to him. Arni swirled round the star like a spinning planet and the whole constellation was heading straight towards Tristan and Harry. The restaurant collectively paused for a beat – looked gratefully at them as they passed. It was the essential part of the deal for everyone in that crazy town. The household gods came down to earth from time to time. Everyone felt vindicated as a result. But not Harry. He just felt jealous.

'The mail room. Why can't I be Matt Dean?'

'His latest film's a stinker, apparently, and he just got fired from that new Zemeckis picture. Three weeks in. So careful what you wish for. He might end up in the mail room.'

Whatever was going on, the star didn't look overly concerned as he laughed and flirted with the geeky girl. Impossible glamour. So near and yet . . .

'Hey, Tristan. My man.' The faces of the whole restaurant turned as one to scrutinise the mortal chosen by God. Tristan stood up.

'Matt. How are you? Geena! This is my friend Harry.'

Harry now stood as well. Arni beamed, rubbing his hands. Tristan and Matt Dean hugged and Harry bobbed up and down. Geena looked at the two English men with barely disguised revulsion.

'How's your dad? How's our picture?' asked the actor.

'He's not speaking to me at the moment, so I don't know.'

'Straight to video I heard.'

'Really? Surely not.'

'Yeah. They're throwing the premiere at Blockbuster. That's what those assholes at William Morris are saying.'

'William Morris?' slipped from Harry's mouth.

'Yeah. You with them?' Matt Dean's eyes briefly focused on Harry.

'I'm thinking about it.'

Puzzled looks.

'Harry is an actor,' Tristan said. 'Did you see *Princess Polly*? He was Lord Botton-Leigh.'

'Lord Bottomy,' sneered Geena. 'Sounds like a great role.'

'It was.'

'Well, don't go with Jacky Battiato,' said Matt. 'He's full of shit.' The audience was over and the couple moved on to a nearby table. 'Catch you later, Tristan. Say hi to your dad.'

Two days later Harry found himself sitting in a booth at Schwab's, waiting for Clive Rich to appear. He thought gloomily of all the actresses who had been discovered sitting at the long bar of the famous drugstore. It had been the destiny he had imagined for himself. To be swept off his feet by a passing producer. In the end he would only be discovered by the mail room. He sighed heavily.

'Well. What about you?' growled Clive as he slid into the booth. Harry had instantly disliked this lizard when he had met him up at the house with Dorinda. He was a poser. 'Takes one to know one,' whipped Dorinda, 'and anyway, he can get you a job'.

With this modified view, which was the first step towards fitting in, biting the bullet, eating it – submerging all personal feelings under an impenetrable twitter of birdsong – have a nice day – you're very welcome – go for Shelley – copy that – way to go – the court vernacular of Los Angeles, he'd put his best foot forward and arrived in good time, fifteen minutes early. One was easily fooled by the laconic tone and look of professional LA. In fact, there was an almost Japanese set of protocols concerning etiquette. This morning, Harry moved from haughty distaste to fawning fascination in one easy step. He was a slut. The finger of fate was firmly inside his arsehole now.

'Great to see you, Clive.'

Clive growled back in a strange mid-Atlantic brogue and got straight down to business.

'Give me one good reason why they should hire you.'

'Je parle un peu français. Did Dorinda tell you?'

'Great news. You won't need it in the mail room.'

'What will I need?'

'Just a natural ability to do whatever is asked. No questions. No complaining.'

Harry loved complaining but just fixed Clive with a dazzling smile. 'Sure. I hate whiners. What are the hours?'

'All hours. If you want to get on. Do you want to get on?' Clive's reptilian hand landed briefly on Harry's knee. Harry neatly converted a gasp into an assertive reply.

'I want to be an agent,' he declared, although nothing could have been further from the truth.

'Good boy. That's the kind of answer they'll be looking for. I'm going to call my friend Peeps Bellevue – he's the head of human resources over there at Morris and he will fix you up.'

Clive moved in closer and slid his arm over Harry's shoulder. 'I'm a photographer in my spare time. I'd love to take your picture.'

'Great.'

Clive's house clung to the edge of a crumbling hill, high above Laurel Canyon, a slide area where the road petered out into a dirt track. Far below you could see the traffic snake down Laurel Canyon. The house was a large room, really – it had been the

studio of a famous costumier – with a staircase up one side to
a kind of minstrel's gallery with doors to bedrooms which led
out onto a higher garden surrounded by banana trees and palms.
It could have been the set for a play. The whole place rustled
pleasantly in the Santa Ana wind, and it was there that Harry
made his first and greatest Hollywood error. Sitting cross-legged
on a large divan, Clive lazily rolled a joint and the two smoked
it before the session. He was an adroit craftsman, fixing Harry
with two jaundiced eyes as his pointed tongue, glistening with
saliva, carefully licked the edge of the rolling paper and his
fingers crawled over the creation, rolling, tightening, talking all
the time as the scented breeze gusted through the open windows. Harry, who compared everything to a film, felt thrilled
to be living a kind of Antonioni *Blow-Up* moment, arching and
pouting as he posed. He was high on the attention as much as
the weed – some validation at last – and he could tell that Clive
wanted him. The Carpenters played on the stereo and Harry
briefly became a star, slithering down the wall when Clive
suggested they do some pictures in the steam room. A pair
of satin running shorts casually appeared and Clive put down
the camera and watched Harry tumble into them, buttocks
and balls on display. The atmosphere was suddenly charged as
the steam hissed and the camera snapped. Harry rubbed his
slippery skin with his hands, and he could see Clive's hard-on
inside his trousers. It was quite substantial. A switch was suddenly flicked and the two men lunged at each other. Pretty soon
Harry was standing in the billowing steam and a naked Clive
was sucking him off. Orgasm was achieved in about a minute
and post-coital regret about a second later. Harry fell over himself trying to get into his clothes while Clive sat nude on the
divan in the failing light, watching and smiling and rolling as the
palm trees scratched against the house like the undead. Harry
hurried home and buried the experience, going straight out to

dinner and getting spectacularly drunk. Clive, meanwhile, got on the telephone to everyone he knew to report the event to the world at large.

News travels light on that hot, dry Santa Ana wind. Visiting Sadie White in her office a couple of days later, she came straight to the point.

'Did you get it on with Clive Rich during a photo shoot?'

'No.' Sweat suddenly pricked all over his chest. 'What do you mean?'

'Nothing. He said he schtupped you.'

'Well he didn't. I'm not gay.'

Somewhere a cock crowed three times.

'Good. 'Cos gay is not the look they want at the studios right now. The bodies are piling up on Santa Monica Boulevard. You know that, don't you?'

'Right,' said Harry lamely, inwardly vowing to kill Clive when he met him again.

At coffee with Dorinda and some of the girls later that day they were all laughing at two dogs sniffing each other's bottoms on the sidewalk.

'Is that what Clive did to you?' whispered Dorinda.

'What are you on about?' was all Harry could think of to say.

'The latest news on the jungle drums. That's all, sweetie.'

'Tell your friend to stop spreading vicious rumours about me.'

'It wasn't a very good idea to choose a publicist as your first Hollywood liaison, was it?'

'There is no liaison. I did some pictures up at his house. That's *all*.'

'Liaison very dangereuse, I'd say. Anyway, that's what Clive says. He says you were HOT chilli.'

Harry looked down the street for a means of escape. There

was a big newspaper stand on the other side of the road. He got up and walked over to it and studiously examined a magazine. His heart was racing. He knew he was blushing. Glancing back, he saw the whole table watching and giggling.

Bad news comes in threes. The next day he had an appointment at Paramount for his second screen test for *Terry Two Million*. Thoroughly coached by a red-headed boy star who lived in an apartment over Tristan's garage, his American accent had been pronounced perfect. He dressed carefully that morning. Harry's physique resembled a wine bottle, all neck and sloping shoulders. He had carefully camouflaged this defect to give himself a more American silhouette. (Shoulder pads.) He was quite clever at this, actually. Possibly cleverer than he was as a performer.

He drove onto the lot, feeling momentous. Could this be the beginning of a long relationship, he thought as he spelt out his name to the doorman. He parked and walked through the lanes of biscuit-coloured offices and sound stages. The whole place hummed with the sound of air conditioners. Golf buggies purred round corners carrying producers and their secretaries. A kind of train pulled two carriages of Roman soldiers towards the wide-open doors of a sound stage. Inside, a slice of the Colosseum glowed in the middle of the vast dark space. Bells and red lights blinked and rang. The big doors clanged shut.

Eventually he arrived at a small Nissen hut tucked away at the back of the lot, beyond it a barbed wire fence and a scrubby hill. Inside he was welcomed by the casting director's assistant and placed in a tiny dressing room. The name of the last occupant was written on the door – another never-known name that someone had forgotten to change. He sat for a few minutes in the small, airless cell. A curtain flapped against an open window. He felt suddenly lonely, unsure, as if he was trespassing. He longed to be home, or at least somewhere familiar. A knock on the door made him jump.

'Time for a bit of maquillage,' said the casting director's assistant.

'Carrie [the casting agent] can't be here today. But she says good luck. I'm MarGO, by the way.'

Two large ladies presided over a long, thin make-up room. They were too big for it, like Alice in Wonderland. Down one side, dressing tables were laid out with the tricks of the trade. Tinctures and powders and sprays, all looking good enough to eat under mirrors surrounded by the obligatory naked lightbulbs. Strange electric chairs faced them, each guarded by one of these gorgons who were chewing the cud, their voices and manners borrowed from cartoons, childish inflections, exaggerated reactions, gapes and grimaces, *Clockwork Orange* eyes and hands on hips. They waggled their fingers like backing singers.

'I heard from Liza.' Gasp.

'You did?' Gape.

'I did.' Wink.

'Oh yeah. How's it goin' up there?'

'Pretty much as we predicted. He's insane.'

'I coulda told her that. Sit down, young man.'

He sat in the chair and the large lady threw a bib around him, like a matador. Then she leant down and looked at his face through the mirror.

'I am Susan,' she said, as though talking to a child. 'I'm going to be doing our make-up. I always bring good luck. I can tell right now. You're gonna get the part. But your skin is dry.'

'She says that to all the boys,' snipped her friend, who was working on a young girl with a blond ponytail. 'This is Zena Dare. She is testing for the role of Terry.'

'Hey,' croaked Zena. 'You wanna run lines?'

'Sure.' Harry was going for the method approach. American

all the way. Zena was in fact vaguely famous already. She'd been in another B-movie hit. Harry was impressed. Testing with Zena Dare!

They looked at each other in the mirrors and started.

'Honey?' he said.

'(Now you give me the flowers.) "Hi. Are these for me?" (Then we kiss.)'

'Uh-huh.'

'Kiss. Kiss. Barf,' she said in a bored croak. And then, 'Oh! Pretty! You hungry?'

'Yeah.'

'I fixed your favourite.'

'Great.'

'Would you like to open the wine?'

'Sure.'

'It's a great year.'

'Huh? Sorry I'm late.'

'Where were you? I was getting worried.'

'Some hotshot tracker they brought up needed spark plugs, percussion caps. They were all bunged up, rusted pure orange, rusted like carrots.' Harry was proud of his delivery of this line and looked over at Zena, hoping for a bit of encouragement. None came.

All she said was 'Bon appétit.'

'Looks great.'

'So do you.'

'Thanks.'

'You're welcome, Sam.'

This was the kind of inane dialogue people had to carve out careers with. Every year a whole unseen ton of this trash was spewed out by the studios. Scratch beneath the fancy Oscar winners and you hit the foundations of rubbish.

Harry had rehearsed the scene in detail, both at home and

also at Peggy Feury's acting class. The red-headed child star –
named Derek, incidentally – had studiously directed the scene,
while Dorinda took the part of Terry, which she drawled in her
own version of an American accent. Born with the plummy scoff
of the British ruling class, no amount of dialect coaching seemed
able to eradicate it. Annoyingly, she had chain-smoked through
every rehearsal.

'Do you think a robot would smoke?' Derek had asked politely, early in rehearsals.

'God. Yuh,' breathed Dorinda, stubbing another butt-end into
an overflowing ashtray. 'At least this one does.'

What she'd lacked in delivery of the dialogue she'd made
up for at the end of the scene. The kitchen sink was meant
to overflow while the two of them made passionate love on
the floor and Terry had to short circuit. Dorinda knew how
to short circuit. Her head banged from side to side. She could
even make her eyeballs disappear. It was the most important
moment in the scene because it was only here that the audience realised that she wasn't just another perfect wife, but a
replicant.

Peggy Feury had craned down as Dorinda performed this
feat, her head turning almost three hundred and sixty degrees.
'Now *this* is good,' she had proclaimed.

On the Paramount lot, the two young hopefuls were ushered
onto a tiny sound stage. Lamps threw a pool of light into the
middle of the space. There was no set, just a couple of chairs.
A smell of dust and carbolic. The director and the producer
sat in the shadows. Harry felt like an animal being led into an
abattoir. He stood there shivering while the director explained
what he wanted the two actors to do. Zena Dare was confident.
She held her own with the director. He wanted her. She knew
it. She stood in front of him tall, eye to eye, no flinching as he

explained to her that basically she was playing an ambulatory blow-up doll.

'There's no Freud in this,' he said.

'Who's Fred?'

'What I mean is that she has no hang-ups.'

'Got it.'

They started the scene. Harry thought it was going quite well. Inwardly he ticked off all the difficult moments for his accent. He passed with flying colours. Coming in for the home run he now got Zena on to the floor and was busily humping her, kissing and thrusting at her when the unthinkable happened. Zena started to laugh. At first, he thought it was part of her acting and so he laughed too. But that made her laugh even more. Then she started crying she was laughing so much. Then she said, 'Sorry. Sorry.' She looked beseechingly at Harry for a second and then literally split herself laughing.

'Cut. What's up, Zena?' asked the director.

'He's so funny. Oh my God.' She fluffed at her tear-stained eyelashes with her fingers, looked at Harry again and began to shake with mirth. 'Sorry. Sorry. Can we go again?'

'Of course. Aaand action.'

'Honey?' cried Harry and Zena screamed with laughter.

'I'm so sorry. It's just you're so . . . so . . . earnest.'

'Oh.' Harry was very confused. Alarm bells. They tried again. This time they got halfway through the scene before Zena collapsed, rolling round the floor.

'This guy . . .' She could hardly breathe. 'This guy cracks me up.'

Later there was a knock on his dressing-room door. It was the director. Looking strained.

'That was great. Thanks, Guy.'

'Harry.'

'I meant guy as in man.'

'Oh. Was it all right?' He didn't really have to ask. He knew it had been a fiasco.

'Sure. It was great. I hear you know Clive.'

'We did some photographs.'

'He really likes you.'

Harry began to sweat. 'Oh, really?' Was all he could think of as a reply.

Needless to say, he didn't get the job.

Two months later, on a wet Monday, he started working in the mail room at William Morris.

The mail room was the chugging engine of the great agency where all the raw materials came in and went out. These were the days before computers and thousands of scripts arrived and were sent out every day all over the world. The mail room was a veritable hornet's nest. At its centre sat Peeps Bellevue (Clive's friend) in a glass cubicle, on a swivel chair, monitoring the workers. His bug eyes never missed a trick and the mail room was run with military precision. Each agent had a box in which scripts and contracts, CVs and rejection letters were retrieved and left to be sent. The mail room was where you started. It was at the bottom of the evolutionary ladder. Maybe you were an outrider and drove around LA taking scripts to the homes of the stars or to the offices of other agencies, producers, directors. On the step above that you were one of those young men (no women in those days) who sorted the mail, retrieved the correspondence from the various agent's offices. This is where you began to learn how to blow smoke, up which arsehole to blow it and when. Manners were everything in the agency and the agency was a fraternity, not unlike a university or a hockey team or the Freemasons.

If you made an impression from the mail room on one of the

agents then the next stop could be to become an assistant, although competition was fierce. In order to scale this particular
ridge, you had to put in a whole lot of extra work, reading all the
scripts that came in from the studios so that at the right moment
(and, by the way, the right moment was everything) you could
venture an opinion. If you misjudged that moment, you could
find yourself back at square one, or even without a job. If you
got it right, things would move fast, and you could start to build
a reputation as someone to watch and then you would have to
read even more scripts because perhaps the head of the agency
would have heard about you and test your mettle one day when
you were delivering his mail.

Harry learnt very quickly that he didn't need to read a
script or see a film because all anyone ever talked about in the
agency, or in the whole of LA for that matter, was this script
or that one, this film or another, so that by the time you had
delivered the mail a few times in the course of a morning to
a few offices, you could glean from the snatches of conversation the whole state of play in that crazy town. The various
opinions could be crafted into one's own individual 'take' and
then you were off, although sometimes he got things wrong.
Example:

'What did you think of *Rumble Fish*?' asked Syd Tucker, the
head of the agency, one day.

'Not much, sir.'

'Oh, why is that?' Syd looked up from his work.

'Well, sir, at the end of the day I thought, so what? Rusty Jane
loves Motorcycle Boy and Motorcycle Boy loves Rusty Jane. So
what?'

'I think you mean Rusty James.'

'Exactly. So gay.' Harry retreated to the mail room, sweating,
while Syd Tucker guffawed contentedly. A narrow escape.

He was repeating verbatim what he had heard the arch-bitch

of the agency proclaim under her breath as she barrelled out of the screening room. She was a handsome woman with a substantial bosom. She could have been one of the great sopranos, according to her. She could certainly hit the high notes, especially when she was dressing down either of her two assistants. She was called Cindy Ridge and she was Harry's favourite. She smoked like a chimney and was extremely rude about all her clients, some of the most famous names in Hollywood. She immediately named Harry Lord Snooty and he was very happy about this. He felt he had crossed a bridge and developed an image of his own. Image was the only thing that counted in that city of mirrors. If you didn't have one you were just a blur, an underexposed negative, and at some point you would have to be reshot or your scene would hit the cutting-room floor. It was all a movie and Harry had scored a cameo. He had been noticed.

'Hey. Lord Snooty. C'mere. I want you to be my secret agent.' Sometimes Cindy spoke in a little girl voice.

'Possibly, Cindy. Why do you ask?'

'I want you to go undercover into Jacket Potato's office.' It was her nickname for the top agent at the Morris agency, the infamous Jacky Battiato. Behind his back. Everything behind the back. The agency was a stage full of asides. In his turn Jacky called her the Avalanche, in memory of her latest trip down the aisle dressed in a wedding cake.

'I want you to go to his office and find out how much Burt Reynolds is being offered for *Gunsling*. Can you do that for me, sweetie?' The little girl voice again.

'What's in it for me?' asked Harry unwisely.

'Listen, asshole. What's in it for you is this: I don't report you to human resources for smoking weed on the roof last week. Now get outa here.'

Harry went red. Miscalculation.

'Don't think you know me,' whooped Cindy at his departing figure.

He made straight for Jacky Battiato's office via the mail room with a fresh batch of scripts. He liked the idea of becoming the agency Mata Hari. He breezed into Jacky's outer office. Sitting on the couch was Matt Dean. Harry looked towards the wall and made for the two poisonous assistants' desks with the scripts.

'Here you go, Byron,' he whispered and made straight for the door. Spying would have to wait.

'Hey,' commanded Matt Dean. 'Don't I know you?'

Harry froze. Mail room people were supposed to be invisible to the talent, like untouchables. The two assistants, Byron and Denis, reminded Harry of the Siamese cats in *Lady and the Tramp*. They arched and hissed with indignation.

'Uh. Not really, sir.'

'Yes, I do. You were hanging with Tristan Hodge the other night.'

Gasps bordering on furballs from the desks.

'Yes. That's right.'

'I have a photographic memory. You said you were thinking of going to William Morris.' Both cats raised manicured eyebrows. Wait until they told Jacky.

'In the mail room. Yes,' answered Harry, flushing, suddenly aware that he was getting too visible in the wrong way. Luckily the conversation was cut short by the inner door to Jacky's office crashing open, and the famous agent himself appeared. Tall with a quiff of white hair, in a pinstripe suit, Jacky Potato looked as if he might produce a machine gun from behind his back. The gun in his pocket, on the other hand, was reputed to shoot only blanks. This was according to the Avalanche.

'Matt, dear. Come in. Hold my calls. Give me a hug.'

Matt Dean obediently grasped the great agent round the

haunches. Like many stars he was pint-sized and the two of
them together looked like some strange vaudeville double act,
ventriloquist and dummy. It would have been an amusing sight if
it wasn't for the fact that Matt, usually so thrusting, hips forward,
buttocks clenched, an Italian stallion all the way from Idaho,
this god of Generation Shoulder Pad, was reduced to a fawning
spaniel, getting down on all fours and wagging his tail.

Harry beat a hasty retreat. Byron and Denis didn't move a
muscle. Just their eyes followed, curiosity mingling with jealousy, and without a word to each other they agreed that when
the first possible opportunity arose, they would do their best to
trip Lord Snooty up in his game.

Inside the great agent's office everything was big and cold as a
freezer. Jacky himself was a giant side of beef with big hands and
fingers like sausages. They hung by his knees, embedded with
rings, and when he sat down they spread over the big lacquered
desk behind which he conducted his affairs. The room was decorated like Mussolini's boudoir or a high-end funeral parlour. Large
backlit vases of lilies certainly made the place smell like a house
of death. Framed photographs of the stars gazed down, saintly,
over a striped L-shaped couch with gigantic cushions. Daylight
was shafted by plantation-house shutters, from the floor to the
ceiling, covering the huge wraparound windows of the building –
whose light Jacky felt had thrown his recent face-lift into rather
stark relief. He preferred to sit in the slashes of light, like Marlon
Brando in *The Godfather*. It all worked. Jacket Potato was one of
the famous agents. A magazine cover featuring Matt Dean ('The
unseen Matt Dean' said the headline) had been casually left open
on the coffee table. Matt lowered himself onto the couch and tried
to regain his allure, legs wide, packet artfully displayed, pumped
arms splayed and cheeky grin in place revealing rows of white
teeth disappearing into the depths of his beautiful mouth.

Jacky didn't like these kinds of meetings. Even though he was a killer he got weepy about his clients. When he had to axe one, as he had to today, he preferred to torture them into walking out on him, rather than expelling them himself. In such a way he had retained a reputation as a kind man while in reality he was the usual assassin, dressed, interestingly enough, as an assassin, but – according to local legend – hiding a heart of gold. Platinum. Jacky had made a lot of money.

These scenes will be the death of me, he thought, popping a Tums chewy into his mouth. It was time for Matt to fly the roost. Despite being a popular star, despite being on the pages of all the girly magazines, this visibility was not translating into offers. Matt couldn't really act. Jacky had better boys who could command better prices and for whom landing a role took considerably less effort. He needed Matt to bail of his own volition. Luckily, agents were trained to disinform and confuse. By the time you had been on the game as long as Jacky, it was second nature. On the other hand, last week's Friday-night party at his house – a celebrated event in Hollywood – had continued until Sunday evening – non-stop – and he was in no mood for lubing things up.

'Hey baby, how ya doin'?' he asked nonetheless.

'Good, man. Good.' It was a script they both knew by heart.

'What did you think of *Hearts of Ice*? Fox really want you.'

'I wasn't crazy on it, man.'

'Oh really? I loved it.' Lie. It was a terrible B-movie.

'I really want *Jump*.'

'You and everyone's mother.'

'Yeah. Except that I really am Chancey Wayne.'

'Let me tell you quite honestly – straight from the heart. It's never going to happen. Creeze's people are all over it.'

Matt frowned. 'Well, what do you think?'

'I think you should jump on board with *Hearts of Ice*. What makes you think you could get *Jump*? It's Warners' big summer movie. They're not gonna give that to you. You haven't had a hit in ... how long? We got to be realistic.'

Realistic? Now that was a word in the Tinseltown vocabulary that was hardly ever used. Alarm bells rang in Matt's head. This was not the usual smoke-blowing and Matt felt it.

Jacky watched him for a reaction. Sure enough, his leg started to bounce up and down.

'Go easy, man. Any minute now I'm gonna think you don't love me any more.' Matt tried and failed to sound casual.

'Love you? You're like a son to me. That's why I can say – I want you to get yourself out there a bit more. Re-engage with the industry.'

'Huh!'

'Get to know new people. Find out what's going on. Stop sitting back. You're cruising. Look over your shoulder – who's coming up? There's a whole new world being born in the mail rooms of LA. That's where the new talent arrives.'

'Wait a minute. I know a guy who works in the mail room here. Harry?'

A scowl of impatience scudded across Jacky's face. 'You know Lord Snooty?'

'Lord Snooty?'

'Harry.'

'Sure. We hung out the other night at Oscar's.'

In the outside office Byron was listening carefully to the conversation. Harry was moving too fast.

Inside, Jacky signalled that the meeting was over by collecting some papers together on his desk. It would only be a matter of time now. Matt Dean looked down at his own body sprawled across the striped couch. Suddenly he didn't know whose it was. His legs closed and his hands clenched at the cushions. The two men looked at each other for a moment.

'I gotta go,' Jacky said finally. 'Tell me what to say to Fox.'

'I need to think about it. Jesus. I made *Crimes of Fashion*, for God's sake.'

'Ten years ago. Bye. Let me know.'

Matt Dean didn't know where the mail room was. None of the talent did. In fact, despite what Jacky said, contact with the agency untouchables was frowned upon. The agency was a show. What went on behind the scenes was a different world.

After a discreet enquiry at the front desk Matt passed through a fire door into the back offices. Faces stared as he walked by – but he was used to that. Eventually he found Harry, sitting in the canteen.

'Hey.'

'Mr Dean.' Harry stood up. It was surnames and rigid formality.

'Fuck that. I'm Matt.' He offered his hand. 'Are you on your break?'

'Yes. Lunch. At eleven thirty! Who can eat at eleven thirty?'

A voice over a loudspeaker made an announcement. 'Urgent pick-up in Ted Tucker's office.'

'You smoke weed?' Matt asked.

'Sure. How do you think I keep sane here?'

'You know anywhere we could go?'

'Absolutely.'

They sat against a wall on the large flat roof, in the warm watery sun. LA was spread out around them. Behind rose the hills, just shapes in the mist. In front the city, block after block, streets, houses, trees, pools (dots of sky blue when you fly in) all melting into the haze. Somewhere out of the smog planes appeared like little lollipops, silent, disappearing over the dimly shining Pacific. It was a typical spring day. The air smelt of rain and metal. They chatted about this and that and then smoked in silence, drifting, strangely at ease, lazily trying to gauge what kind of conversation – if any – was applicable. Harry closed his eyes and listened – the drone of air conditioners, the far-away wail of a siren, the constant rumble of traffic.

'My agent is trying to get rid of me,' Matt's voice cut in.

'What do you mean? He loves you. You're Matt Dean.'

'Maybe.' He was silent again.

'What's your next picture? I heard they were getting you that *Hearts of Ice* role over at Fox.'

Harry was proud of himself. He could speak the lingo now.

'Did you read it?'

'Sure.' A lie.

'Well, what did you think?'

'Actually, I didn't. But everyone says it's a stinker.' He decided to come clean about his methods.

'You didn't invent that game, dude,' Matt said once Harry had finished explaining. 'Everyone plays it.'

'Some better than others. Most people don't listen to what anyone else is saying over here. Are you going to do it?' Harry wasn't particularly interested but he knew how the conversation was meant to go. He also knew that, despite the informal smoking of a secret peace pipe, this was still work. Work in LA started the moment you woke up and only stopped when you passed out, and sometimes not even then.

'I dunno. I'm totally broke. So yeah, I guess. I need the money. I got a mortgage. I got alimony. I need ... ' Matt broke off and stared up at the hills (from whence cometh no help). He looked at his watch. 'Hey. I gotta go. Look, let me give you my number. If you ever read anything you think I should have a try at, let me know, huh? You would be really helping me out. And if you hear anything from Jacky's office—'

'I'll fill you in,' finished Harry, smiling inwardly.

*

Time slides by in LA and the jacarandas seem always to be in bloom. But it was several months later, during a cold front, when all roads led to Tony Perkins on that fateful Friday in December. Mount Baldy was covered in snow. You could see it when you drove east on Sunset, like the Paramount mountain, before turning up Benedict Canyon on the way to the Perkins house. They were giving a dinner for Andy Warhol and that whole New York crowd had blown in on the snowstorm that howled down from the east. Worlds would collide tonight, which was unusual in that hall of mirrors, that inverted glitterball called Hollywood, where every twinkling light on the dark hill was a separate galaxy of planets and suns, cliques and gangs, rocks and comets revolving exclusively round each other, micro versions of the whole, replete with their own hierarchies, rules and codes of conversation.

Tony's crowd was international. Bohemian. Bicoastal. Bisexual. Anything went. It was the least Hollywood of the Hollywood scenes. It had an effortless chic. Partly due to his wife Berry, who was a blue-blooded European. Partly due to the fact that he famously lived a secret double life. Partly because he was extremely funny and so were all his friends. They liked stars and drop-outs, society folk and drug cowboys and anybody who could crack a joke. The result was a kind of salon/saloon reminiscent of something in France at the turn of the century.

Meanwhile, down on Hollywood Boulevard Dorinda was rushing in heels and tumbled down the stairs, landing hard on her coccyx at the front door. She was collecting her treasured Sultana, who had just flown in from Geneva and was staying at the Beverly Hills Hotel.

Pause a moment for a happy snap. The Sultana. She was not in fact the wife of a sultan. She was actually called Mrs Oya Benici, the second wife of the disgraced Turkish billionaire Aagha Benici, who owned a chain of supermarkets called Sultan Benici.

(Pronounced Benigee. Not Bernice, or Bikini, as Dorinda had called them both for the first five years.)

It had been a stroke of extraordinary luck, or destiny, that Dorinda just happened to be there on the fateful day that Mr Bikini was arrested in Istanbul. There had been a lunch party at their home – a wonderful wooden house on the very edge of the Bosphorus – and Dorinda, a friend of a friend on holiday, had managed to get invited. They had never met.

It was a grand affair: twenty guests, liveried staff, an amazing table, a glinting blur of cut glass on fabulous damask and the reflection of the waves outside, ripples of light on the ceiling and walls. Careful conversation was made in eight languages. Too careful, for Dorinda's taste. However, after the first course, instead of lobsters, the police arrived, bursting into the room, armed to the teeth, arresting Mr Bikini and dragging him away while everyone else sat in stunned silence. Things were looking up. Then the screaming began as the police ransacked the house. Suddenly lunch turned into breaking news. Sultan Benici owned supermarkets across Turkey and was famous all over the world. A live feed(ing) frenzy ensued. Helicopters circled the house like killer mosquitos, paparazzi on speedboats, journalists climbed the drainpipes and the guests melted away, their hurried kisses blown from retreating hands and brightly painted lips as they escaped through back doors or on boats across the Bosphorus to the relative safety of the European side.

By about half past three, Mrs Bikini found herself alone, abandoned by all. Only Dorinda remained, still hoping for a lift back to Bebek, where she was staying in a small hotel with a friend. She was enthralled as she held her hostess's hand while a SWAT team blew up the safes. They were empty. The Sultana nearly fainted. But not quite. Suddenly, a complete stranger was the only person left and she grabbed on to her for dear life. And so Dorinda was beside her when she finally emerged, her elegant Valentino dress shrouded in a flowing cashmere burqa. They were chased to a private airport outside Istanbul from which they flew to freedom aboard Mr Bikini's jet – destination Geneva. No questions were asked about Dorinda's luggage, or the friend she had left behind at the small hotel in Bebek. Luckily and tellingly she always carried her passport with her.

All this was a lifetime ago – ten long years to be precise and Dorinda had provided invaluable support during that time, sliced in half in pictures, just a hand holding tight to the Sultana's arm while the Sultana herself achieved international notoriety as she was arrested and imprisoned for smuggling priceless Coptic Bibles and a tenth-century Quran out of Turkey.

Tonight – what a scoop – Dorinda was taking her to Tony and Berry's house in the Hollywood Hills for dinner with Andy Warhol and she couldn't be late. She clambered to her feet like a crazed replicant and hobbled out into the rain.

Dorinda drove like a fiend, the beams of her headlights darting from left to right through the rainy mist. She couldn't fuck this one up. She was always *this close* – to getting an acting job, to getting her production company off the ground. (Daddy Long Legs Productions.) Now she was *this close* to getting the Sultana a Hollywood deal. There was no doubt that tonight was the perfect setting for her patron's introduction to Tinseltown. Oya Benici was already known to the Warhol crowd. She was their type of oddity and they had good noses for money. They longed for her, and she longed for them. Dorinda had thrown double sixes. Now she was a registered mover and shaker. Soon, if the prevailing winds stayed in her favour, Daddy Long Legs Productions would be a weaving its web around the Sultana at the centre, its poison spider.

Like most people of extreme wealth, the Sultana was a tough

cookie. She'd been around. These days Mr Benici was under house arrest in Istanbul. The scandal, the abduction, prison, the courts, the publicity had drained the colour out of him, and he had been forced to dye his hair a russet black. Beneath it his skin was sallow. Banished children from his first wife were snapping at his ankles – trying to make arrangements barring the Sultana from any more of his wealth than she had already managed to syphon off.

Luckily for the children, the marriage had been barren – and not for lack of trying. The Sultana knew the missing link was a child and so she buzzed back and forth, from Geneva to Turkey, desperately trying to fertilise, but the clock was ticking. She had several friends/slaves dotted around the world who could be counted on to drop everything and follow her. Dorinda was her *amie nécessaire* in North America. Finally, the wind was in her sails. Of course, it was all a matter of timing, and it would probably go wrong. It always did, but like many chaotic depressives Dorinda was an eternal optimist. She had been trying to get the Sultana to LA for five years and now she was finally here.

Matt Dean called Harry. 'You wanna do something?'

'Sure. What?'

'There's a party I'm invited to.'

'Great.'

'I'll collect you at seven.' Conversations were short and to the point.

They drove to the party in Matt's sports car. It was like being in a rocket. The dashboard blinked with lights. Rubies and emeralds throbbed to the fashionable music that waved from discreet speakers.

'So many pretty lights,' was all Harry could think of to say.

'That's my graphic equaliser,' declared Matt proudly. He

adjusted a dial and the backing singer wailing behind the samba seemed suddenly to be coming from under Harry's seat.

Matt Dean's profile was heroic against the rainy canyons flying by outside. A powerful nose, straight, with flared nostrils, a high forehead, thick black hair and one deep-set eye staring unblinking at the road. He wore a black jacket and a white shirt. Matt's was a carefully achieved image, although Harry got the feeling that the actor personally subscribed to no particular taste. In music, in clothes, he happily followed. It was all designed to confirm and enhance his status. Beyond that, he was rudderless, lost. Tonight, his face was gaunt and coiled in the street lights. The fact was, the wind had changed and he had become the angry young man he had played at being for the last ten years. Now that he was it, there was nothing left to play. He was behind on his mortgage, behind with his alimony, behind the curve. When you got cold-shouldered by one of the great agencies you usually had no idea what exactly was going on. Word was out in the deep-pile corridors of power. Footsteps were receding; doors were quietly and carefully closing. But nobody told Matt Dean. And so the long and lonely process of burning out began. It was like screaming in space. Nobody heard you. Not even you heard. But strangely, Harry heard. Something touched him, watching this nice simple farm boy, unaware that he was being torn apart, like an old robot, for spares.

Harry knew because he heard all the talk at the agency. In Hollywood they swarmed like wasps when they wanted you and turned like a shoal of fish when it was over. And once they had turned it usually took a fatal car crash to bring them back, and by then, of course, it was too late, except for your back catalogue. It was Looney Tunes. Up until now it had never occurred to Harry that the odds were stacked against people like Matt Dean. Living in the stark black and white environment of the agency with its reductive world view, it became clear how most people floundered, how only a few flourished, and why. Without knowing it, Harry was being radicalised. Soon he saw him and Matt as one against the agency, against the world. Maybe it was love. They both felt it, although Matt kept up with the endless stream of frustrated girls who, try as they might, never managed to get their hooks into this slippery fish.

Actually, there was nothing to hold on to, Harry thought, during the dull dinners with one of these croaky (from crying) actresses. Nothing to hold on to and no one reaching out. Just ghosts passing through the light at fifty frames a second. If only he could find a script, one that was good enough but not so good that one of the sharky reps to some hammerhead star would go after it, then maybe Matt Dean's career still had a chance.

Matt, for his part, was touched. 'You really care about it all, don't you,' he said to Harry in the car that night.

'Of course. Don't you?'

'Hell yeah. It's all I have. Who am I if not Matt Dean? I got to stay hard. But you: why?'

'It's making me hard. The challenge, that is.' And that was the nearest he got to a declaration. In the soft moment that followed, Harry sighed. 'Don't you think there must be another world out there?'

'Sure. But what's your point?'

'I don't see how you can ever win. It's too tough.'

'Well, try going back to Idaho. That's tough.'

Matt concentrated on the road, round and round, higher and higher, over the rainbow to the Perkins house tucked away in the hills on a little street with a brook flowing over it, a trickle really. The road ended abruptly in nothing. Black, like the edge of a flat planet. Harry was expecting the Bates Motel. In fact, the Perkins house was a long, low barn hidden behind a wooden

fence. You walked through the door and you were there, in some
great hall from medieval times, but a hippy version – wooden
floors, wooden walls, rugs from Kathmandu and a huge log fire
crackling at one end. Christmas cards were stuck everywhere
and a large tree leaned to one side in the corner, drunk, draped
in silver tinsel. On one side of the room was a long, thin table
like the Last Supper. In the middle sat that week's Christ, the
anaemic Andy Warhol in his lopsided silver wig. Bianca Jagger
was next to him, dressed in her treasured silk Halston from back
in the day, dark and dewy, listening carefully to Berry, Tony's
wife, and her sister Marisa, granddaughters of the Italian designer Schiaparelli, who huddled and talked earnestly in French
and Italian, stabbing at one another with their pointed, perfectly
manicured fingers. Everyone smoked. Fred Hughes, Francesco
Clemente, Helmut Newton and June his wife made up a sacred
centre, with lower dignitaries further beyond the salt on either
side – Clive Rich, Tristan Hodge, some young actresses, sitting
like mermaids on the rocks at one end, combing their hair with
conch shells and wailing.

It was a world within a world and its man in the moon was
Perkins himself, thin, wrung out, the funniest person anyone
knew but the sense of humour came with a sting and so did
the double life. A family man in the Hills, a confirmed bachelor on the Santa Monica strip. The only person who didn't
know was his wife. Or did she? Watching him now as he got up
to make a toast, her gaze was impenetrable, steady, amused,
reserved. Perkins stood up and clinked on a glass. 'Tonight's
been one of the great nights,' he breezed. 'BUT. If the Grim
Reaper knocked on my door right now – I'd just say gimme five.
I'm ready.' Everyone laughed; bellowed, actually. They were
laughing at the truth because the Grim Reaper was at the door.
He hadn't knocked yet but it was a doomed affair for many of
the people sitting there that night. Andy, Fred, Helmut, Tony

himself, even Berry, they would all be gone in extraordinary circumstances and quite soon. Maybe they all knew it. Or at any rate felt it. Or maybe it was still too early. There was a frenetic charge in the air. That's what happens when the Grim Reaper stands outside your house.

At any rate, neither the Sultana nor Dorinda were thinking of death that night, so they barged past him – and burst onto the scene. Everyone stood. The Sultana was a frosty beauty along the lines of Snow White's stepmother in her prime, or Norma Desmond in hers, turbaned and cloaked, her priceless jewels winking in the candlelight. She held her head high to avoid germs and her hands out, also glittering, as if she was about to fall. Actually, it was to clear her airspace. Seats were vacated next to Andy. Bianca, Marisa and Berry were pushed along the table and fell off the edge, laughing. They got up, still locked into each other, and stalked off down a long passage to Berry's bedroom, leaving the table to Dorinda, victorious, to sell her wares.

Mrs Bikini was immediately the centre of attention. People who kissed tried to kiss her and she drew back. 'No kissing. Sorry,' declared Dorinda, like a policeman, honking with laughter. It was all a game to Dorinda.

'We're very scared about diseases,' explained the Sultana. 'Especially in the winter.'

Everyone wanted to know how she had smuggled the famous tenth-century Quran out of Turkey. 'In my vanity case of course. Underneath my creams.'

Everyone screamed with laughter.

'What a shame you got caught,' said Andy in that flat voice he used when he was really interested.

'It was really very simple. My maid called the police. It turned out she was working for a newspaper. I know pick 'em to how!' she confessed.

' "How to pick 'em",' explained Dorinda.

'Did you get paid for it at least?' asked Helmut Newton.

'SHE got paid,' continued Oya. 'We, unfortunately, did not. My husband is under house arrest as the result.'

Everyone groaned with compassion, while Andy and the Sultana were soon engaged in planning her portrait. 'In national costume. Please say yes, Andy? Is sooo important for my country.'

Dorinda made a great show of eavesdropping and kept the table amused. 'The Sultana is going to wear national costume,' she chirruped. 'In chains,' she added for good measure.

'Gee,' mumbled Andy. 'Like a whirling dervish?'

'Andy just said gee!' screamed Dorinda, a hand behind one ear like a character in vaudeville, or a silent movie. 'I hope you've brought your chequebook, Oya. Andy doesn't take credit.'

Dorinda was wild after a few drinks. 'It's my Crohn's disease. No intestines. The alcohol goes straight to my brain.' Her tactics were unsubtle and unknown to LA. She came from the school of country house party games, and she loved being the centre of attention – like a child. At the same time her performance neatly camouflaged her real vocation in life, which was to enable and procure anything she could – preferably at a knockdown price (pourboire included) – for her benefactress. She was enthralled by the Sultana. The Sultana could do no wrong. If life had been a cartoon (it nearly was) the Sultana would have been a boa constrictor in a veil with a pair of large psychedelic eyes, giving orders to Dorinda, her mesmerised goose, in a gentle coo.

Dorinda was quite good, though, thought Harry, as he watched her operate. Nobody could make out if, like her heroine Holly Golightly, she was simply a fake, or a fake fake. In fact, she was the real thing. An upper-class nutter – and her outlandish performance gave Harry a shot of courage. If she

could make a splash, so could he. Already, Matt was introducing him to everyone as one of his agents, and he suddenly felt
flushed, pleased to be himself, to such an extent that when
Clive Rich arrived, the man who, after all, had outed him so
fatally just months ago, he had managed to rise above the
initial panic and combine a casual and knowing friendliness
with his newly learnt greeting – that agency three-point turn:
the assertive handshake, the affectionate shoulder bonk and
the hearty backslap. He even managed to say 'My friend' in
a squeaky voice. In fact, in the wake of the Perkins evening,
he and Clive became close friends and, as Clive said later,
quoting Wilde, it was better to be talked about than not.
Nobody in Hollywood could argue about that, although they
did, endlessly.

And then – quite suddenly – fate played its card. Barely
had Harry sat down next to Clive when the Sultana shrieked.
(Norma Desmond.) The table fell silent. Andy took a photo –
her eyes and mouth wide open.

'That's the portrait,' he said to no one in particular.

'This is the one,' the Sultana wailed, pointing to Matt. 'This is
the man with whom I wish to have my baby. Look at the profile,
Andy. Like my husband but better. Don't worry, you can leave
once you have spermed. I don't need man any more.'

Matt was thrilled. 'Just let me know when,' he said, turning red.

Watching him, the flimsy foundations upon which his happiness was built, Harry quietly and protectively fell in love.

As the evening progressed, the table was slowly abandoned
and the young agent found himself alone among the rubble –
bottles, plates of food, glasses, napkins. (This often happens
to agents and he'd better get used to it. They are suddenly left
on some mountainside while the talent takes the last train to
somewhere else.)

Harry didn't care. He loved to watch. Someone turned the lights down and, looking round in the dim light, he felt finally – and momentarily – that he had found the Yellow Brick Road after all. He had arrived backstage in Hollywood. There was music. Ella and a piano. An after-dinner crowd arrived in groups, falling into the room, actors and producers, directors and dealers. Almost immediately Matt got embroiled with the usual type of girl, an emaciated wraith in smudged eyeliner. The fragile rocks were the type he usually got wrecked on. Dorinda had disappeared. Harry, feeling alone now, suddenly longed for London. He wandered down a long corridor, encrusted in framed drained holiday snaps, happy faces fading, bleached to ghosts by the desert sun. Open doors led to children's bedrooms. A glitterball hung from a ceiling and shards of light moved across the room, past the twittering faces of guests perched on beds and beanbags, past a giant stuffed bear slumped in the corner. People emerged from bathrooms, deep in conversation. There was an underwater feeling, as the guests flitted through the gloom and the party spread all over the house. The music, the muted conversation, the far-away doorbell that never ceased – and Harry kept moving, drifting from room to room. Someone had given him a hit on some magic weed and he felt invisible. A voice close by said, 'John Travolta's about to arrive.'

'So is Pee-wee Herman,' said someone else. A girl danced for two men sitting on the floor. Slow, half-hearted and then laughing. A huge mouth flung open. A group of industry guys smoked and huddled in the usual secret conversation, who's doing what at Universal, the weekend bomb, etc. Tony himself held forth to two enraptured studio wives. Their hands were clasped in prayer and punctuated his every phrase with applause and gales of laughter. There was something biblical about it. The actor seemed to be hovering above them and they adored from below, their eyes gleaming with affection and their lips twitching with longing to slip that miracle meat, so near and yet so far, into their mouths. Harry looked for an inviting gesture from any of these groups, but none came.

He opened the door to a bedroom at the end of the long corridor. The Sultana was sitting on the bed, leaning over a small man in a white suit and slicked-back hair who was lying back on the pillows, hands behind his head. They were talking with lowered voices. A single lamp threw them in shadow against the wall. The Sultana's was a predatory silhouette. They stared at Harry as he came in.

'Sorry,' he said, making to leave.

'Come in. You look interesting,' said the man in the white suit.

'Shut the door.' The Sultana patted the bed. 'What do you do, Boney?'

'I'm Matt Dean's agent. One of them.'

'You selling him?' Her eyes gleamed and she had a lop-sided grin.

'I'd like to.'

'You'd like to?' laughed the man in the white suit, imitating Harry's accent.

'Yes.' The door to the bathroom opened and a dishevelled woman peeked out.

'Oya,' she hissed. 'Are you coming?'

'One moment, please,' said the Sultana to the woman, and then, 'Would you excuse me?'

'Aren't we coming too?' asked the man in the white suit.

'Women's problems. Be here when I get back.' She blew a kiss at the man, got up, went into the bathroom and the door slammed shut.

'I guess we're not invited,' said the man in white. He got off the bed and left the room without a further word.

Harry sat on a bed and leafed through a magazine. He had hoped to be invited to join someone's expedition to the loo, but so far, no luck. Then the door opened and the Sultana's voice came from inside. 'Hey! Boney! Get in here if you're coming.'

The Sultana was perched on the edge of the bath. The dishevelled lady, a famous producer's daughter, sat on the loo with an upturned mirror on her lap and a rolled-up dollar bill in her hand. The usual story. 'I haven't got very much,' she said cautiously. It was never the truth. A great pile had been divided into huge rails of snow on the glass and like a serving maid she offered the mirror to the Sultana. Another biblical scene.

'Ugh,' said Oya Benici politely. 'I'm sorry, but I only take my own. God knows whose nose that dollar bill has been stuck up. Give it to Boney.' The Sultana opened her bag and extracted an amber vial. It had a little spatula attached to the top on a chain. 'This spoon is platinum. Amusing, non? There is a shop in Geneva that sells this sort of thing. For rich junkies. Très drôle, non?' She flicked it with her fingernail, then took two brief sniffs and returned the vial to her bag. The producer's daughter proffered her dirty bill to Harry and he gratefully hoovered up a substantial pile of powder.

'Now,' said the Sultana, relaxing into the high with a little shiver, 'let's get down to business. What's the price?'

'There's always a price,' warned the producer's daughter in a high squeaky voice.

'It depends what you want.' Harry had no idea what she was talking about.

'His child, of course. His genes.'

'Oh. You mean Matt.'

'C'mon Boney. This is all you're getting.' Harry was leaning forward for another line and the producer's daughter winked. 'We haven't been introduced. My name is Patty and I'm an addict. I hadn't been sober for two minutes when ... ' She hoovered up a line.

'I'll pay him a million bucks. That's good for one ... What does one call it?'

'A wad.'

'A wad?' Oya looked at Harry for confirmation.

'Yes, I believe so,' said Harry, trying to sound professional as he wiped the coke from the end of his nose.

'A million for one wad.'

'Two. No strings. We're talking about Matt Dean's wad.'

'Now that's what I would call a happy ending. For Matt Dean,' giggled Patty.

'We've got lawyers who can tie it up nicely,' reasoned Harry.

'But do you really want a baby, darling?' Patty pressed. 'All that sacrifice and then they kick you in the teeth. Mine haven't talked to me in years.'

'It could be something extraordinary,' said the Sultana thoughtfully. 'We'll talk about it in the cold light of day. Let's do another line.' Bang bang bang went someone at the door.

Patty opened it up a crack and Dorinda barged in, guns blazing.

'Where have you been? I've been looking for you every-where.' She was almost screaming. These signature fits of rage were often her undoing, but Mrs Bikini didn't seem to mind.

'I've been here. Don't worry. Your friend has been looking after me.'

'I bet he has.' Dorinda flashed a warning sign at Harry. He knew her temper. Perhaps the Sultana knew it too because she got up quickly, checked herself in the mirror, applied lipstick and washed her hands.

'OK, the party's over. Let's go.' She turned to Harry. 'Now, Boney. Don't forget what I said.'

Dorinda looked at Harry, eyes like smashed plates. 'What did she say?'

'Relax, honey. I'll tell you about it in the car.' And the Sultana swanned out, followed by her irate lady-in-waiting. Harry was about to follow but Patty locked the door again, leant against it and looked intensely at him.

'Fuck me,' she demanded.

'Oh dear,' he said to himself.

'Did you just say oh dear? That's so cute.' And she straddled him as he sat on the edge of the bath. She looked kind of like Debbie Harry if you screwed your eyes up. And she clearly had an unending supply of coke. They began to kiss, dry mouths, tongues like budgies, lost their balance and fell together into the bath, laughing. Harry banged his head quite hard. Now she was on top, looking down, hair everywhere, a crazed grin on her face, a dribbly nose. She sniffed noisily. 'Maybe bumping pussies is not such a great idea.'

'Look. At this point, I can't even see straight,' he replied. And they laughed again.

In such strange ways friendships are carved. Patty and Harry became PH on the scene and went everywhere together for at least a decade.

They were driving home, smoking silently. 'By the way, thanks for calling me one of your agents. It felt great,' said Harry.

'I'm counting on ya. That's why, dude.' Dude, man, bro, guy – these names thrilled Harry. Matt put his hand on Harry's knee and squeezed for a second, passed him the smoke.

'I think it took me on to the next level.' Harry exhaled dreamily. 'At the party. I ended up trying to sell your sperm. I told that Arab lady a cool two million and no strings.'

'Oh yeah. That would fill the hole.'

'I wonder how we'd do it,' said Harry to himself.

The next day Dorinda threw herself down on Harry's bed.

'What the fuck is going on?' she demanded, blowing a stream

of smoke in his face. He came up through the mist, crash-landing into the morning, with a gruesome close-up of Dorinda leaning down, hair falling over her puffy scrubbed face, dead eyes wide.

'Hi, Dorinda. I don't know – what's going on?' he spluttered.

She grabbed him by the neck of his T-shirt.

'Look here, darling. All pleasantries aside, Oya is *my* Sultana. Capeesh? Stop trying to work her.' She looked insane.

'I'm not trying to work her.'

'You are. She wants to meet you to talk business. She's just called. At eleven in the morning! And that's what she told me.'

Harry hid beneath the sheets.

'What business?' Dorinda screamed and stripped the bed.

Later in the kitchen over coffee and cigarettes they came to an agreement.

'Everything changed for me last night,' confided Harry.

'What do you mean?' Dorinda was sulky, perched on a chair, arms and legs knotted up.

'I mean that when I looked at you operating that cash cow I was impressed by you in a totally new way.'

'Fuck off, darling. Get to the point.'

'The point is that I have a possible two million dollars' worth of sperm on tap and you and I could carve a neat five per cent each out of that.'

Dorinda's lips twitched with concentration as she tried to do the simple arithmetic.

'It's a hundred thousand, idiot,' Harry snorted, lighting a cigarette.

'She won't go for it. And nor will he.'

'Don't worry about Matt Dean. I'll handle him. He needs the money. No one will ever know. We'll make a contract. I know a lawyer from the agency who just retired. He can do it. All we need to do is to convince her. Make her feel confident about the idea. It could take some time. But that's the one thing we have a lot of.'

'Not that much,' said Dorinda, thinking hard. 'She's here for a month. We need to get it done by the time she leaves or else it could be years before we get the opportunity again. You know how these people are. Or maybe you don't. They have one idea in one place and then move on to the next place and have a completely different idea.'

'About what?'

'About everything. Anything. They're drifters. From Doha to the Dorchester via the bank.'

'And now the sperm bank.'

Dorinda was silent for a moment. 'Oh my God! We could be on to something. She has talked about having a baby – needing a baby – but I never thought she was serious. You see, she's not remotely maternal. She never looks at other women's babies. They don't even register. But she wants to consolidate her position with her in-laws.'

'She might. He might. We might. Together we might be able to pull it off. Look, let's go and meet her and see what she says.'

'OK. But she's mine, OK? Everything you do is through me. Is that understood? On your honour.'

'As a gentleman.'

Dorinda scoffed. 'No. As a lady. A lady in love, I should say, if last night was anything to go by.'

'What do you mean?'

'What do you mean, what do I mean?' she whined. 'Everyone noticed. You are in love with your client, Mr Dent. Naughty. Go back to square one.' Looking at Harry's shocked face she started to laugh. She honked like a goose in flight. It was her signature noise.

Now they were sitting in Bungalow One at the Beverly Hills Hotel, having tea. Harry and Dorinda on one over-stuffed sofa

and Mrs Bikini on the other, swamped in silks, shawls, pash-
minas, handbags, magazines and make-up, all scattered around
her within easy reach. It was a cold day outside, grey and damp.

'Last night. What confusion,' declared the Sultana.

'It really was. We left very late.'

'Did the stud take you home?' she simpered knowingly.

'Not all the way. But to my front door, yes.'

'Ha! Now he really is a good-looking guy.' She appraised her
fingernails. There was an awkward silence. No one knew if now
was the right moment.

'I know. He really is,' ventured Dorinda cautiously, lighting a
cigarette and blowing out a stream of smoke. She leant forward,
a mad smile on her face. 'So how about it, Oya? Are you ready
for that big sausage?'

The Sultana's eyes widened slightly and her sleek feathers
ruffled in shock while Dorinda honked with glee.

'No sausage,' corrected Harry smoothly. 'I am not offering up
my client for prostitution. Let's be clear about that right away.'

'From the go-get.' Dorinda was a parrot, proud of her
Americanisms.

Harry breezed on. He really had learnt, in just a few months
at the agency, a good line in bullshit. 'We are talking about
something much more profound. Much more complex as well, I
think. Am I right, ma'am?'

Ma'am worked a small soothing miracle. The Sultana fixed
her kohl-rimmed eyes on Harry and her hackles went down.
She burped discreetly and laughed. She certainly had a magnetic personality. He felt his eyes going round in circles. 'I'm
not interested in sausage, as you call it, Dorinda,' she said. I'm
not buying cock. Don't worry, Harry.'

Dorinda and Harry nodded solemnly.

'So far, I have no child. My husband ... something doesn't
work. Since the tragedy. This is the record off, huh?'

'Totally.' Our two procurers looked saintly.

'I have forty years. I must move. I have been moving. Too much. All the time, like the crazy bird, but time is running out.'

'That's not true, ma'am. You are looking sensational.'

'Anyone can look sensational, Harry. With the right money. But in here.' Now she pressed her hands against her stomach, fingers stretched across the sacred space. 'In here time is running out. So, let's talk. I have flashes. Dorinda will tell you. No, sweetie?'

'Hot flashes?'

'No. Flashes. Of inspiration.'

'Totally,' agreed Dorinda. 'Once you set your mind on something.'

'I have to have it.'

'Yuh. Or you leave town and forget it.'

'That's not fair, Dorinda. I may be drifting but it's because I have not been facing this.' Again, she hit at her stomach, with little fists in the operatic style. 'If only I can give my husband a son ... he will be so happy. Believe me, that's all I want.'

'I believe you,' said Dorinda. She didn't bother to sound very convincing and watched Oya through big, sceptical eyes.

Harry nudged her ankle with his foot.

'You don't need to kick me under the table, darling. I know what I'm doing. Don't I, Oyly?'

'She knows everything,' confirmed the Sultana, beaming at her friend and reaching out across the coffee table for Dorinda's hand.

'So, let's talk about Matt Dean,' said Harry.

'Can you get him?'

'For the right money.'

'And the right deal. I get copyright on the kid.'

'Of course. And equally, the kid will have no recourse to my client's estate.'

'What estate?' said Dorinda annoyingly. 'I thought you said he was broke.'

'Dorinda, please! Of course he's not broke. I'm just signing him to a great deal over at Fox. Are you crazy?' He believed it as he was saying it. That's what happened in Hollywood. You created a fantasy narrative and then you fell for it even if no one else did.

Luckily the Sultana wasn't paying attention. She was engrossed in cleaning her hands with surgical spirit. Then she waved them back and forth to dry.

'You think I'm crazy? I am very afraid of disease. I hate germs. I never want ... all those things. Kissing. People touching with me.' The very thought of it made her retch. 'That's why this could work. Provided my husband lives to recognise the kid. How much?'

'Two million.'

Silence. The atmosphere got thin and everyone gasped for breath.

The retired lawyer lived in a house on stilts, hanging over the edge of a cliff. The whole city lay below. A dizzying effect, and the view bounced slightly when you walked across the floor. Charles Ronson was small and sharp and evenly tanned. He had thick white hair, slicked with pomade and sprayed to hurricane-resistant levels. He was smartly dressed, in pearl grey and pink, and his house resembled a silent movie star's dressing room. Photographs by George Hurrell and Clarence Sinclair Bull smouldered on the leopard-skin walls. Douglas Fairbanks Junior as the Grand Duke Peter dominated the lounge and his uniform from the film hung on a defeated mannequin by the fireplace. 'This costume was made by Adrian,' said Charles with wide, wonderstruck eyes, fingering the moulting velvet. (It wasn't.) Low couches, large pillows (a soothing touch in case a star gets

chubby – they still feel petite nestled against them). In the bedroom Greek nudes painted in stucco stalked over the mirrored
bed. Charles Ronson swished through the atmosphere like a
comet waving coasters, slipping one under the beer that Harry
was about to put on a lacquered table, coming to rest breathless
on one of these low couches upon which he comically draped
himself.

'It's not as simple as it sounds.' Like all lawyers in showbusiness he enunciated every syllable. 'We would have to get the
money in escrow, of course. Favoured nations for all sperms.
Kidding.'

Harry was feverishly writing everything down.

'For the actual shot – the merchandise – the wad – we have to
make sure that the "actuality" of it is signed off by both parties.
Otherwise – afterwards – she could ask, how do I know it's his
sperm? And he could say, "She didn't tell me she was having
triplets." We need two independent observers.' He wagged his
finger like a metronome to the beat of his voice. 'Selected by both
parties to be present at the ... er ... seed transfer. You better get
on top of this, medically speaking. Shall we talk about my fee?'

'Two per cent.'

'Three.'

'Two.'

'In that case, we should look at doing it abroad for the tax
implication.'

'We have to do it here in LA.'

Christmas came and went. Harry and Tristan Hodge spent
a rainy night at Oscar's seeing in the new year. Arni played his
favourite records from the seventies (Boney M.) on a clapped-
out stereo. There were only a few odd drifters in the restaurant.
Exiles who didn't have anywhere to go. It suited their mood, and
their thoughts drifted to England. Arni had a recording of Big
Ben striking midnight and they drunkenly waded through 'Auld

Lang Syne' several times before the old year ended. Some girl had a Super 8 camera and was going round the room. When she got to Arni, leaning on his elbows through the hatch as usual, she asked 'What're you hoping for in 1984?'

'Death.' Was the great restauranteur's placid answer. He got it. But that's another story.

'This is the year I become a serious player. Otherwise, I'm going home.' Harry was sloshed and maudlin.

'You need to find some more stars to milk. Pardon the expression.'

Harry had explained everything to Tristan. 'Maybe I can put an anonymous note in all the in-boxes at the mail room. Wanted: celebrity sperm. They need to get their heads around the new world.'

'What new world?'

'Deregulation, Tristan,' breezed Harry loftily. 'That's the name of the game. I've been reading about it. They've got to wise up – follow Wall Street – learn to asset-strip the talent.'

'What do you mean?'

'Well, there's a lot of spare meat on some of those old car-casses. Look at Matt. Who knew his jis could be worth a cool two mil?'

'What assets could you strip? Apart from sperm? Which, you might find, doesn't go down very well with the community at large. Let alone the Screen Actors Guild. Or the theatre owners. Don't forget about them.' Tristan started to laugh.

'OK. Maybe not sperm. But books. Perfume. Advertising. Home furnishing. I don't know. All the things they secretly go to Japan for now. They could do it here.'

'But in the States the movie star is like a virgin. She can't be sullied.'

'Not yet. Wait until I get my teeth into her.' Now Tristan really laughed 'What's so funny?'

'You are. You've really done it. You've been bitten. You got the bug.'

'What do you mean?'

'You've jumped into the sewer and you're loving it. Careful, though. You don't want to drown in your own bullshit.'

At that moment Big Ben rang out again.

'This is it,' shouted Arni. 'Good luck, boys. Here's to another year we're all going to fuck up.'

Of course, Harry had been offended. He didn't see himself in such a stark light, but actually he was part of a gradual shift. He had merged with the spirit of the city. He woke up in the mornings hungry for his deal and soon a contract was drawn up between lawyers. A specialist nurse was employed to gather the seed. Matt Dean was contracted for five shots over two days, no action replay if the seed didn't take. Matt himself was tested for sperm strength – good results – he was put on a special diet and a date was set for the impregnation.

On the day the fee went into escrow they had a celebratory lunch.

'We need a name for the company,' said Charles Ronson.

'Cuddles. Let's call it Cuddles,' suggested Dorinda.

'And Associates,' added Harry.

'This all remains at crypt level, by the way,' continued Charles. 'It will kill us all if it gets out.'

At work, Harry was promoted to the office of Cindy Ridge. He was out of the mail room, on his way to the middle, if not the top. Lord Snooty had become a fixture. He had confidence, he was funny, deferential when he needed to be, and had managed to score a small independent film for Matt in the fall.

*

The impregnation of Oya Benici of Sultan Supermarkets took place in Bungalow One at the Beverly Hills Hotel one teatime in late January.

The whole group was assembled. Charles Ronson paced up and down in a dove-grey suit and a matching tie with a thick knot. (Everything was grey except his eyes, which were bright blue on brilliant white, due to that killer eye drop, Collyre Bleu.) He was consulting some notes on a clipboard.

'OK, ladies and gentlemen. Listen up,' he snapped. 'First and foremost – good afternoon. Welcome.' He paused, surveyed the group. The Sultana had ordered beluga and champagne and raised her glass. Someone handed him one.

'Later. Thank you. This is a highly sensitive mission. I don't need to tell you all that. Non-disclosure forms will be distributed when I have finished. Any questions, come to me or my associate Ivan Laslow' – he put his arm around the other lawyer – 'and remember: signing the NDAs is only half of the job of keeping this at crypt level. I am telling you. C R Y P T. We are dealing with reputation here. Its value is priceless – so go figure. Notwithstanding, I would like to go through the order of the day and how we are going to approach the whole ... ' he paused, lost for a description ' ... affair.'

The Sultana lay back on the cushions, dressed like a ghost, a white turban on her head. Only her fingernails and toenails were flesh and blood red. It was hard to know what she was thinking. Dorinda was like a nervous husband, drinking champagne and chain smoking. Two nurses, like angels in white scrubs and hats, stood to attention. The doorbell rang and a troupe of waiters appeared, pristine in white jackets. Charles threw up his hands in frustration. Trolleys with starched white cloths were wheeled in, artfully converted into round tables by the waiters, laid with plates of burgers and fries and drinks and salads. The Sultana signed the bill with a careless scribble. The waiters left in a line.

'May I continue?' asked Charles Ronson.

'Sorry, Charles,' cooed the Sultana, ignoring the acid tone. 'Do keep going.'

'Right. The boys will get set up in the other bedroom and Mrs Benici – you will stay in your room.'

'Thanks.' Now it was her turn to be acid.

'Each of you has an assigned nurse. Welcome, Shania and Lucas.' The angels waved. 'They both have a lot of experience in this field – and no champagne for you two, please.' Laughs. 'The whole process will be filmed, and the film will be destroyed after it has been witnessed by both the participants and their representatives – all of us together, please. This is so there can be no doubt about the provenance of the harvested seed.' He looked at Matt and winked. 'Straight after, we will burn the film. The seed will be extracted manually. Harry Dent has been designated to operate the camera. At the moment of jouissance – as they say in France – the nurse – yes you, Lucas – must be in the room to harvest the seed and it will be taken straight to Mrs Benici's bathroom to be folded into the binding agent – Fertigel QO5 – plus a vitamin serum that Shania will then infuse into ... er ... Mrs Benici. We will repeat the process twice more today and once again tomorrow, in the morning. Now, any questions?'

'Yes. Can I have a drink? Please. My nerves are in shreds,' giggled the Sultana.

The love affair – if it was a love affair – had its beginning, middle and end that night. Harry lay on the bed pretending to read a magazine. Matt shut the door. Took his shirt off and prowled round the room closing the curtains. Then he put on a CD. He gyrated over to the bed, singing along to the song. ('Sister Morphine' by the Rolling Stones.) He opened Harry's mouth with one hand and put a small pink pill on his tongue with the other. 'Body of Christ,' he whispered. Harry began to protest. Matt put a pointed finger up to his mouth. Then he took a pill himself, watching Harry as he swallowed it down with a bottle of water next to the bed. 'Let's make it a party. Just us two. But no words.'

'The nurse has got to come in. And the lawyers.'

'Yeah. At the end. Just say nothing. You talk too much.' Then he sat cross-legged on the bed, rolled a joint, got up to look for a lighter and opened the door to the hall. Outside sat the two lawyers and the nurse, their heads together, eyes wide, whispering. They stopped dead, looked up guiltily.

'Ready?' asked Charles.

'Not nearly,' replied Matt, slamming the door again. He blew out a jet of smoke that formed a large lazy question mark over his head. The ecstasy was beginning to come on. Waves of pleasure, affection, the sudden need to touch. Inhibition evaporated and Matt ran his hand along Harry's shoulder. 'Take off your shirt,' he commanded.

Harry obeyed. Matt stroked Harry's clavicle with his thumb while his fingers circled his neck. Nothing this intimate had ever happened to Harry and time suddenly stood still. Swaying slightly to the music, they came together, flesh on flesh. Matt put his head on Harry's shoulder, his arms round his waist and sighed. They moved round as slow as the planet for a while and then Matt laughed. 'OK, let's start filming.' Harry was spellbound, his eyes locked into Matt's. He picked up the camera and put it to his eye.

'OK. Lights, camera, action.'

Matt knew how to give it his all – through the lens. 'You want me to start.' He rubbed his hand over his crotch. Unzipped his fly.

'Oh my God.' Harry spoke before he could stop himself.

'You like it?'

'I think so.'

'Think so? Come on, Sister Morphine. Make my nightmares into dreams.'

And so Matt Dean pleasured himself while Harry stood in front of him with the camera, their eyes locked through the lens. It would always be the strangest coupling either of them would ever have.

'OK,' said Matt finally in a strangled voice. 'It's gonna happen.'

'Could you come back in,' shouted Harry to Lucas the nurse, zooming in with his camera. He thought he might faint. Lucas reappeared in rubber gloves and scrubs, holding a little cone, like the ones they have next to water coolers. The two lawyers stood in the doorway, leaning in.

Matt didn't seem to be put off his stride. The performer in him had arrived at the ultimate revelation and he leant back on his hips and watched himself with a proud grin on his face. Harry zoomed in and got the shot in close-up, while the coiled body of the nurse in his shower cap and blue gloves harvested the seed with wide, horrified eyes, adding a comic element so that Harry got the giggles. Then Matt laughed. And then the two lawyers. Lucas looked upset and stormed off holding the cone in front of him. Harry followed – still filming.

In the white marble bathroom, Shania had set up a portable laboratory. She mixed the cocktail in her new-age cauldron, added various ingredients, drew the infusion up into a gigantic cartoon syringe and took it through to the next room, where the Sultana lay on her bed, legs akimbo, talking on the phone. It looked like a dose for an elephant. Stifled giggles again as the men leaned through the door, and the nurse raised the huge syringe to the light and squirted out a little bit. 'Is that really necessary? We're not mainlining it,' barked the Sultana. 'That's ten grand right there.' It was like being in some weird theatrical farce, everyone making exits and entrances, each one more comic than the last. 'Hang on, darling,' whispered the Sultana into the phone. 'I'm just having my baby.' She put the receiver down and took Dorinda's hand. 'Here we go.'

'Can we have you on your front, please, Mrs Benici,' said Shania.

'On my front?'

'Yes. All fours is best.'

The Sultana rolled over and planted herself on her knees and elbows. 'Come on, then. If you're coming.'

The nurse inserted her syringe carefully. It reminded Harry of an eighteenth-century oil painting he had seen of a maid administering an enema to her delighted mistress on a four-poster bed, observed by a rake hiding behind a screen. The Sultana moaned a little but Dorinda stroked her hand. After it was done, the two of them lay against the wall of the room, legs in the air.

In the adjoining room, Matt had crashed back onto the bed. 'Come here,' he commanded as Harry returned. 'Lie down.'

Harry felt shy without the camera. He lay down on the other side of the bed. Matt rolled over onto his side. Their faces were close. And then Matt leaned towards him with a lazy smile and kissed his mouth, tenderly, deeply, for the first (and last) time. Little tears like diamonds glittered in the corners of his eyes. Then he fell asleep. A tear oozed from a closed eyelid and slid down his cheek. Harry, wide awake, watched, not moving a muscle until his arm went dead.

And that was the entire spectrum of their relationship as lovers. One kiss.

*

Ten years later. Harry was a powerful agent. He had single-handedly resurrected Matt Dean's career. Matt was the jewel in a crown of good clients. Harry was the real thing now. Less fun, less spontaneous. He had that thing that killers get. He always thought before he spoke, and he never interrupted. He just let you go on and on and gave nothing away. His language and vocabulary drew on the agency phrase book, that he had sworn at the start he would never adopt. However, it was impossible to deal with wave after wave of phosphorescent star quality crashing against one without some decent decoy mechanism in place, or else they simply wore you out, ate you down to the bone like a pet shoal of piranha fish, with their big lips and dopey eyes and bone china teeth and flashy tails. Harry wondered now, how could anyone deal with their anxiety, their anger, their diminished view of themselves on Monday, their syphilitic perspective on Thursday, without using every trick in the agent's manual?

The wages of sin. Harry had a great house in Malibu Canyon. Matt had been nominated for an Oscar.

The story of the Sultana was more or less forgotten. The pregnancy was a thing best left alone. They realised after the event – like people who have narrowly avoided a fatal car crash – just how dangerous it could end up being for the Sultana, who brought up the child as the son of her husband. They kept up with her in the gossip columns and looked with interest – but no more – at the picture of Matt's little son. The whole business had been sealed in concrete long ago. CRYPT.

But one mistake had been made. Charles Ronson had not been able to resist keeping the tape of the infamous evening in Bungalow One, and little by little it was beginning to get a reputation. At parties in his house for those guests who were apparently at crypt level – other vile queens from the business – Bob and Jacky, hairdressers from hell; Larry and Walt, actor and production designer; Gene and Laurie, first assistants from the silent days – these lucky people got to see one of the most scandalous porno singles of the decade and, naturally, at some point someone was going to snitch. It was a young front-office queen from Warner Bros. who made a film from the film and sent it to the *National Enquirer*.

Mayhem ensued. The Sultana fled from Turkey. Harry was fired from William Morris. Matt Dean too. They were on the cover of every tabloid the world over. Matt would never work again. Harry was going to be sued by the agency. And that was how it all started.

He was having breakfast with Dorinda in the aftershock. She was nearly forty, still unmarried, still drifting, this close to everything, still friends with the Sultana.

'Sometimes I think we should just be what they say we are,' he wondered out loud, head back, eyes closed, drinking in the warm winter sun.

'What do you mean, exactly?'

'I mean, let's start an agency. Sperm. Eggs. Wombs. It's the future. After all, NO female star wants to have her own baby these days. They want to keep working. We could sign up a roster of high-quality surrogates – the real dairy product – we could find the perfect person to carry our client's precious eggs. *We* could even have an egg bank. Buying and selling. We can realise people's dreams. It could be huge. Let's talk to Oya. She has two hundred million dollars to play with, remember?'

'A lot more now that she has an heir. She nabbed all the supermarkets.'

'Great. So, let's be what they say we are. Matt can front it. We can turn him into a kind of preacher. Maybe a dog collar, even.'

'We could call him the Revered. Like in *Travels with My Aunt.*'

They laughed hard but within a year the agency was formed. In two years, Matt Dean made the famous ad for Cuddles, shot by Bruce Weber. It exploded. Shirtless, with a baby. 'You know it makes sense,' he growled at the end to the baby who gurgled back in agreement. The response was incredible. A tidal wave of demand.

'This close to everything,' said Dorinda on the telephone that Christmas, describing another failed relationship. She was at her beachfront property in the South of France. Harry was at his farm in Bahia, Brazil.

'Not any more. You were finally in at the kill.'

'And what a kill.'

'Do you regret it?'

'The agency?'

'The whole thing. The debasing of our parents' value system for one thing, the merchandising of motherhood? Having a baby. Creation. I don't know.'

'Oh, pull yourself together, Harry, for fuck's sake. Why are you always such a wimp? You do it. And then you regret it. What kind of life is that? Anyway, we haven't trivialised anything. We have made life easier for some people. We are a part of progress. You can't stand in the way. Where is Matt, by the way?'

'With a new girl in Aspen. He's working again. Can you believe it?'

'What is he doing?'

'Some old wizard fell off their broomstick and he got the part. It's a superhero film. Tristan is producing.'

'So they lifted the fagwah?'

'They had to. What we did seems like nothing by today's standards.'

'Make your mind up.'

'I mean, what Matt did. A sex tape is your calling card these days.'

'It's a whole new world. I hate it.'

'You started it.'

*

Outside the stock exchange they stand on the sidewalk for a moment. Strangers now. Money has pulled them apart. It always does. Harry is heading for the airport. Dorinda and the Sultana are seeing a show on Broadway. Matt Dean is in love with a new girl. They have all gone hard, set, like plastic models. Soon they will have security guards. But meanwhile the show goes on.

THE LAST RITES

In 2017 I was shooting an eccentric film in Jodhpur about the Rani of Jhansi, her band of lady warriors and their struggle during what the Indians call the First War of Independence and what we – for now – call the Indian Mutiny. It was a privately made film, a family affair, and starred the daughter, directed by the mother. As part of my research, I began to read about the Mutiny and I couldn't stop. I am not one of those people who thought they were Cleopatra in a past life (this life, maybe) but I felt as if I was walking on my own grave. God knows why. Perhaps because I am historically tied to empire. Either way, I was immediately enthralled and horrified. Would I ever be able to figure out exactly what happened and why? William Dalrymple's book about Bahadur Shah, *The Last Mughal*, was particularly vivid. *Our Bones Are Scattered* by Andrew Ward was another. Historical novels abound. My favourite was Julian Rathbone's *The Mutiny*.

One stitch in that terrible tapestry of 1857 that I couldn't get out of my mind was the story of Margaret Wheeler, the daughter of General Wheeler, who disappeared in the fatal retreat from Kanpur – presumed dead – but was found in 1907, living as a Muslim.

My own great-grandmother left Northumberland for India, to marry a man she hardly knew, at around that time. Hers was another story that moved me. She had been a free spirit, from a large, exuberant family who adored amateur theatrics. She found it difficult to settle into the rigid life of the cantonment. Her husband, Donald Maclean (not the spy), seems to me to have been a sour-tempered man. According to her, they had 'terrible altercations but wonderful reconciliations'. I think she was being kind. In my mind, he was unimaginative, unyielding, certainly racist, whereas she – my great-grandmother – was curious, sympathetic and eccentric.

Making the film about the Rani of Jhansi – I was rather good as General Sir Hugh Rose – I started to dream of my own story, a series. The heroine on the English side would be a collage made from poor Margaret Wheeler and my great-grandmother, Gwendolyn Hope. The story of a girl who leaves home never to return and the sepoy who loved her.

I am a camera, but not the single-shutter box Brownie through which Christopher Isherwood observed Berlin. I am a twenty-four-frame drone moving through the Indian night, flying like a ghost train down a labyrinth of grainy lanes and alleys, twisting and turning, through courtyards and archways. Not a soul abroad. Just a small figure in a ghostly niqab fluttering through the deserted streets. The only noise – her breath and her footsteps, the sounds of snores and odd dreams from the flat roofs above.

She runs out into the bazaar, into the orange glare of the street lamps. Her billowing robes make an impressive shadow as she flits across the empty square. Bells ring out the quarter hour on the clock tower, a miniature Big Ben, as she passes. She disappears through an arch, down dark streets, picking her way over sleeping untouchables, men and women in rows, past rickshaws parked in lines, their owners sleeping at the wheel, arms and legs piled up. She runs through the Tikonia Garden, past the Wind Palace, the heavy-set government buildings. A December night in Lucknow. 1921.

She hears the faraway sound of a hymn – a Christmas carol, in fact – and she runs into the cantonment, past the guards – they know her – the parade ground, the officers' mess spangled in light, into streets called Sunningdale, Reading and Cambridge Circus. Christmas firs sit in the windows of bungalows that might have been transported directly from Bournemouth, all pebbledash and frosted glass, framed in tropical foliage, palms, creepers, gigantic leaves looking in bewildered at the candlelit tree. She runs up the hill to Christ Church, that heavily rusticated fortress of God where Christian blood was spilt during the Mutiny in 1857. On a slight hill, looking up, it might be some village church in Shropshire. Looking down, on the other hand, from its bell tower on a hot afternoon, the whole subcontinent seems to be laid out, shimmering in India's peculiar dust-cut light. The city, the plains and the distant mountain range blister and buckle in the heat. A steam train labours through it all, the black smudge from its funnel melting into the haze, its whistle moaning softly, like a mechanical turtle dove, as it heads towards Lucknow, which falls like a dirty skirt onto the rusty plain.

Tonight, the bells ring. Their message flies through the cantonment as the faithful spill from the church. Men in uniform, women in evening dress negotiate a steep flight of steps. Cars and carriages (still many carriages) wait in line at the bottom. The general and his wife first, the rest hanging behind. An organ wheezes through a voluntary and an old vicar stands at the door wishing his flock a happy Christmas. The girl hangs in the shadows, her eyes fixed on the holy man. She waits until the last parishioner has left, and she darts over to the priest, tugs at his robe. The padre looks round, raises his arms. A reflex. The girl holds an envelope.

'Is this for me, child? Yeh mere liye hai?'

The girl nods. He opens the envelope and a medal falls to the ground. He picks it up and looks closely. It's the cross of a Knight Commander of the Order of Bath. He turns suspiciously to the girl. 'Where did you get this?' She smiles, gestures with one hand, pulling at his cassock with the other. He looks in the envelope. A piece of paper with three words, in a spidery scrawl. Please. Come. Urgent. Followed by an illegible signature.

Her eyes are wide and beautiful, the colour of hazelnuts. The vicar has been looking forward to a little supper and bed – tomorrow is a big day – but his resolve melts in the mute appeal in the child's eyes. 'I can't go like this, young lady. I shall have to change.'

'Jaldee. Jaldee,' she insists.

'And where am I going? Who is this personage? I can't read the writing.'

She nods her head in agreement but offers nothing more.

With his heart in his mouth, he follows her through the Tikonia Garden into the bazaar, but his nerve falters as she leads him into the unlit lanes behind the clock tower. Three times he stops. Three times she urges him on. 'Jaldee. Jaldee.'

He is a good vicar, not a typical sahib – he loves India, at odds with the workings of the British, still haunted by the fresh memory of Amritsar. She pulls him by the hand and together they plunge into the dark. He clutches comically at the crucifix round his neck. What a mess it will be if I am killed here, he thinks, looking up to God, but where is he? The question has been gnawing at the old vicar for some years. British India does that to you. The moon appears through the clouds, briefly crosshatching the minarets of Bara Imambara in silver. The vicar is wonderstruck each time – by the wonderful chaos. Tonight, the great mausoleum looks lopsided, like a sinking ship on a sea of rooftops.

Finally, they come to a dead end. A door in a wall. She puts a finger to her lips for silence and smiles to encourage. She can see that the vicar is deeply uncomfortable. He has never been this far into the interior and he's frankly afraid. He is about to speak but she hisses quietly, offering him instead her hand, which he willingly takes, their roles neatly reversed. She has a key and unlocks the door, slips inside, shutting it behind her, leaving him for a moment alone.

'Jesus Christ save me,' he prays. Is this an elaborate trap?

But what can he do now? He won't be able to find his way back
to the bazaar. So he waits and watches the moon climb across
the sky. It seems an eternity before she is back, beckoning
from the open door. He breathes a sigh of relief and follows her
into a large courtyard. There is a pool and the sound of gently
splashing water. On the far side a verandah stretches from one
corner of the yard to the other. Beyond it, electric-lit rooms
under humming fans and a group of men sitting cross-legged on
the floor, five or six of them, bearded, pristine in white, round
a cloth spread with food. Servants stand behind them. All men.
The vicar can hear his heart pounding. 'If I am discovered
here – but don't think. Just follow the girl.' They creep through
the shadows to another door. She pulls him through and locks it
behind her. She is nervous too.

It takes a moment for the vicar to adjust his old eyes to the
dim light but when he does, he gasps. Three blue-shrouded
figures sit in a row against the wall. Their faces are covered. Just
three small squares of gauze to see through. They are like statues in the half light, or blue ghosts, or the barge ladies of Avalon,
thinks the vicar. He is in a harem, a thing utterly forbidden to
anyone – let alone a firangi – beyond the husband of the women,
their children, some close female family. The vicar nearly faints,
puts a hand against the wall to steady himself.

The girl says something and one of the figures rises, gestures
for them to follow, past these gatekeepers, down a passage and
into a large bare room, lit by a single paraffin lamp. Somebody
coughs and the vicar strains to see. In the far corner a figure
lies on a divan covered by a sheet, like a corpse. Another blue-
shrouded figure sits on a stool next to the bed and presses a
cloth against the corpse's forehead. As he becomes accustomed
to the dark, the room slowly emerges from the shadows. Now
he can make out an old woman's face, grey and ghostly, drawn
but not dead, breathing with difficulty. The other woman dips

the cloth in water, wrings it out carefully, presses it again to the head of the old woman. Whispers of encouragement. The scene is mesmerising, primitive, sacred, and the vicar marvels to himself. 'Nothing has changed in this room for a thousand years.'

The faraway sound of the men at their midnight meal makes the silence echo deeper through the halls of purdah. From somewhere the sound of dripping water. The air is thick and sweet. It smells of incense, but also of dung. A thin plume of smoke snakes lazily from a brazier of coals to a blackened vent in the ceiling. The old woman struggles to breathe and for a moment the vicar is struck by the extraordinary simplicity of death, slowly pulling life away from its moorings onto the invisible current. It can't have been much of a life, he thinks, looking around, these rooms in which women have lived, waiting for a man to arrive or for death to release them.

The corpse coughs again and gestures with her hand for the other woman to leave.

'Aap bhi,' she says to the girl who brought the vicar. The girl bows and they both leave the room. The vicar turns to follow them. He definitely doesn't want to be found alone with this woman. He will be killed.

'Sit,' she commands – in cut-glass English.

Shaking slightly, he moves the stool around so that he can face her.

She raises herself with difficulty on the pillows, drawing the sheet to her neck with long, skeletal fingers. The effort exhausts her and she lies back. Closes her eyes. For a long moment nothing is said. Her shallow breath clatters inside her chest. Her hands clench and unclench at the sheet, the fingers searching for something – but it's not there. Finally, she groans and opens her eyes, looking straight at the vicar, and regards him steadily. Still not a word. She reaches for his hand.

'Don't be afraid,' she whispers. 'You will not be discovered.' Each word takes its toll. Her eyes are startling, bright blue with rings of grey around the pupils. Her throat clicks and she points a shaking finger at the confused vicar. Click. Click. Click. She might be laughing. He can't tell, but the hairs on his arms suddenly stand erect, static with fear. A tear slips over her drooping lid and makes its way slowly across the tracks and tributaries of her hollow cheeks.

'Who are you?' he asks.

She answers with difficulty, one word at a time, but he can't hear. Just a crackle, like an untuned wireless. There's a jug of water by the bed. He pours a glass, lifts her head, puts the glass to her lips. She drinks gratefully and then lies back on the pillows, looking up to the ceiling (and beyond).

'My name is Lydia Saunders. I am the daughter-in-law of Brigadier Saunders of the 24th Rifle Brigade.'

Somebody is walking on my grave, thinks the vicar as the thin hair on his head bristles with electricity and beads of sweat appear all over his body. There are many legendary names in the sad annals of British India, particularly from the Mutiny. Canning. Nicholson. Wheeler. And Saunders. Lydia Saunders. The vicar only came to Lucknow in 1895 but the memory of '57 is still fresh in the cantonments. The men still swear by Lydia Saunders at the officers' mess at Meerut.

She'd disappeared during the retreat from Cawnpore on 27 June 1857, when the survivors of a two-month siege were routed as they tried to escape to boats on the Ganges. Indeed, there is a plaque to her memory that says as much in the transept of All Souls' Church. But a body was never recovered. Legend variously recounted her being abducted by the mutineers, or killing her assailants, three men, before fleeing north to Kashmir, never to be seen again for the shame of it all. To that end there had been a famous cartoon in the *Illustrated London*

News of Lydia with a gun, dispatching three sepoys, a tattered Union Jack wrapped around her like Liberty at the barricade. Most probably she was simply butchered along with the soldiers and their families during that tragic morning on the river of blood.

Either way, the vicar is speechless.

'My dear lady. It is not possible. Mrs Saunders died years ago. In 1857. It is now 1921.'

She thinks for a minute.

'My name is Lydia Saunders, Brigadier Saunders's daughter-in-law. Do you see that box under the table?'

He reaches down for it.

'Open it.'

In the box is a letter. And a brooch. The letter is addressed to Miss Lydia Hope.

'It is from Captain Saunders, the man I married. He died during the siege. They are all I have left. Read.'

The vicar opens the letter.

'Out loud.'

'"Dearest – may I call you dearest? – Miss Hope. We are all leaving for Darjeeling in two weeks. My mother and my sisters would all be delighted if you could join us. I believe Mama has talked to Captain Hope but of course the last word is with you. I sensed a disinclination at the club on Sunday. You seemed distant. Have you changed your mind?"'

'I had not,' whispers Lydia. 'But how I wished I had.' She freezes, eyes suddenly wide. Is she going to drop dead? Now. Before she has finished. He waits, hardly daring to breathe. He can feel her need to talk. At the same time, he can see that it's almost impossible for the words to emerge. They battle with her lips, trying to find form. She opens her mouth, but nothing comes. Just the strange clicks. A kind of death rattle, perhaps. Her lips and face have learnt not to give anything away. She has

built a dam inside but now it is breached. Soon the words begin
to tumble out and the years fall away in the flood.

'I am eighty-three years old. I was born in 1838. Listen carefully. This is my last chance to talk. My only chance – to set the
record straight.'

The girl comes in with a tray. She places an iron pot on the
brazier and squats beside it, raking the coals, pouring tea from
the pot into small bowls. She helps the lady to drink – a thick
oily liquid – offers another bowl to the vicar, which he takes.
'Careful,' says the old lady. 'It's poppy seed.'

Too late. The vicar drinks it. As far as he is concerned the
world has crashed to a halt. What is one poppy tea, more or less?
When in purdah ... etc. He stands. 'I shall finish this and go
straight to the general. Fear not, Mrs Saunders. We'll have you
out of here by morning,' he says, borrowing the gallant attitude
from his flock of troops.

'I didn't ask you here to rescue me. I want to confess. That's
all. Tell someone my story. So that at least I am remembered,
if only by you. I am very happy where I am. Do you imagine it
would be pleasurable to be saved? At this stage? Paraded across
the cantonment like a jungle creature?'

The vicar sits again. Luckily, because he feels a little
unsteady.

'You don't look comfortable.' She gestures to another mattress on the floor. The vicar collapses onto it, grunting slightly,
panting, laughing to himself at the extraordinary turn of events.
Lydia lies back on the pillows. They sit for another moment in
silence as she gathers her strength. Then in a hoarse whisper
she begins her story.

'It started on the night of the big party at Shoreston. I was
eighteen. My brother John was back from India and we had a
ball, you see. Not a terrifically grand affair but I can remember
every second of it. We put on a play after supper. Five brothers

and me. Plays were the thing at home and what fun we had doing them. We became quite famous. Our *Christmas Carol* was reviewed in the *Newcastle Times*!' Her eyes glow – unseeing – in the dim light.

She's back there, back at Shoreston, thinks the vicar. It's funny, she had seemed Indian propped up on her pillows and yet, the more she talks, the more obviously English she becomes.

'We had planned a new play to celebrate my brother's leave and we were instructed by him to be sure of a "whacking good role" for his friend Captain Saunders. We knew Captain Saunders. We knew him well. In fact, it was generally assumed that he would propose to me that summer. And he did. Almost as soon as he arrived in June. I hesitated. To be or not to be. To stay at home with my adored family or to strike out and begin a new life in India. To see the Ganges. The maharajahs, with their ropes of pearls, the panthers, the white elephants, the sacred temples. I longed for the adventure. My brother had written so much about it. His letters were read after dinner by my father, who always wept at the end.' She pauses for thought. 'My brother was another reason for going. My dearest friend in the family. But that friendship died in India.'

'Did I love Captain Saunders that summer? My sister Lillie kept on at me. What does it feel like? How does the world look now? To be sure, he was handsome and light-hearted, sweet and attentive, but I think, looking back, he fell in love with our family, not me. At Shoreston he was full of life.' A cloud of frustration scuds across her face, taking the light from it. Her lips draw back, revealing a mouth void of teeth. She waves off the invading thoughts with her hand. Then she covers her face and weeps. 'It's like looking through a kaleidoscope, always the same pictures, revolving, shrinking, reversing, night after night, year after year. Trying to find out why.'

'Why what?'

'Why did it all happen? Why did I make such a huge mistake? I keep looking for clues. I watch the same scenes. Over and over. Playing croquet with my brother and Captain Saunders on the lawn, seeing the strength of their friendship, wanting to be part of it, watching his hands on the mallet in the half light, strong, manly. Do I want them around my waist? Did I? I can see the dusk gathering in the woods. I can hear the noise of the mallet against the ball. The woods are dark and silent. They are trying to tell me something, you see, but I am too young to hear. Often, I am sitting with them, before the lamps are lit, watching their laughing faces, just black shapes against the dusk outside, or walking with them by the river under the summer moon. All memories of darkness and darkening. Strange, isn't it? But it wasn't love. And it turned to . . . '

'Captain Saunders was Brigadier Saunders's son?'

'Yes.

'That night at the ball Papa tapped his glass with a spoon and stood up. You could tell everyone liked him because of how they all smiled and laughed. The men in their stiff shirts like armour, the women rigid in their corsets, their hair piled up. He said he hoped everyone was having a wonderful time, but that for him it was a tragic occasion because he was losing his best friend. You see, Mother died in '46.'

She falls silent for a moment. The vicar tries to think of something to say.

'I expect you ran the house for him.'

'Indeed. And that was why I felt compelled to leave. I knew I would never get away if I waited too long. Buried alive, I thought. What a fool. What a terrible bloody fool I was. I didn't look carefully. I just danced into the abyss, blind in my white dress and drunk on Captain Saunders's attention. Round and round. Faster and faster.'

She groans. It is heart-rending to watch the grinding of memory inside her head. Finally, she calms herself.

'Everyone was jealous. And I loved that. So it was agreed that I would join my brother in Cawnpore with a view to getting married to Captain Saunders at Christmas in Calcutta, in the presence of Lord Canning, the governor-general. Do you see? My head had been turned. Twisted, actually. Saunders himself had sat for what seemed like hours in Papa's study. They both came out ashen-faced but a contract had been drawn up. I will never forget my father's eyes. Those eyes have watched me through ... all this. He knew he would never see me again, that he had lost me. But I was so sure. The dream felt real. My future husband was attentive and patient. The idea of India thrilled me. Even the journey. Anything to get away from Shoreston. Never trust yourself when you feel sure. You are bound to be wrong. But it was that night, when we danced, that I suddenly realised I had signed a kind of death warrant. I was laughing and waving to my friends as they swirled by, talking as we passed one another in the dance – I felt giddy, like a child, but at the same time not like a child, it was terribly intoxicating – but when we left the floor, he took me outside on to the terrace and said – kindly, not in anger, although there was an edge to his voice that I was to get to know later – he said, "You know, Lydia, if we are to be married, you must behave yourself as befits the wife of an officer when you are with him on the dance floor."

'"What do you mean?" I asked.

'"We are at a country party, so I do not scold you. But when we dance at the governor-general's ball in Calcutta you will look only at me. Is that understood?"

'"Why, yes, dear. I'm sure I never meant to vex you." It was something in the way he spoke. Intransigent, perfect, kindly but icy, suddenly lifeless. I excused myself and went up to my room and cried. How I cried that night. But it was too late. I couldn't stop. The wheels were already in motion.

'So a few weeks later I set off with my father for London. I remember every moment of that parting as if it were yesterday. The coach being loaded up. And the traps. Five trunks. I remember thinking – this is my mass worth. Everyone came out onto the drive that morning and we all cried. Cook gave me a picnic basket and a bunch of flowers. Rawlings – the butler – presented me with a framed photograph of all the servants. It was signed by them all and inscribed "We will never forget you. Don't forget us." I could hardly speak and had to look up so that the tears didn't fall from my eyes. *Face the future*, I said to myself but as we drove down the lime grove I turned. There they all were, the dear people with whom I had passed my entire life, going back into the house, going about their business, and I felt a sudden chasm open in my heart. Their world was going on. Mine had stopped dead. I studied the old house for the last time, juddering up and down through the back of the carriage. Every window held a memory but now it was a picture, a kind of screen. I would never go back. In that moment I knew, one of those terrible certainties that happen a few times in a life. I looked at Father and he knew it too.

'"It's not so easy having daughters," was all he said.

'"Do you think I shall ever come back?" I asked him.

'He took my hands in his. His face said no but his lips managed to lie. "I hope so my child. I hope so. Our plays will not be the same without you."

'We headed south to York. More heartbreaking goodbyes. Our grooms and stable lads had been like family to me. We stayed the night at the Station Hotel and the next day went by train to London and then to Dover, where we caught the packet to Calais. Crossing France, scorched in the late-summer heat, we forgot ourselves briefly, lulled by the motion of the train, the comfort of our compartment and the view of France through the windows, of hay ricks and cart horses, roads flanked with plane trees, honey-coloured towns built into the sides of great winding rivers. We stayed at Lyon, on a hill looking over the city, and the Rhône was a pale blue snake.

'The light changed as we barrelled south, through fields of lavender dotted with poppies, past the sharp rocky hills of Provence, their long blue shadows thrown across the plain, and finally into the station at Marseille on a muggy afternoon, myself, my father and five trunks, my dowry: china, silver, paintings, clothes and books, everything I had been, now reduced by marriage to boxes of memories. Smashed, as it happened. All the china was broken when I unpacked it.

'We spent two nights in a boarding house above the port and wandered about on the steep streets, arm in arm, like a married couple almost, engrossed in one another. There was so much to say but we didn't have the words. We talked about everything except for the one thing. He could tell I'd had a change of heart. We were very close, you see. The night before I sailed, we were having dinner, he took my hands in his and asked me if I still wanted to go. I didn't, but I said yes. I couldn't bear the idea of failure, of letting him down.

' "Well, you know you can always come back. If you don't like it out there." He kissed my wrist and we both cried.

'In India my brother and Captain Saunders were different people. Hard, calculating, humourless and pompous. I lived with my brother in a bungalow called Jacaranda on a repugnant street of identical houses. We were served, the two of us, each morning at breakfast, each evening at dinner, by twelve men. In our small home we had a cook, an undercook, two houseboys, a man to operate the fan. Two men to mow the lawn, weed and water the grass and marigold beds. (The garden drew none of its inspiration from India. Its dogged, withered borders came straight from Tunbridge Wells.) I can see the hard faces of my brother and Captain Saunders. All around, a blur of smiling eyes and lips. The natives. They were never cross at one, as I should have been. I remember thinking that. They seemed to accept their servitude and probably the contempt of a sahib was no worse than life in service to some local nawab. I remember thinking that too.

'My brother gave me a book called *Housekeeping in India* and told me I was in charge. Then he went off to work. Alone all day, only them, smiling and bowing. Of course, I adored them all. They were the only people who talked to me. Until the terrible evenings in the club, where the memsahibs sat in kid gloves and evening dresses on the verandah, drinking tea. I disliked them all on sight and the men made me afraid, glimpsed far away in the bar, smoking and drinking together. A bell would ring and they turned as one – like a herd – and strode through all those double doors to the verandah where the ladies looked up and summoned every particle of allure. It almost made one laugh, except that it didn't. When the general appeared, flanked by his ADCs, the sea parted. It was as if God or a great saint had stepped down from heaven. Everyone stood and watched in wonder as he made his way to his table. A widow called Mrs Seymour played "God Save the Queen" on a badly tuned piano.

'As for Captain Saunders, in the orbit of his father, the briga-dier, he went down on all fours and fawned. Out of his father's sight he was tyrannical. Quite soon I hated him. Once I tried to talk about it – the change in him – to reignite the carefree intimacy we had once shared, but he simply replied, "You don't seriously expect me to behave as if I was at a house party in Northumberland, do you? We have an example to set. These people have to see that we are superior to that ridiculous puppet show, their maharajahs and begums and nawabs. Ha!"

'There was no escaping marriage. I quickly realised that.

One night at dinner, I broached the subject with my brother. He flew into a rage, like a mad child, stamping his foot. I might have laughed, but in fact I was suddenly afraid. He was barely recognisable, purple with fury, spittle flying from his mouth, stabbing the air with his finger, bearing in on me for at least an hour, while the punkha wala watched – expressionless – pulling his cord. The creaking of his fan sounded like a listing ship in the rare moments of silence that punctuated my brother's outbursts. According to him, I would disgrace the family, myself, him. In short, I would never be able to show my face again.

'We got married in Calcutta. The reception was at Government House. Lord Canning stood with Brigadier Saunders greeting the guests. It looked as if they were the married couple. It was beautiful but empty. The ballroom, candlelit, the huge windows open and the dancers swirling round, blood-red uniforms, gold shoulders, white gowns. But it was a pastiche. Everyone overacted. The memsahibs were more English than the English. They had forgotten what it was actually like in England. They were proud and particular and puritanical and poisonous. I was transferred from my brother's house to Captain Saunders's – almost identical, except that everything was in the other direction. The door to the bedroom was on the right whereas it had been on the left in my brother's bungalow. Otherwise, the same garden, the same mementoes from home on the walls, on the tables, military prints and potted palms, lamps from the Army and Navy.

'I fell in love shortly before the wedding, not with that man to whom I had been manacled but with a sergeant in his regiment. Nazim Ali Khan.'

She opens her mouth again, as if to say more. The same crackle rises from her throat, the same tear, the same short breaths. The vicar thinks of a fish drowning on a riverbank.

She clutches at his hand. 'We don't have much time. I did fall in love – but it was a schoolgirl's dream. My father-in-law sent him to take me riding. He was an esteemed soldier. In the regiment. A native who could be relied on. Every morning he arrived at our house before dawn, when it was still cool. I had a wonderful mare, given to me as an engagement present by the brigadier. She was called Maud. As the sky turned pink we rode through the cantonment, into the countryside. Every day. We stopped in villages. We saw a panther. I was happy. I knew it was nothing more than my secret fancy and I had no illusions. These kinds of feelings evaporate fast in the harsh sun of empire. We were advised endlessly about not engaging with the natives, that each time someone did, calamity ensued, and I could see that it was true. The gulf between us was simply too huge. The firangi had made sure of that. For me, the secret was strangely liberating. I was inviolate.

'He wore kohl round his eyes. His beard was the deepest black. His brow also. His cheekbones were high, and his eyes hid behind them, inscrutable, deep. Wrapped up in his turban and uniform he seemed to be quite simply a god. He certainly had the grace of a god. What a contrast to the pink and blond pigs of the 24th in their puttees and pith hats, waving their sticks and cantering around the parade ground in their steel-capped boots, barking orders and blowing whistles. Never for a moment said I a word to the man in question. You must believe me. We looked at each other. Oh yes. There was an intensity in his regard that froze me to the marrow, but both of us knew and accepted our roles. Only occasionally did our eyes suddenly lock and our defences might have slipped. But they didn't, and after my marriage he came no more with Maud.

'Three nights after we returned to Cawnpore the Mutiny began in Meerut. I can add nothing to what has undoubtedly been said. All I can tell you is – suddenly the fear of God was in the eyes of the English. After some simple calculations General Wheeler realised how outnumbered we were and ordered everyone to the entrenchment at the edge of the city. Very quickly news of the Mutiny spread and suddenly there were seven hundred of us there, sleeping on the floors of the half-built barracks either side of the parade ground. And then it started. The mutineers had found a house that looked right over us. Nobody could move without being killed. For three weeks we crouched there, waiting for reinforcements. But nobody came.'

She stops, closes her eyes, but the picture is still there, like the image of a light bulb one has stared at for too long. After a few moments of inner turmoil, she sighs deeply and comes back, her eyes opening slowly, glassy with tears. To speak is costly.

'Try to be quiet,' says the vicar, taking her hand again. He is leading her to the Styx but she must finish her story before she gets there, and so she fixes him with her eyes and takes his strength.

'The well was in the middle of the yard.' It's a whisper now, and the vicar leans his ear towards her mouth and can feel her breath. She touches his head with her fingers. 'They shot anyone trying to get water. Sunstroke. Dysentery. Cholera. Anguish. The endless shooting and screaming. Blood and brains. Bodies stinking in the heat. Just a mud wall between us and three thousand sepoys. My brother was killed first. Then Captain Saunders.' She gasps as the memory hits again, razor-sharp.

The vicar wants to pinch himself. He's beginning to dream. He can almost hear the voices, the explosions, the screams of the women. He rubs his eyes. The poppy seed tea is taking him further into the woman's story than he wants to go. Her whispers echo in his head. He looks down at her and sees her as she once was, a child. She must hardly have been a woman when all this happened.

'How old were you?'

'Nineteen,' she answers. She pulls herself up on the pillows. She has found another pocket of energy and her lights flicker on again. She even smiles toothlessly. 'Nineteen and quite pretty, I think. Have some more tea, vicar?' She cracks with a hollow laugh and the hairs stand again on the vicar's arms.

'Thank you.'

She motions for the girl, who is sitting on her haunches in the shadows, looking from one to the other with profound interest, listening without understanding. She pours the sickly dark liquid into his cup and hands it to the priest with the same sweet smile. The vicar smiles back.

'One by one they picked us off, but when Captain Saunders was killed the brigadier lost his mind. General Wheeler surrendered the entrenchment and sued for safe passage out of Cawnpore. The morning dawned. A cloudless sky. We had buried the dead as much as we could and were organised into groups for the retreat. My father-in-law was in a kind of trance. He hadn't slept for days. None of us had. What a picture we must have made as the gate opened from the entrenchment. India's rulers reduced to a limping, ragged, stinking exodus. Barely recognisable. Less than three hundred of us were left. Our clothes were filthy. Our faces cut and bruised. We stank of the latrine. The children were starving. Everyone was starving. They watched us walk past. The looks on their faces. I will never forget. Blank, inscrutable, waiting. Nana Sahib had agreed to provide boats that would take us down the Ganges to Allahabad.' She presses her hands over her head and groans.

'This is harder than I thought. Forgive me.' More tears leak from her drooping lids. 'My God, sir, it was terrible. The river was low and blinding in the sun so that one could hardly look at it and everything glittered and seemed to turn upside down. I got onto the first boat and as we set off – almost immediately, twenty or thirty of us, tightly packed, some standing – the sailors jumped overboard, running and swimming for the bank. For a moment nothing happened. We watched them, not understanding. And then we noticed a strange glimmering in the woods. What was it? It looked supernatural. Actually, it was the blades of sabres catching the sun. Behind them a thousand sepoys moving forward out of the darkness, and when they broke cover they charged.

'It felt like a dream. I couldn't move. They came at us in a slow crashing wave, across the river and on to the boats, slashing at anyone – women, children – cutting us down. I saw Mrs Murdoch's head fly through the air and just as I was about to faint, a hand closed around my face and it was him – Nazim.

'He lifted me up and fought his way from the boat through the carnage and carried me off into the woods. At some point I must have fainted because the next thing I knew I was on a mattress in a hut. In the forest. He was beside me. Complete silence. Just birds singing. No echo. Two other men were behind him. He told me everyone was dead and that I was now to be his wife. I bit and screamed and refused but he married me anyway. That's how it was. That's how it is.

'After a while – a long while – I realised that resistance was pointless. Of course, I no longer loved him. How could I? I hated him for what they had done. He moved me here to Lucknow and at a certain point I decided I had to make the best of it. I converted to Islam. I had three children. I gave him a son. He took three other wives. They're good women. I have been in charge as much as one can be in a cramped purdah like this. He never hit me. He treated me with respect and soon I forgot who I had once been.

'Now I watch the English and I can't help laughing. If only they knew it was me behind the veil, walking so closely by. No. I am eighty-three years old. The only thing I regret is coming to India in the first place. I never saw my father again. My darling family. My home. But I know it's still there somewhere. And I'm still there. Somewhere. Some of them, some remnant must be hanging on. I suppose there was the war. I missed that. But now I want absolution. And I have this brooch. Diamonds with a ruby pendant. It was my grandmother's. Please see that it gets home to Shoreston Hall in Northumberland. Tell them you saw me and that I was happy. There was no other way. I could never have gone back. Society draws invisible lines. Once you are on the other side there is no return.'

She puts the brooch into the vicar's hand. 'Please. Absolve me.'

'Of course.' He kneels by the bed and begins to pray. 'Lord Father almighty, ruler of heaven and earth, look with pity on your servant Lydia that she may find solace in your bosom and life everlasting by your side, world without end, Amen.'

He glances up. Lydia has her hands joined in prayer and tears pour down her cheeks. She begins to sing. A small, faraway sound. 'Lord for tomorrow and its needs I do not pray.' It is almost unspeakably moving to the vicar. He anoints her with water and holds her hands as she talks and drifts, fainter and fainter, still determined to remember every detail, every room, every flower in that endless summer garden of her memory. It is as if she is there and has taken him with her. 'Walking down the lime grove at dusk. Behind us the house. Look how pretty the light is through the open windows. Is the hall table covered in lilacs?'

When he wakes, he is in his own bed. 'It's a dream,' he breathes. 'Thank God. A Christmas dream.' It's as if he is falling from a great height, gasping as the familiar things come into focus. A print of Jesus, gilt-framed. Thin chintz curtains – closed – blow slightly in the open window. Fluttering light over the linoleum floor and the sounds of talking outside. The chatter of India. The vicar smiles with relief. A monkey sits in a tree, watching. Two women talk in Urdu. It's a dream.

He gets up, rubbing his head, but on his way to the bathroom something glints in the periphery of his vision. He looks down and on his dressing table is a brooch. Diamonds and a ruby pendant.

TEN-POUND POM

'Sign here,' said the solicitor, Jim Macarthur, sitting comfortably at the familiar desk. 'And here. And here.' Bony fingers slid the pages of closely typed paper towards the young man on the other side.

The young man was called Tom. He pretended to read, sifting through the pages aimlessly, the deeds of sale in front of him. Three hundred years of what? Suffering? Signed away in a second.

'Please initial every page.'

Tom looked up. How easy it was to be Jim Macarthur, enabling the manacles of centuries to be broken, without a thought, just a few easy jokes, while Tom was hardly able to move. The world stood still. The papers blurred in front of him, and he turned away towards the window. Tears slid down his cheek while the old lawyer discreetly rummaged. Through the window life was going on as usual. It was the day of the poultry sales in Bunclody. A summer's morning from childhood, a mirage almost, framed by the panelled gloom of the lawyer's office. Ruddy faces in the sunlight, strutting cockerels in cages, hands, voices, screams and whistles, seen through a blur of tears.

Tom Forley Walker was blond, clean-cut, reasonably good-looking with pale blue eyes and a little chin. He held himself like a soldier. He was the last in a long line of impoverished Walkers. The chin and the eyes could be seen in all the family portraiture since 1685, when they arrived in Ireland with William of Orange and later shone at Boyne. Their blue eyes flickered and flared across the eighteenth century but – instinctive rather than inventive – the Walkers were quite simply befuddled by the Victorian age, so that by the time the old queen died they were considered half wild and their home, Rathdown Abbey, glimpsed only at the end of its majestic lime grove (the longest in northern Europe), was southern Ireland's answer to Dracula's castle. Its parapets, its tottering towers and the pointed skeleton of its ruined church made terrible black shapes against the winter dusk while rooks cackled like witches in the misty woods. In short, few people had the courage to take the short-cut to the village by the river (Laney) and up the drive, where it was rumoured revolutionaries could still be seen hanging from the trees.

A shot in the withered arm of the Walker family came in the shape of Miss Victoria Forley, the thin-lipped heiress to a cotton mill who fell in love with young Black Jack Walker on a water-colouring holiday in the spring of 1901.

Victoria was brought up progressively. Her mother was a disciple of the great Annie Besant and she had been educated in the church of Theosophy, but she was certainly not fanatical. Far from it. In fact, she was heartily sick of the whole thing and had been itching to abandon her mother's strict vegetable regime for years, so that after one of Bearded Mary the cook's game pies at Rathdown and a couple of smouldering glances from Black Jack at the other end of the table she began to formulate a plan, and within six months the couple were married.

It was the wet summer of '02 when the Forleys arrived for the wedding. It was then, as they shivered and whispered in corners about the collapsed state of the castle, that the plan for a new wing was hatched. It was proposed by Victoria's father during a long, dull speech at the wedding lunch. Any qualms he might have had about wounded pride were unfounded. The Walkers couldn't believe their luck. As Oscar Wilde said, there's nothing like an Irish tinker once he gets into his stride.

And so Rathdown enjoyed a sort of Indian summer. The new wing was built. The old house was renovated. Windows were replaced. Hot running water was installed. A central heating system gurgled and hissed into large new-fangled radiators. Twins were born. Merlin and Iolanthe. By the beginning of the Great War they were eleven and running wild. They waved their flags and screamed as Black Jack and his brothers marched through the village, over the bridge to war.

All three brothers were killed before the end of 1914. The shock waves of grief somehow extended to the actual fabric of the place, the stones of the Abbey, the gardens. Like a fairy kingdom in a children's book, Rathdown fell under the spell of tragedy and a permanent winter set in. The parents of three dead boys could not be roused from their torpor and hardly moved again. At the armistice a band played in the village. It could be heard in bursts on the breeze and yet Rathdown remained shrouded in silence. Grandparents and one great-aunt pottered around, failing and falling one by one until suddenly the house was empty. Just Victoria and the children, nearly grown up, lost and longing for something to happen. It was the dawn of the roaring twenties.

One morning, looking out at the rain, Victoria made a decision. The next day they left for Rosslare, took the ferry to Pembroke and the train to London. The furniture was covered in dustsheets, the shutters were closed and the ancient house turned in on itself.

Life in Wimbledon was not without excitement. They lived with Victoria's mother in the magnetic field of Annie Besant and the Theosophists. There were séances and cleansings, sightings and predictions. One of those predictions was that the new messiah had just arrived, and he was called Krishnamurti.

Strange years for the young ones, as they watched their mother
and grandmother being sucked out of themselves into the frenzy
around the young Indian guru. Krishnamurti was good-looking,
dressed by a Savile Row tailor, and seemed to like nothing more
than flirting with the young rich girls and boys who hung on his
every word. The twins were captivated and competitive.

Victoria died of malaria in Madras after the scandalous
Theosophist convention of 1923. A year later the children – of
age now – rich but alone in the world – returned to Ireland,
where Merlin had his 'turn', his astral awakening. He fell badly
on a stone spiral staircase, crashing his head several times as
he tumbled down. He was unconscious for two weeks. When
he came round, it was with a message for humanity. God was a
woman and he – Merlin – was here to spread the word. Along
with his sister he launched a new religion from the dungeons
of Rathdown. In those post-war years people were looking for
alternative spiritual solutions and Iolanthe went into wonderful
trances. Pretty soon they had gathered around them a group
of like-minded loons and the pendulum kept swinging. The
siblings were keen to get their religion out to a broader public
and so they sold the paintings, then the land, and finally the
gravel pit at the end of the park to pay for all the literature they
published.

Merlin married a local woman, Sylvia, ten years older than
he. Six years into a barren marriage they had a son and named
him Tom Merlin. Sylvia was encouraged to hold him naked at
the font while Iolanthe took on the role of godmother, or Mother
God as she called herself, and neatly reorganised 'à sa façon' – a
pagan christening in the dungeon. Tom's strange shyness probably dated from this eccentric event.

Victoria's ebbing wealth kept them fed from beyond the
grave but with the arrival of the second war the family found
themselves penniless again. Merlin grudgingly joined up, was

packed off to India, captured in Burma and returned in 1945, un-hinged. In 1952, against everyone's advice, he removed the roof of Victoria's wing for tax reasons. The large rooms were exposed to the heavens. He died of a colossal heart attack a month later. Death duties wiped out what was left of the family's wealth. Her husband's death left Sylvia an empty shell, like the wing.

And so to Tom. His childhood was lived largely in an Irish harem, comprising his mother, his aunt and Dolly, his doting nursemaid. Merlin flitted in and out. They froze happily through the long winters, cut off from the world. Sylvia was loving, but vague, wrapped up in her husband. Iolanthe was busy in the dungeon with her druids, but Tom and Dolly were a team, tucked up together in the sanity of the nursery as Rathdown was slowly reclaimed by nature and began to fall down again around them. At the age of seven, on the advice of well-meaning cousins, he was sent off to boarding school in Scotland and Dolly retired to Southsea, to live with her sister. The grief at leaving the ladies and his home was something he never overcame. A crack he never managed to paper over, a certain loneliness and reserve that somehow managed to be the dark star by which he charted his whole course through life, so that whenever an opportunity for intimacy, for communication, arose, a brick wall magically appeared, impenetrable to any oncoming vibration. After school he decided on the army and was soon a captain in the Household Cavalry, and that's when our story starts.

The papers were duly signed. The castle now belonged to a chain of rest homes. The land was sold to a local developer. The roof of Victoria's wing was to be replaced. Tom bought a small cottage in the village, to which the old ladies would have to acclimatise themselves.

*

He shook the lawyer's hand. The two men looked at one another for a long moment.

'Well, that's it. Thank you, Jim.' He wasn't one for unnecessary words.

'There was nothing else you could do. Today was always waiting in the wings.'

'I know. It will be a release of sorts. And yet ... '

'What will you do, Tom? That's the main thing. You have everything ahead of you. A little cash to get yourself started. You have the army.'

'I left the army.'

'Why? If that isn't a rude question.'

'I've decided to go to Australia. Start again.'

'In Australia?' The old lawyer was aghast. 'Will you be taking the ladies?'

'No. They will stay here. I am also going to leave them all the remaining money. They pay you ten quid to go to Australia. Did you know that?'

'I read something of the sort. Mary McGregor's son went. No one's had sight or sound of him since.'

'That's just it. You can melt away. That's what I shall do. And I have to do it now. While I still have time to—'

'Do they know?'

'Not yet.'

'Will they understand?'

Tom looked away again. He wouldn't cry in front of Jim.

'Of course they will.'

'What is it with Ireland? Sons abandon their mothers. Mothers dying alone.'

'That's not fair, Jim. They'll have enough money. I'll be back. Maybe I'll make a fortune and buy the Abbey again. They'll understand.'

*

They didn't.

'How long for?' asked Iolanthe for the fourth time.

'Where is he going?' chimed Sylvia. She had gone deaf and spoke slowly since Merlin's death, like a medium in a trance.

'Australia.'

'Will we see you at the weekends?' she sang.

'No. It's quite far.'

Iolanthe was sharper than her sister-in-law.

'He's not coming back. Are you?'

'Not for a while.'

'In other words, you're emigrating.'

'I suppose I am.'

'Your son is emigrating.' Iolanthe shouted the words close to Sylvia's ear.

'I'm not deaf,' said Sylvia.

No one knew what to say next. Or maybe there was nothing to say. He was abandoning them. In the ensuing silence Iolanthe began to weep.

'Are you crying, Io? Whatever is wrong?'

'Tom's leaving.'

'I expect he'll be back at the weekend.'

And so it went on. Round and round, in and out, until the last day.

On the morning before he left the sun shone like a child's drawing over the hills above Rathdown. A big round fireball in a cloudless sky. He walked through the woods for the last time. The familiar trees creaked goodbye, the breeze moaned and the sunlight flickered through the branches. The buzz of a scooter on the high road sounded like a bluebottle on a windowpane. I will see this on my deathbed, he thought dramatically, walking to the top of the hill where he used to hide as a child. The woods swayed and billowed around the rooftops and turrets of the castle and for a moment it looked as if it was tilting, a sinking ship in a green sea. In reality it was Tom who was sinking.

He made a last tour of the house, the furniture sold, the carpets taken up or burned. His footsteps echoed across time and the empty rooms. Strange shadows were seared into the walls where once the family portraits hung, pale shapes on old wallpaper. With a shiver from the top to the bottom of his spine, one of those spasms that sets one's head nodding, he realised that he and the house were inseparable, indistinguishable – the stone and the flesh. He was the house and the house was him. Would he ever be able to get these ancient slabs off his back? Or would he buckle under the strain of them for ever? He leant his face against the cold stone wall. 'I'm a ghost,' he whispered. 'Let me go.'

He rose before dawn. Pillars of cold blue light already fell through the windows as he walked quietly down the stairs and into the old kitchen. It too was shrouded in shadows, creaking quietly like a galleon on the ocean floor. He put the kettle on the Aga and was suddenly conscious that he was not alone. Sitting in the corner – at their usual places – were the two ladies, upright, dressed, statuesque. He blinked to make sure they were actually there.

'I thought we said goodbye last night,' he said.

'Did you think we would just lie there in bed as you drove off out of our lives?' said Iolanthe. The two women glared. Their eyes glittered with tears.

'Iolanthe says you won't be coming back for the weekends,' sighed Sylvia. 'I'm your mother and I'm the last to know.'

Tom looked helpless. 'I did tell you, Mum. I'm just going to have a look,' he lied.

'Well, you forgot May.' She produced a dog-eared donkey

from a bag. 'She would never forgive you if you left her behind.'

He took the toy and looked at it for a moment. One eye was gone, and the stuffing had come out so two of the legs were withered. Suddenly he didn't have any more courage and so he sat down at the kitchen table and held his head in his hands. 'Well, you'll be coming over to see me in Sydney in no time and I'll be back before you've even noticed I've gone.'

The two women were silent. They both looked at the floor.

'Let's all face it, darling,' clipped Iolanthe finally. 'This is it. We shall never meet again. Except in our dreams. We realise that now. It's not your fault. This family was born under an unlucky star. So, let's be serious and not push it all under the carpet in the English way. We're half Irish after all.'

Her voice sounded strong. Tom looked up. Both women reached out a hand and he took them in his. They sat for a few minutes in silence.

'This is what they do in Russia. At the beginning of a long journey. And now go. We release you. Don't look back. Don't worry about us. We'll be fine. Just remember our faces and we'll be together.'

He kissed them both and went outside. They didn't follow.

Just two figures in the window, only half there in the early-morning light. He blew a final kiss and got into the car. Don't look back, he said to himself as he drove for the last time down the lime avenue but at the last minute, as the car passed through the gates, he couldn't resist. There it was, through the rear window, standing defiant in the summer dawn as the last Walker threw in the towel.

Joe McKenna from the garage took him to Rosslare. The ferry carried him across the sea to Wales, where he caught a train for London, and he was sitting in a small hotel room in

Paddington by eight o'clock that night as if his whole life had
never happened.

That night he drifted across London like a ghost. He took a
bus to Hyde Park Corner and walked through the park to the
Knightsbridge Barracks as the warm night drew in and the
lamps lit up one by one along Rotten Row, like a necklace
draped around the park. From the shadows of the big plane
trees he watched the soldiers come and go. Life with his regiment felt like another dream, something that had happened to
someone else. An old friend appeared from the entrance and
seemed to look straight at him. He didn't move a muscle. The
friend whistled, as if calling, but a taxi drew up and he climbed
in. Tom breathed a sigh of relief and set off for Piccadilly,
drifting with the crowds into Soho. The soot-stained buildings
seemed less austere and forbidding, on one of those muggy
summer nights in London. He dined at the Lyons' Corner
House.

The next morning he set off for his meeting at Australia House.
    The man behind the desk did not glow with frontier spirit. He
was the usual careful official with slicked-back hair, tortoiseshell
spectacles and tobacco-stained fingers.
    'Household Cavalry?'
    'Yes.'
    'Rather unusual.'
    'Why?'
    'What does Australia have to offer a person like you?'
    'What do you mean?'
    'An officer. A gentleman. Most of the people who come to us
are from, let's say, the professional classes.'
    Tom thought for a moment. 'I saw a poster. It said "Walk tall
in Australia." I liked that. I've been crouching.'

'Do you have anyone there? In Australia?'

'No one.'

The man looked at him carefully, as if trying to picture him in the outback. 'It will take a couple of weeks to process your application. Assuming you pass the medical.'

'When do I get my ten pounds?'

'You pay *us* ten pounds,' laughed the man unkindly. 'That's the whole point.'

Actually, it took longer. Finally, one rainy morning in November, he set off from Waterloo to Southsea for one last goodbye. Dolly.

Dolly lived on a street of small terraced houses, yellow, pink and white, just behind the front. Seagulls wheeled and screamed all day and at night you could hear the waves crashing against the breakers and hissing back to the ocean across the pebble beach. Dolly rarely left her tiny front room where she sat in the bay window watching the comings and goings in the street. If she leaned out, she could see the sea. In such a way she watched Tom appear round the corner from the station carrying a small bag. (His trunk had been sent in advance.) She got out of her chair with difficulty and had arrived at the front door as he was about to ring the bell.

'Don't be in such a rush, lad.'

'Sorry, Dolly.'

'Come in then.'

She shut the door behind him.

'You're too thin.' She always said it.

'I thought I was getting rather fat.' He always replied.

He was a poor lost soul as far as she was concerned and she always resolved to be tough, but now she held on to him as if she was about to fall. They stood there for a moment, two people unable to make words. Finally, she undid herself with a sniff and turned towards the kitchen.

'You'll be wanting to have a wash. I'll make the tea.'

He took his bag up the tiny attic staircase to the familiar room under the eaves. A large dormer window was carved into the ceiling and looked over the rooftops at a sliver of sea. As a teenager he would sit there at night with the window open and a blanket over his pyjamas, dreaming about the future, watching the fog roll in – or waiting for the lights of the two piers to flicker on at dusk, their domes and towers and fairground rides blinking at the falling night, sketched in stars almost, reflected on the oily black waves below. Now the future was actually happening, and the room seemed smaller.

The visit followed the usual routine. They had tea in the bay window. Dolly plodded in with the pot wrapped in a knitted hedgehog. There were teacakes. 'Millie brings them in. I don't get out much.'

Millie was Dolly's niece and the focus of the old lady's frustration.

'She's nothing more or less than a slattern. She'll go wrong. You mark my words. She has that hair, all built up in a cloud over the fake eyes.'

'Fake eyes, Dolly?'

'You know what I mean. Them stick-on lashes. A disgrace. Ivy must be a turning in her grave, poor soul. You're right to be getting out. This place has gone to the dogs.'

They sat in comfortable silence watching a man park a small car on the other side of the street.

'Shall I read the leaves?' Dolly asked with a sly wink. She fancied herself as something of a clairvoyant.

'Go on then.'

Tom sat back and sighed pleasantly as she went through the familiar routine. Draining the cup. Staring at the leaves. Breathing heavily and clicking her tongue.

'Well,' she said finally. 'Fancy that. I see a bride. But no

groom. Don't you be living in sin over there, young man.' She
scraped a bit at the cup. 'Oh well. You won't. There's another
man. And a wife for yourself. Thanks be to Jesus.'

'Will I ever come back?'

'I don't need the tea leaves to answer that question.'

'Well?'

'Come on. It's past my bedtime.' It was six o'clock. 'Now. I'm
leaving you this key. Don't lose it. It's the only spare after that
idiot Millie dropped hers down the gutter. I expect you'll be
taking a turn and getting yourself some fish and chips before
you turn in.'

He wandered the deserted streets and the light drizzle stood in
for tears. He felt nothing, as if he was in one of those dreams
where the air was greasy and you could hardly walk through
it. Everything was familiar and yet he might have been on the
moon. The lights of the fish and chip shop bled into the mist.
Inside, the usual scene. 'What can I get you, love? Cheer up. It
might never happen.' The promise of sudden eye contact. He
looked down, walked with his fish down to the front. The lights
on the two piers were smears in the smog and he watched the
last ferry leave for Portsmouth. Its horn sounded like a birthing
cow, bouncing across the harbour. Somewhere out there was the
ship that would take him away.

The *Oriana* had seen better days but still it towered over the
pier, white and stately. There were two gangplanks. It was operating as a commercial liner and there were ordinary travellers
as well as emigrants. A band was playing, and crowds had come
to see off the ten-pound poms. It reminded Tom of a musical
he had seen. The rain came in bursts but there was the same
festive feeling that you could see in a thousand films. Dolly had
been forced to bring Millie, 'to help on the way home'. They

had bought visitors' tickets and so the three went on board to find Tom's cabin.

It was three decks beneath the waves, no porthole, eight bunks, four on each side.

'Six weeks in here?' gasped Dolly.

'It will be fine.'

He thought quickly which would be the best bunk to get and decided on the top. That way he could keep out of the way of whoever else was billeted with him, for he wasn't planning on making any friends. 'I may try to chat a bit with some of the Greeks when they get on board. I learnt it at school.'

He left his small case on one of the top bunks and they went up onto the third-class deck. A crowd had gathered and there seemed to be a kind of riot brewing.

A small man in a bowler hat was shouting and stabbing the air. Beside him stood a woman, presumably his wife, and their two children. Before them an ashen-faced purser.

'I'm afraid it's company policy, sir. There's nothing I can do.'

'Oh yes there is,' shouted the man, a cockney with the husky voice of someone long used to shouting. 'You can get my trunks out of the hold presto cos I ain't going.'

'Come on, Pat,' said another man sagely. 'Six weeks with your feet up. You're looking a gift 'orse in the mouth.'

'How very dare you?' chipped in Pat's wife.

'Don't get involved, Nat,' shouted Pat, swinging round on his wife.

'No offence meant, lady. But we could all get a rest. How long've you been hitched?'

'Seventeen years, thank you very much.' Nat was about to cry.

'Shut it, Nat. Don't start with the waterworks.' Pat was beginning to see his friend's point.

'And another seventeen in Oz. Just a lovely holiday from 'is snoring for six glorious weeks.'

'Oh no,' said Pat. 'Why did nobody inform us?'

'What's going on?' said someone else.

'It stinks. That's what's going on. It's segregated. You can't be with yer own missus.'

Some younger families seemed to be seriously upset.

'We only got married last week,' said one boy to no one in particular.

'Stop making trouble,' suggested a reasonable man in glasses.

But now the man called Pat got violent. 'Who you calling a troublemaker?' and he swung at his accuser, knocking a pair of tortoiseshell spectacles off his face. 'I'll give you trouble.' At which point the third-class deck erupted into violence. A brief British scrummage ensued, but it only lasted a second. The women screamed and the sensible men held the combatants at bay. Pat, his bowler hat at a comic angle, was carried back on a wall of arms holding his flailing body. They dropped him and he brushed himself down, strutted off like a pigeon in rut to find his segregated cabin while the poor man he had attacked searched blindly for his glasses, a wife standing over him, hands on hips. 'You and your big mouth. There they are. Thank God. Oh no, Trevor, look, they've got a crack. He doesn't have a second pair,' she added to the crowd.

'Oh dear!' said a sympathetic woman. 'Then 'e won't be able to see the pirimids.' Everyone laughed.

'Worse'n that. He'll think it's 'is missus in the next-door bunk an' it'll be 'im in the bowler.'

'I'd like to be a fly on the wall for that!'

'I hope Australia knows what it's in for,' whispered a sensible man to his wife.

Dolly and Millie watched with fascinated horror. Not a moment too soon the liner's huge horn blasted three times. Long metallic roars that made your bones shake. The echo bounced across the port and a sailor appeared ringing a bell.

It was time for the visitors to leave and Tom accompanied the two women to the gangplank. There, a concentration of grief had blocked the way and another crowd swayed, this time with affection. Mothers with red faces covered sons with kisses. Fathers with fond looks and clenched jaws shook hands for the last time. Sisters and brothers, vicars and friends stood glumly by. Nobody knew if they would ever see each other again. That was the world in those days. It was a huge uncharted place and a journey to Australia was a trip to outer space. Once you had left, it was very hard to come back. Everyone knew it. You became a myth and the old world zipped up behind you.

By comparison to the others, Dolly's leave-taking was subdued and controlled, but nonetheless heartfelt. They loved each other but the boy she was bidding farewell to was a coiled-up creature, too hurt or too closed to accept easily the embraces that others took for granted. He felt – and Dolly probably sensed it too – that if they put their arms around each other he would never be able to let go, and so they kissed each other gently.

'Take care of yourself, dear boy,' was all she said, tapping him on the chest with the flat of her hand. Millie knew her role too. She bubbled with laughter. 'We'll miss you. But I bet you won't miss us.'

'I will. I will,' was all that Tom could say, looking down, blushing, and he held their hands before they finally turned and walked down the gangplank. 'You'd better be on deck waving,' shouted Dolly. 'Cos we're going to stay until we can't see the ship no more.'

He ran to the deck, suddenly afraid he was going to miss them, found a place to stand and searched the crowd below. Where were they? There seemed to be thousands of people. The boat began to move off from the quay. People threw bunting over the sides. The band struck up with 'Rule, Britannia!' and the crowd below seemed to roar. For a second the panic of not being able to see Dolly was unbearable but then suddenly there she was, waving a handkerchief. Millie stood beside her crying her eyes out. And so they waved and blew kisses and the boat pulled further and further away, as if being slowly released from one magnetic field to another. Tom kept waving until the crowd were dots on the shore. The liner took the tide and soon they had disappeared behind the Isle of Wight.

He went back to the cabin and the man called Pat in the bowler hat was strutting back and forth, defending himself to two young men who were already lying on their bunks, one on top of another. Tom introduced himself and the two men stood up.

'I'm Ross Morris. And this is my brother Finn.'

'Tom.'

'And this is Pat. You probably saw him take a swing at that poor bloke upstairs.'

'Yes. I did.'

Pat offered a big hand. 'It was 'is fault. You don' goad Pat Hannaway.'

'Is that a warning?' laughed Finn. 'Where do you fancy?' he asked Tom.

'I put my bag up top there. Is that all right with everyone?'

'Just so long as you don't expect me to serve you afternoon tea,' sneered Pat, lifting his leg and making a rude noise. The two brothers laughed. 'You should be in vaudeville.'

Tom climbed up onto his bunk and lay down. His arms behind his head. It wasn't so bad. This underwater metal box suited his mood precisely. The other three talked about their wives. The Morris brothers were nice-looking boys, thickset, with dark hair and identical upturned noses. They loved each other and had decided to leave for Australia together. 'Things are shite in Northampton. I don't care if I never see England again,' said Ross. 'And my wife feels the same.'

'Mine doesn't,' warned Finn.

'You've got to tell her what's what, boy.'

'She'll come round.'

'Some people don't,' said Pat. 'I knew one couple who came back a month later. Said the Aussies were always complaining.'

The door opened and another man came in.

He was fifty, tall, wearing a large mackintosh coat with the collar up so that his face only just appeared over it. He breezed into the cabin and came to a standstill. 'Jesus Christ,' he muttered, looking around. 'Is this me?' he asked in a high, breathy voice.

Pat made goggle eyes at the two brothers. They sniggered and got back onto their bunks.

'Not much left, I'm afraid,' said Finn, introducing himself.

'Well, I'll get vertigo up there. I need to be near terra firma.'

'Who's she?' asked Pat.

'Who indeed? I am bound to get seasick. My name is Trelawny. Not of the Wells. I am escaping everything I know. Which includes you,' he said, wheeling on Pat. 'Are we exporting our pub culture to the Antipodes? Or do they have that sort of thing over there already?'

Tom looked down, intrigued.

'What sort of thing?' growled Pat, ready for the next altercation.

'Brainless brawn. Or prawn, should I say? Hahaha.' He gestured grandly at Pat's diminutive stature and scored a laugh from the two brothers. If he was intimidated by this distillation of Merrie England, he was not showing it. Instead, he sauntered over to the remaining bottom bunk and edged himself in. 'Well that's five of us. Where are the other three?'

'Probably getting on at Naples.' This was Tom.

'Naples?'

'Yes. Hello. My name is Tom.' He reached down with his arm. A thin, weak hand took his from the bottom bunk. 'Hello, Tom. So, we stop in Naples. Good. That will provide us with some variety at least.'

The next hours were spent unpacking. Space was in short supply. Trelawny quickly took charge. Even Pat was mesmerised. He allocated everyone places to put their clothes. He summoned a purser to explain where the washing machines were and how often the 'inmates' – he kept referring to the group as inmates – were allowed to use them. He found out when meals were, how drinks were paid for, how telegrams were sent.

'Oo's 'e going to be sending telegrams to?' whispered one of the boys.

'I heard that. Your mother. In case you are swept overboard. My great-aunt was holding her baby one day on a boat from Hong Kong. Whoosh. Just like that. An enormous wave. A blessing I thought, knowing my family! It was saved from a life of horror.'

There were two sittings for all meals and soon everyone was signed up.

'We can all sit together,' suggested Ross.

'Is that wise? Do you think?' asked Trelawny.

'I'm sitting with my missus and the kids. That's flat!' said Pat.

'And we're a four,' said the boys.

'That leaves us,' said Trelawny, looking at Tom. 'Can you take me for six weeks?'

'I can try.'

And that was that. Teams, tribes, even armies were formed in the course of the afternoon. The bell rang for dinner and they moved as one from the cabin. It would be us against the world, us against each other, us against ourselves.

*

The restaurant had seen better days, although for the man seeing it through cracked glasses it probably had old-world glamour. The saloon stretched from one side of the boat to the other, flanked by large windows. It was long and low with rust-coloured carpet and wood-panelled walls. You only noticed how threadbare the carpet was the first time you dropped something on the floor. There must have been a hundred tables of varying sizes, each spread with pink cloths and napkins standing in cones, all pretty from a distance but blotched with indelible stains and frayed edges up close. Upon these cloths were placed those kinds of knives and forks peculiar to trains and boats, badly laid, scattered around the tables as if they had been interfered with by a poltergeist. Overexcited children screamed around the room, Messerschmitts and Spitfires, arms outstretched, attacking one another, going down in flames with piercing shrieks. Families had lost control, such was the fever engendered by being let loose aboard a gigantic ship. Some couples had dressed up. Others had not. The noise was deafening but not unpleasant. Some common purpose lit the room with a strange celebratory atmosphere. Everyone was at sea, destination unknown. They had taken their lives in their hands and the mass exodus had a religious tone to it. Everyone locked eyes in fraternity.

Outside the large windows the deck could be glimpsed, tables, chairs and couples taking the air, looking and wondering at the sea stretching out on either side, grey and silver and sad, unwelcoming. Many of them had never seen it before. The boat throbbed. Everything shook slightly. The bones vibrated and the marrow quivered. The effect was subtle yet intense, perhaps the thing that Tom liked best. He could feel years of tension being shaken from his joints and he wondered if everyone else was feeling the same.

A steward in stained white led him across the room. People

stared. Perhaps it was Trelawny who was following behind. 'Let's try to get a table for two, for God's sake,' he said. 'If I have to sit with a group of troglodytes I shall commit a murder. Here's ten quid.' He gave it to the steward. He obviously knew the ropes because the steward changed course and the two men were guided to a corner and a small table for two. Trelawny didn't think to ask Tom if he wanted to be stuck alone with him for six long weeks. He had simply assumed the two of them to be cut from a different cloth than the rest of their cabin mates. 'Don't worry,' he said, reading Tom's thoughts. 'We can bring our books.'

They settled down to the dog-eared menu and ordered soup, sardines and jelly. The ten-pound tip went a long way and the steward – named Dylan – was attentive. Drinks arrived and they drank in silence for a few minutes. The Morris brothers waved from a table in the middle of the room. 'They're not bad, actually,' sighed Trelawny. 'The wives, I mean.' They were sensible, pretty, similar. 'I wonder if they're sisters too.'

'They do look alike,' agreed Tom.

'The best of a bad lot, anyway,' snorted Trelawny. 'What a crowd. I wonder what they are all going to do in Australia. Straight to prison, by the looks of things. Like in Monopoly.'

'I wonder what I'm going to do, actually,' said Tom.

'Yes. What are you doing here?' Trelawny turned and fixed his wide grey eyes on his dinner companion. 'You look to me as if you were in the army. A good family. What happened?'

'I ran out of luck.' Tom was in no mood to tell his life story. Not yet anyway. Trelawny had no such scruples.

'I couldn't wait to get out. I don't know why it took me so long. We had a big blow-out when I was sixteen. Me and my father. And I said, Goodbye, Charlie. Never went back.'

'Where have you been since then?'

'Oh, knocking around. I was a performer before the war.

Cabaret. When it broke out – the war – I thought this really isn't for me, so I got a job with ENSA, booking acts to go overseas, working for Basil Dean. What a cunt he turned out to be. And then . . . I had a friend. We shared digs. He got TB. Went to one of those fancy clinics in the Alps – everything paid for – never came back. Dead at thirty.' He paused for thought. Someone was having a birthday and the whole room joined in the sing-song. 'Jesus Christ. Is it going to be like this every day?'

'What will you do in Oz?' asked Tom, to change the subject. As much as he didn't want to tell his own story, he also didn't want to hear too much about anyone else.

'Oh, I've got a job, dear. I'm a dresser, you see, these days. In the theatre. I have a friend who works at the Sydney Theatre Royal. He's promised me something.'

Later, Tom sat in his greatcoat on the deserted deck. He couldn't sleep, trapped in the bowels of the ship. There was a fetid, breathless feeling and Pat had begun to snore. A blue emergency light on the ceiling shone day and night, and it threw a grim glow across the cabin. The sleeping figures looked like bodies stacked in a crypt. He crept from his bunk and climbed the stairs, floor after floor, to the deck outside. It felt magnificent to be sitting there in the stiff ocean breeze. The ship ploughed through the night. The moon was a toenail-clipping hanging over the sea. He felt weightless and epic at the same time, in his rightful place at last, no longer posturing as a landed ruler of a forgotten clan. Somehow, he felt he could at least hold his head up here at the bottom of the food chain, sandwiched below the waterline between the engine rooms and the third-class deck. The second-class deck above that had been given over to the emigrants as well, and they were allowed in to its saloon, its bar and its little cinema, but beyond that the poms could not go.

Their circle of the Inferno ended at the stairs to the first-class decks. It was fun to think of the rich travellers having cocktails in their evening clothes while the rest of them howled and drank and slept and their children screamed around being Nazis, nurses, battleships and doodlebugs.

Through all this, Tom felt the first deep peace he had ever known. He realised he had not a care in the world. The past was dead. He had done what he could. The future was unknown. Just the present, looking out to sea, lulled by the hum of the boat, lost in the crowd, with six wonderful weeks to forget everything.

Everyone fell into a lazy slow-motion routine, listing and lurching on the clanging, humming ship. It was still only a third full so there was a feeling of space despite the crowded underwater cabins. People lacking inner resources at first found life at sea claustrophobic. Some were desperately seasick. One woman never left her bunk. There was often a smell of vomit on the wind and the lavatory floors were at times awash with puke. There was nothing much to do if you couldn't read a book and so the English fell back on their main area of expertise. They drank all day in small groups that got larger as the journey progressed. The men talked while the women watched, looking up with tough, beady eyes from their knitting. In general, the ten-pound poms were social and curious and keen to make contact. Tables for four spiralled outwards as people joined the fray. 'Old Bill will know. Come here, Bill. Take a pew. Nancy – Bill. Fred – Bill. Johnny – Bill.' Handshakes and another round, bursts of laughter from inside clouds of smoke. Cliques formed quickly. Raucous. Genteel. Clever. Less clever. 'Where you going tonight then, Ben, skulking past like that?'

'I thought I would check up on the Bradys.'

'Not good enough for you, are we?' But it was mostly all fun.

The group was united in a common preoccupation. What were they going to do when they got to Oz?

For two days there was no land in sight. People craned over the side looking for it. The endless ocean made them feel uneasy. Then Portugal appeared one morning out of the mist. Many on the boat had never left the north of England, let alone been abroad. The idea of going ashore in Lisbon, where the ship was to dock for two days, was exciting and horrifying in equal measure, and the travellers worked on each other's nerves with worries and concerns.

'I'm not eating a thing.'

'Can you get draught Bass?'

'They don't have soap, apparently.'

'That's what I hear.'

'I'm staying put.'

'You have to stand over the bog.'

'And rats come up and eat your shit as it comes out.'

'Stop it, Barry.'

Tom rose early, went to bed late and kept largely to himself. He often fell asleep during the day, wrapped up in his army coat and a woolly hat on a deckchair. The cold wind on his face and the warmth of the coat and hat made him smile and sleep dreamlessly. He did push-ups and sit-ups and ran around the deck at dawn, starting a trend among the more active of the men. He'd packed *David Copperfield* to remind him what he was leaving behind, but the book sat on his lap and the pages fluttered in the wind unread. He was transported by this new feeling of freedom and wondered how long it would last. He spent hours looking at the sea, at its changing face, watching it break against the prow. Sometimes dolphins played in the wake or swam alongside the ship, jumping out of the water and winking.

Battles blew up in the bar, squabbles in the dining room, drunken altercations that spun out of control like whirlwinds, sucking everyone into the eye, where, more often than not, Pat Hannaway was to be found. Pat rose late and rolled into his bunk at closing time. The brothers spent a lot of time in their wives' cabin. One day they took Tom and Trelawny to meet them. Down a labyrinth of bolted metal passages and stairways to an identical cabin where gigantic bras and bloomers hung from pipes under the ceiling to dry. Johanna Morris was a spirited Irish girl with jet-black hair and forget-me-not eyes. She was married to the younger Morris brother – Ross – and Jane was the bored and bespectacled lady wife to Finn, the elder boy. There were three other ladies: an actress, single, called Zeena Flyte and two spinsters called the Miss Larches. The ladies had somehow managed to get a table in their cabin and they sat around it drinking tea and talking.

'We've heard all about you,' said Johanna, looking the two visitors up and down.

'What have you heard?' asked Trelawny.

'Nothing,' giggled Johanna.

'Nothing will come of nothing, speak again.'

'Eh?'

'Shakespeare, dear, but don't worry about it,' breathed Trelawny. Tom realised that he and Trelawny were seen as some kind of ungodly couple. Since they ate at a table together it was assumed that they were both of a certain persuasion. The girls looked at them as if they were about to scream.

'How long have you two known each other?' asked Jane, straight to the point, sharp-eyed behind her glasses.

'Just as long as we've known you. We met in the cabin,' replied Tom, hoping to set the record straight.

'Humph,' grunted Jane, unconvinced.

Tom ploughed on. 'How are you enjoying the trip so far?'

'So far so good, though God knows what we'll do when the wops arrive.'

'And then the Greeks. Don't forget the Greeks,' screamed Johanna.

'Well, let's enjoy the last days of peace then, shall we? When it's just us?' suggested Ross.

'Who's us?' asked Trelawny with thinly disguised sarcasm.

'Us Brits.'

'Jesus Christ.'

'We're having a party. It's tomorrow night. Will you both come?' asked Zeena Flyte. 'We have a gramophone.'

'I'm afraid I hate parties,' declared Trelawny cleverly. 'Forgive me if I decline. I'm deaf, you see.'

'Well I never,' said Jane. 'Fancy turning down a knees-up. You'll come, won't you?'

'I would love to,' said Tom, inwardly groaning.

The whole ship seemed to have been invited to the knees-up in Cabin 316 on Deck 5. By the time Tom arrived, the party had spilled into the passage and the next-door cabin. The girls had decorated the place with fairy lights and tinsel. There was a kind of punch in paper cups and the record player had a very limited repertoire. A song called 'Sugar Bush' played over and over. Zeena Flyte, the actress, was drunk. She pinned Tom to the wall and leant against him. Looking down, he could see the false eyelashes glued to her lids. They were heavy and kept her lids hanging, half open, giving them a strange sultry effect. Her lipstick exceeded the perimeter of her mouth – like Bette Davis – and overflowed into the small surrounding wrinkles; her teeth were yellow but she had a funny smile and an owl's hoot.

'The other girls think you're a pansy,' she said drunkenly. Tom knew better than to rise.

'Oh, really?'

'I told them no. You are just one of those men who don't mind being with pansies. Am I right?'

'What pansies?'

'Oh, you know perfectly well. Boy Trelawny. It's perfectly obvious. We're making a list of the whole lot of them and putting in a request to the captain that they be put in a cabin of their own.'

'With the slaves? In the galleys?'

Zeena Flyte's face was granite. 'We don't want them infecting our men. But I told the girls to leave you off the list. I can smell a pansy and you aren't one.'

Luckily for Tom he didn't have to respond, because at that moment the music stopped and the lights snapped on. Three officers with whistles appeared.

'Everyone out,' someone shouted, and the women giggled and shrieked.

'Come on. Don't dawdle.'

'It's like school.'

''Ere. Hands off.' Another brawl looked set to begin and Tom escaped from the actress's vice, elbowing his way out of the room, tumbling into the corridor where an officer took his name and soon he was back on the deck under the moon, where he sat until dawn. At a certain point a ridge of pink cut through the night sky, the ship ground into reverse, shuddered and turned towards the harbour of Lisbon. Two large white columns rose from the land on either side of the sound, little by little. Green and red lights flashed in the darkness. As the dawn broke the sea turned from black to blue and four small tugs appeared, cartoon beetles in the half light, buzzing towards the ship, more green lights blinking, the smoke from their funnels like black hair blowing in the wind. They circled the liner and came alongside, two on either side. Ropes were thrown from unseen hands below, caught by men balanced with the casual elegance of sea folk, standing like statues in the bows of the little boats on the bumpy waves, and soon the flotilla began to make its way in convoy around the corner and into the bay. As the sun came up the ship gave three blasts of its horn and as if by magic there was Lisbon spread across the hills, white and ochre in the dawn light.

Tom set off to explore as soon as the ship docked. He hadn't slept but wanted at all costs to avoid the possibility of getting hitched to some group for sightseeing. So he strode purposefully through the city with his collar up and his hands dug into his pockets, braced against the sharp wind, and as the rain began to pour down took shelter in the cloister of a monastery. He sat on a stone bench, a solitary figure in the deserted quadrangle, watching the rain cascade between the pointy arches and spew from the mouths of the gargoyles straining from the walls on extended necks. He was nearly asleep when a door opened on the opposite side of the cloister and a monk scuttled out, a little black mole, sniffing at the rain. The noise of his footsteps echoed round the courtyard, then silence. Tom smiled, settled into his coat and pulled his woolly hat over his forehead. Again, the new sensation of peace fell over him, in waves this time. Waves of love flowing at him that made him laugh out loud. He squinted up at the towers of the church beyond the cloister, medieval skyscrapers, almost moving, swaying in the wind. He had a sudden conviction that his destiny was being rewritten as he sat there. Everything started now. That if he wanted to change it, he must leave the cloister. He didn't move. Instead, the noise of the rain sent him into a kind of trance, and he dreamt of the two old ladies in Ireland, looking out at the same rain. They smiled at him and pointed towards a young woman, standing alone, a little way off. He couldn't see the girl's face, but he knew she was beautiful. Church bells began to ring, jolting

him back to reality. He grabbed the stone seat as if he was about
to fall. The bells in the towers were clanging at each other as if
a war had ended. The image of the beautiful woman lingered a
moment but then he forgot the dream.

Another bell was ringing, in another church a thousand miles
away, somewhere in Greece, a high faint quiver across the mountains from a town called Arachova where a girl stood alone in
front of the altar, dressed in white and veiled, a bride, in fact,
but without a groom beside her. In the pews of the peeling nave
three or four women were gathered, watching gloomily. One of
them cried in silence. All of them wore black. There were no
men. A priest flanked by two acolytes appeared through a door
carved in a wall of painted saints, waving a silver pot billowing
with scented smoke. The altar boys held open his encrusted
cloak so that he looked like a sort of pantomime peacock as he
advanced on the solitary bride, singing mournfully.

Wedding rings were produced on a cushion.

'You are being married in the sight of God.' But out of the
sight of a husband. In fact, he was a man she had never met. He
had emigrated to Australia before she was born. But things being
what they were in Greece in those days – too many mouths to
feed, no secure work – the girl, called Amara, was considered
lucky to have landed such an offer. So tough were the times that
the church even allowed marriages to be conducted without a
bridegroom.

'What God has tied together let no man untie,' sang the priest.
'I now proclaim you man and wife.'

The ring was slipped onto her cold finger. The veil was lifted
to reveal a tear-stained face. No lips to kiss. Everyone sang and
then the priest disappeared back through the door in the sainted
wall, like a weathervane announcing in this case a stormy season
of hardship.

Amara Argyros turned uncertainly from the altar. Looking at her mother and sisters, she felt a sudden chasm had opened up between them. She reached towards them, but they were somehow strangers to her now and kissed her carefully before leaving the church. Outside, the bell began to ring again. She looked up at the tower. Would she remember all this in the years to come?

There was no wedding party. A horse and trap arrived. They all climbed up and set off on the long journey to Athens. It would take three days. She had only a small suitcase. Her luggage had been sent on ahead. They were quiet on the journey. Too much had been said before the wedding and there was no going back, not enough time now to untangle the crossed wires. It was better to stay silent and avoid any further conflict. There had been six months of war in the house since the day her mother had announced to Amara that she would be marrying a distant cousin, recently widowed, twice her age, already living in Australia. That day – the day her world fell apart – she had simply thought her mother mad.

The family were poor but close. They had striven together in the wake of the war, with no men – all killed by the Nazis. A bond beyond the normal family ties had been formed as they fought for survival and the women had been happy, happier perhaps without the overbearing weight of the patriarchy breathing down their necks. Amara's mother had her own mother and two further daughters to feed and clothe. The offer of marriage had come like a gift from God. Money arrived with another distant cousin from a village on the other side of the mountains. This lady, who called herself Madame Kasta, inspected Amara's teeth as if she were a horse up for sale. Satisfied, Madame Kasta acted as broker, beadily pinching the merchandise and reporting back to Sydney. She came back several weeks later with a photograph of a small fat man with a moustache. She explained that he had

a respectable business. He was forty-eight years old. At first
Amara flatly refused. She threw herself on the mercy of the
local priest, who advised her to accept her destiny and to see her
marriage as God's work. She was a deeply religious girl and returned home chastised. She hardly spoke again. Colour drained
from the small house carved into the hill above Arachova. In the
last evenings they sat and worked in silence. Waiting. Amara
had been the life and soul of the family, spirited, loving and
hard-working.

In the trap, passing through the hills for the last time, she
tried to raise the spirits of her sisters.

'Look, it's going to be so exciting to be in Athens.'

'Well it's a chance in a lifetime,' said her mother evenly.

'That's true. Everything paid for. We will never have such an
opportunity again.'

The girls got excited and Amara felt guilty.

From then on, she was determined to enjoy the journey. They
would arrive in Athens, where they had a hotel room with two
double beds. Two more nights until the ship docked.

Meanwhile the *Oriana* docked at the Bay of Naples. Everyone
stood on deck as the city came into view. It was evening. Lights
twinkled around the bay. Half-sunk warships reached out of the
water. Vesuvius was pink and peaked with snow. The war-torn
city, stacked up against the hills, was like a mouth of broken
teeth, laughing in the face of fate, swarming with life in the
rubble. Everything and everyone was for sale that evening in
the bombed-out galleria. Tom went to the opera. He visited
the ancient cisterns under the city, honey-coloured, hewn by
the Greeks thousands of years before Christ. There was indeed
a pagan spirit to the place and the people were wild-eyed, their
language a guttural song that sounded only vaguely Italian.
The next day he visited an old marquesa, a schoolfriend of his

grandmother's, who lived in a collapsed villa at the water's edge in a village outside Naples called Posillipo.

'How is dear Iolanthe? And Seeelvia,' she asked as she led him down an endless passage towards her front door. 'It's been so long. We have not meet since before the war.' She was a tiny creature, all in black, with a cadaverous face and white hair scraped off a low forehead. 'Do you know Oscar Wilde?' she asked. 'He lived here.' And she opened two large double doors and led him through a suite of darkened rooms overlooking the sea. 'I must open to see,' she exclaimed as she wrestled with enormous shutters.

In the shafts of light, marble like slabs of rotting flesh covered the walls and the sea's shadows danced on the ceiling. Outside, the bay and the volcano seemed unreal, creamy and vague in the morning sun. In an empty salotto a little girl practised the piano. 'My granddaughter. She weesh to be a concert pianist,' said the marquesa. 'She may weesh. She must practise.' And she closed the door.

He was given tea and strange Neapolitan cakes which he ate while the dizzying rounds of scales and arpeggios echoed through the house. In the pauses between exercises, little waves could be heard giggling and slapping against the walls of the villa. 'One day soon we will sink,' remarked the marquesa grimly. 'But not yet.' He could picture Oscar Wilde sitting there and for a moment he missed Ireland. He was driven back to Naples in a pony and trap with tractor tyres.

The next morning the Italians came on board. The English were horrified. They stood about on deck with scandalised faces as the Neapolitans flooded in. Even the children eyed the invaders with distrust.

'Terrible smells.'

'Will you look at that woman's beard.'

'He's got three whole salamis in his pockets.'

'And a stove.'

Three men – Aldo, Maurizio and Gianni – came into the cabin and it became immediately clear that they intended to cook.

'Now look here,' growled Pat Hannaway. 'There's no cooking in this cabin. All your filthy greasy muck.'

'Wait a minute,' said Trelawny. 'Italian food is delicious. Why do you always cut off your nose to spite your face? Wait and see. You may get some cooking tips.'

'Don't you start telling me what's what, ya bloody—'

'Bloody what?' demanded Trelawny.

'You know what.'

Tom was lying on his bunk looking down. He introduced himself in Italian.

'Look who's trying to grease up to the wops.'

'Shut it, Ross.'

The three sisters and their mother arrived in Athens late at night. The bus station didn't look much like the cradle of civilisation. The ride from the mountains had not been comfortable and they felt lost and shaken in the crowds as they looked for the cousin's cousin who had been engaged to guide them through the city to the hotel reserved by the groom's family. None of the sisters had ever seen Athens. Their mother only twice. They were all overwhelmed by the smell, the din, the dust. They instinctively formed a circle, holding each other's hands, their heads looking back and forth for the cousin who had still not materialised an hour later. The crowds slowly drained from the station. The newspaper kiosks rolled down their shutters. The night buses clanked out into the void. Soon only a solitary café remained open. The ladies adjourned to it and studied the menu, amazed by the cosmopolitan prices, and cautiously settled on coffee and bread. The mother looked across at her eldest daughter and regretted. Poor old woman. She was only a peasant.

She couldn't imagine anything that hadn't actually happened, but here, in the deserted bus station, she suddenly had a clear picture of her daughter's loneliness. Momentarily overcome by a kind of animal fear she reached out for Amara's hand. The young girl took it, looking up in surprise, wide-open eyes, brown and innocent. Nothing was said – the masks remained in place – but a kind of peace was established.

They were finishing their meagre snack when the cousin arrived. He was a tiny man in a straw hat that came off with a flourish. He wore a dirty linen suit and had a bunch of parched flowers that he presented to Amara with a courtly bow that made the girls giggle. 'May I offer my hearty congratulations.' Amara couldn't think for what but then she remembered. 'Thank you. How beautiful.' They all laughed, and a party atmosphere suddenly lit up their frightened faces, including the mother's – the cousin was her favourite relation, not seen since childhood – and the tiny man led them out of the bus station, the mother on his arm. They were a cartoon couple, his thin bandy legs and gesturing arms and her sturdy figure, feet squeezed into her best shoes, being crammed by him into a borrowed car, and soon they had all bundled into it with Amara's luggage on top of the three girls in the back seat. It started to rain. They craned out to see Athens passing. So many cars. They were entranced by the headlights, the black-slicked streets, the horns and the people, women in evening dress in the backs of cars, men on scooters, the odd donkey pulling a cart, the Acropolis wobbling through the rainy windows, the whole pandemonium delighted the country folk, and they briefly forgot the grim purpose of their mission.

The pensione was on a long, low street of brightly coloured houses in a kind of village that nestled at the bottom of Mount Lycabettus. It had closed for the night. The cousin banged on the door, finally rousing the owner's wife, another sturdy woman in a dressing gown, who seemed to know and dislike him. Introductions were made. The landlady looked the women up and down, at the same time blocking the entrance with her arm. The cousin talked but she looked sceptical. He had a high, womanly voice and it shrieked up and down the scales like a badly played fiddle.

'Uh-huh,' was all she would interject (bassoon) at various pauses in the cousin's explanation. After five minutes of this odd duet the women were allowed to enter and the landlady stomped peevishly up the stairs, showing them to a room in the eaves of the house with two beds and a sink. 'Look,' she commanded. 'You can see the Acropolis from the window.'

They ducked down and could just make it out. 'It's better from the bed,' she said and left, pushing the cousin ahead of her. 'Next thing you'll be telling me is that you are staying here with them, I don't think.'

The door slammed shut and they listened to the retreating footsteps and a reprise of the duet.

Exhausted and dirty, they undressed, washed and fell into bed. Three sisters together. The matriarch alone. The girls slept immediately while the mother sat on the side of her bed listening to the noise of the rain on the roof, watching her daughters' faces on the pillow, neatly laid out in a row, ghostly in the street light, flecked with the shadows of raindrops. She thought they looked like weeping angels. She could remember giving birth to each of them. Amara had been the first and hardest, tearing her apart. Perhaps that was why she had always been hard on the girl. The other two had been easier. Selene, the last, had come out on nothing more than a sigh and the mother had always loved her best. But now she wanted to save Amara from the fate she had inflicted upon her. Looking at her now, she saw for the first time how beautiful her eldest daughter was. She craned forward to look closer. 'How could I have missed it?'

she whispered to herself. The girl was a stranger to her and now she wished she could cry. As the sky paled, the rain ceased, she was still watching.

Amara woke long before she opened her eyes. She was determined that their last hours together would not be spent in mourning. She shook her sisters awake and they both started to cry.

'This is it,' sobbed one.

'I can't move,' wailed the other.

'Let's not be sad. What's the point? Let's remember this day as the best day of our lives.'

'It's the end of the world.'

'Well, let's make it a happy ending then. Please?' Amara put her arms around their necks, pushed her forehead into their faces, and they snuggled close like puppies and drifted for a time in silent communion. Then they became high-spirited, hysterical. Screaming and laughing, they set off to see the sights. Only the mother kept her executioner's frown in place. Try as she might, she was unable to change it. They saw the Acropolis, the Theatre of Dionysus, the Parthenon. At the Temple of Zeus, they were the only visitors, just an old lady selling postcards, the whole place to themselves. The ruins felt sacred on this day of days. The broken columns, lying where they had fallen, hundreds of years ago, gave them a fresh focus, a sense of perspective that drew off some of the poison inside. The stones looked somehow alive, standing up to time, for thousands of years against the rain and the wind under a million new moons. Today the sky was bright blue. It didn't matter what happened to her. If she fell. She would always love her sisters. One day they would possibly meet again. Or maybe not. It didn't matter. There was no future. Just now. And so she felt a kind of peace, walking off from her sisters, climbing a scrubby hill, panting as she reached the top, watching them below, moving about the

ruins. This is how she would picture them when she was thousands of miles away. She waved and shouted their names. They
looked up and waved back – and she felt light-headed. There
was no such thing as distance where love was concerned.

But as the day drew on, they instinctively drew close, brush-
ing past one another like cats, touching, looking into each other's
eyes. Childish games turned wistful. Smiles shone with tears.
Soon it was time to make for Piraeus and put Amara on the ship.
They went back to the pensione. The rest of the family would
be staying there that night. They collected Amara's trunk and
set off in a taxi for the port.

Madame Kasta, who had initially brokered the marriage, was
waiting for them at the customs house. 'I thought for a moment
you weren't coming,' she laughed brightly, but the eyes were
steel.

'She's here,' confirmed the mother frostily.

'Isn't this exciting?' gushed Madame Kasta, ignoring the unhappy faces. She was cheerful and practical, happy to be leaving
the hardship of Greece. 'I shall be living with the newlyweds
for a while, so don't worry, cousin. I will see that everything is
all right. Now don't keep calling me Madame Kasta, child. You
must call me Cousin Semina. We'll stick together.'

The family stood awkwardly on the quay, the vast ship
towering over them, hundreds of faces leaning over the rails.
Boisterous groups made for the gangplanks. Other Greeks stood
on the dock. The favourite cousin arrived with his wife and their
children. It was an event, an honour: a Greek girl was leaving
Greece. Introductions were made, pleasantries exchanged. The
family, so obviously from the countryside, were like four black
nuns blown about by the sharp wind coming in off the sea. They
watched as Amara's trunk was hoisted on board and her papers
were checked and stamped. They looked up at the great ship
twinkling in the dusk. None of them had ever seen anything

like it. It was as if they were small children, even the mother. Then the ship's horn blew and it was time to part. 'Come along then, dear,' commanded Madame Kasta.

'Well, here goes,' said Amara. She looked down, trying to hold back her tears, waiting for some miracle. The sisters stood their ground too and for a moment nobody moved. Then all at once they reached out, all four of them, and crashed into each other's arms. 'I'm sorry,' cried the mother. 'Forgive me for everything, Mama,' whispered Amara. 'Don't forget me.' They held on for a minute or more while the cousins watched. Finally, Amara broke away. She wiped her eyes with the back of her hand and without looking back walked up the gangplank and on to the boat. Cousin Semina followed. The mother collapsed and her daughters carried her to a bench. They sat there scouring the decks with their eyes as the funnels smoked and the horns blasted across the sound. 'There she is,' cried Selene, and sure enough Amara had appeared, her tiny face squeezed through the crowd. They saw each other and waved frantically, shouting as if they could hear each other.

'Don't worry about the donkey.'

'Write soon.'

'Mama misses you already.'

'Look after her.'

The ship began to strain on its moorings. Sailors released the lines, waving at others on the ship who hauled the thick grimy ropes from the frothing sea. As the ship groaned and throbbed at a snail's pace from the quay, the ladies' eyes were fixed on Amara's face, moving slowly but surely away from them, getting smaller and smaller until it was barely discernible, yet still they waved, tears pouring down their cheeks. The liner slowly turned and she disappeared from view.

'Oh, she should have stood at the back,' sobbed the mother. 'Then we could have seen her.'

As if by magic, she appeared. She must have run the entire length of the boat. Now she was at the back blowing kisses, shouting something, but they couldn't hear, and the family stood up and reached for the departing stern of the ship. They stayed waving until the boat was just a dot of light against the oncoming night.

How does love come about? Does it happen in an instant? Is it pre-ordained? Do two people move blindly towards each other at the command of some inner voice that we no longer hear, the same one that drags whales across oceans and birds south in winter?

Watching this Greek tragedy from the third-class deck, Tom fell in love. He was ready. His heart and mind were empty and craved to be filled. He could read the body language of the family on the dock. He had seen all its gestures with his own mother and her sister. He felt completely what they were feeling. Every movement the girl made, he understood. Her beauty was extraordinary to him. Was it her physical beauty? Or was it some kind of inner dignity that set her apart? When she turned away from her family and started up the gangplank she looked up and their eyes met. For Tom, time stood still. For the first time in years he felt sure. He also knew that this girl loved him. Strange but true.

The ship made for Alexandria across the Mediterranean, and it grew warm. The passengers sat on deck. The English were pasty and bleary eyed. The Italians were coffee-coloured and stripped down to their vests, playing games. The Italian men were appraised discreetly by the English women from behind their knitting. Expressionless faces, only the fingers and needles moving, balls of wool unwinding slowly on sensible laps. The Italian women giggled behind their hands. The British made

them laugh till they cried. Only the Greeks were beneath contempt, ignored and avoided by all. Despite all this, there was a
lift in the air, a drama in the light, that slowly began to dissolve
the tribal prejudices of the British. The wind blew them away
and the sun struck them dumb. They had never really seen
it before. When it set, the sea seemed to boil. A shimmering pathway unfolded – from the sun directly to them – first
silver, then orange then grey before the final fade to black. It
left them breathless and struck a chord much deeper, much
richer than the contemplation of a sunset in Wigan, or a misty
day in Motherwell, a universal connection which southerners
took for granted. It was moving for Tom to see his compatriots
in the sunset, their faces washed briefly of care in the golden
light. Soon they were even to be found up early to witness the
dawn as the sun came up from the east. It dragged with it the
scent of India and Persia. The nights were clear. The heavens
stretched out and yawned, so that you could see the curve of
the Milky Way.

Over the next few days Tom observed Amara from a distance.
He discovered her name reading over the shoulder of the purser
in the restaurant. He repeated it like a mantra all that day, under
his breath.

'What are you whispering for?' asked Trelawny in a dangerous
voice at dinner.

'Was I?' He had no intention of making a confession. Not yet.
He revelled in his secret.

'Yes. You keep whispering. It's quite irritating. I think you're
asking me something but you're not.'

'Do forgive me.' He looked sideways and could see her
eating her soup. As luck would have it, she and her companion
had been put on a table in the restaurant quite near to theirs.
Madame Kasta never took her eyes off her charge, or if she did,
it was only to scan the horizon for predators. Tom was discreet

in his attentions. He watched Amara walking down passages. He found out where her cabin was and guiltily followed them back to it one evening after dinner. He walked on the deck near to where she sat but he didn't make a move. She looked at the sea. He looked at her. Her face was so full of feeling. He knew how she felt about everything.

One morning he was running round the deck and she appeared. She smiled. He smiled and bowed as he ran. Contact had been made.

A few days later there was a party. A band played after dinner in the restaurant, a ragged group of five musicians in dirty livery, with a singer. Tables were moved and a dance floor was revealed cut into the threadbare carpets. The Italians leapt to their feet. A few English couples swayed onto the floor. Tom took his life in his hands and got up.

'Are you asking me to dance?' laughed Trelawny.

'I haven't been at sea that long.'

'I'll ask again at Aden.'

The two men laughed. They had developed an easy marriage of convenience. They talked at dinner or did not, depending on their mood. Sometimes one talked and the other read.

Tom made for the Greek table with his heart in his mouth. Ten Greeks looked up as he arrived, and he made a sudden decision. He asked Madame Kasta to dance. It was an inspired move delivered in flawless Greek. The lady was bowled over. She coloured and refused but the whole table was indignant.

'Go on, Semina. It might be your last chance.'

'Don't have a heart attack though,' said a younger man in the party.

Finally, she got up and they took to the floor. She was surprisingly good as she swirled and wiggled around. Conversation was easy. She was thrilled by his Greek. And it was even she who suggested the next move.

'Why are you dancing with an old woman like me when there are so many young ladies in the room? I know what you men are like. You would like to dance with my ward. Huh? She is married. But we are on the ocean, and I don't see why we shouldn't all have fun.'

His legs almost buckled at the news but with a last extravagant swirl they arrived back to the table and he helped her into her seat. The table applauded. He could see Trelawny laughing and made a discreet v-sign in his direction.

Then he turned to Amara and blushed.

'Would you like to dance?'

She laughed, looked to Madame Kasta, who clucked her approval, and got up.

The band played a brassy introduction and the singer explained with a gigantic smile 'Sugar bush I love you so ...' It was the popular hit of the year and half the room rose. Couples converged on the dance floor like bumper cars, all elbows and laughing faces. Suddenly it was very tight. For a minute they danced in silence, both of them hardly daring to breathe. He could feel it in her. She looked away and he looked over her head. He smelt her hair. He was pressed too close and felt a surge in his groin, and moved back so that they were finally face to face.

'I saw you with your family at the port.'

She said nothing, merely acquiesced.

'Why are you going to Australia? All alone?'

Still she said nothing. Perhaps he was going too fast.

'Is Madame Kasta some kind of relation?'

'You are very curious.'

'I am.'

'Why?'

'I'm not sure. I felt so sorry for you at the port. You were so far away but I could feel how sad you were. It was odd.'

'It is odd. I don't know when I will see my family again.'

'We're all in the same boat, I suppose. That was why it was easy to understand.'

'Have you left your family?'

'Yes. Two old ladies.'

'But you don't mind.'

'I do. But I had to start again.'

'I never dreamt of leaving home.'

'For me there was nothing left.'

'Where?'

'Ireland.'

They danced in silence for a moment. Tom felt confident now to move closer. The touch of her body against his was electric.

'I'm married,' Amara said. 'Did she tell you?'

'Yes, she did. Where is your husband?'

'Australia.'

'Has he been there long?'

'About thirty years, I think. I don't know exactly.' She looked up at him and he could hardly breathe. Black, sad, steady eyes looking into his for the first time.

'So you have been visiting home.'

'So many questions. No, I have not been visiting home. I am going to Australia for the first time. I've never been anywhere. And you? Is this your first time away?'

'No. I was in the army. I went everywhere.'

'Lucky you.'

He wanted to reply – to have found you, I'm lucky – but he didn't. Instead, they danced on for a minute and then she abruptly stopped. 'Thank you. I'd like to sit down again now.'

Later, he felt flat. She was cold and distant. He could see her across the room. He hoped, waited for a glance, but it never came. The music stopped and there was a tombola. A starched officer stood behind a table pulling numbers from a hat. A barrel of beer. Dinner for two. A night out in Alexandria. Tom won two tickets to the captain's cocktail party in the first-class lounge.

Two days later.

'But I won't understand a word.'

'I will translate.'

There was a summer storm and they were sitting on the deck out of the wind. He had been on his morning run and she had appeared. She smiled suddenly. 'You are kind. Yes, I will come. But I must ask Madame Kasta first.'

They climbed the stairs to the first-class deck. Everything was different, hushed, tidy. Sensible couples read books on comfortable deckchairs. The women had rugs wrapped around their knees. Children sat with their nannies, doing sums. The restaurants and bars were glossy and low-lit, shiny teak walls and thick honey-coloured carpets. Early diners looked up as they passed. They felt their nakedness like Adam and Eve. Tom smiled at Amara to reassure her. He wanted desperately to take her hand but knew he could not. They were ushered into a saloon filled with people drinking champagne. They all seemed to be English. Tom took two glasses from a passing waiter. They sat down and watched the party. Amara had never seen such a collection of people and she was fascinated.

'Would you like to walk around?' he asked.

'Oh no. I prefer to watch from here. You go.'

'No. I'm happy here.'

She laughed suddenly. 'They all have so much to say. How can they hear?'

'They're not listening.'

'Really. How do you mean?'

'They're just talking. They don't wait for the reply.'

'How interesting. Is that the English way?'

An old man sitting nearby began to laugh. 'I'm sorry. I

couldn't help overhearing.' He spoke perfect Greek. 'You are perceptive, sir.'

'Thank you.'

'I was looking at your shoes,' continued the man. 'Very smart.'

He had bought them in Jermyn Street. 'I went on a spending spree before I left England. Good shoes last a lifetime.'

'Are you away for a lifetime?'

'Yes. We're both emigrating to Australia. What about you?'

'I'm jumping ship at Aden and going on to Bombay.'

An officer appeared. 'Mr Forley Walker?'

'Yes,' answered Tom.

'Would you like to come and meet the captain?'

'Very well. Come along, Amara.'

'You go. I will wait here.'

'Forley Walker. I can't think when I last heard that name.' The man looked after Tom for a long moment, giving Amara the opportunity to study him, and what a strange creature he was. Ageless but ancient. He turned to her, as if answering some unspoken question. His hooded and bagged blue eyes, penetrating, unwavering, looked right into hers and made her gasp. His patrician head was crowned with bright white hair. He was obviously bald, but the hair had been artfully arranged over the top of his head into a kind of helmet. As if reading her thoughts, he touched it with long, delicate fingers. He wore a beautifully made suit. His tie was carefully knotted and he too wore a pair of brightly polished shoes. He sat upright, like an owl. There was something about him – a wall, almost – of warmth and Amara felt suddenly elated.

'Forley Walker,' the man repeated slowly, studying her carefully. 'How odd. I once knew a lady of that name. Years ago. In India. I wonder if she was a relation of his.'

'What is your name, sir?' asked Amara.

'They call me Krishnamurti. Jiddu Krishnamurti. And you, dear lady?'

'Amara Achoeva.'

'Amara. You look very unhappy.'

'Do I?'

'You are embarking on a long journey. Alone. That man—' He pointed at Tom, who was now talking to the captain and a couple of ladies. The old man laughed. 'Look at him. Yes. It is he. He will never forget you. He has waited for this moment for a long time. But—' Here he stopped, and his eyes rolled back slightly in their sockets. 'But now is not that moment. He likes you very much. Be kind to him.'

Amara smiled. 'I'm sure he is very nice, but unfortunately I am already married.'

'Details. Just one of those things. I must go.' He touched her shoulder and it felt like an electric shock. 'There. Tell your friend that I invite him and you to dinner tomorrow night in Alexandria. And a concert. Umm Kulthum is singing. Will you come? I think we dock at around teatime.'

'Oom who?'

'Kulthum. She's only the greatest singer in the world.'

Amara thought she might get the giggles. 'I will tell him. For myself, I must ask my guardian.' He didn't seem interested in her excuse and waved it aside.

'Goodbye. Say goodbye to Forley Walker and ask him if his grandmother was called Victoria.'

And he left. Not just left but disappeared. One moment he was here. The next he was not. Tom returned. 'Where's our friend?'

'He left. He thinks he knows you.'

'Impossible. How would he?'

'He asked if your grandmother was called Victoria. Was she?'

What a strange place to hear a forgotten grandmother's name.

He looked down at Amara sitting there. Her face seemed sacred to him already. It glowed with inner light. He didn't want the past to invade.

'What's wrong?' She looked concerned and for a moment he was deliriously happy.

'Nothing's wrong. Did you catch his name?'

'He told me. But it was not a normal one. Krish . . . something.'

'Krishnamurti?'

'That's it.'

He shivered and the hairs stood up on his arms. He hadn't given a thought to his family since leaving England and now a name was mentioned, one that was carved into the heart of his entire clan. The kind of name a medium stumbles on during a séance. He felt faint. Winded, actually. He got up and clawed his way from the room. At least that's how it felt. Outside on the deck he leant against the balustrade and held his head in his hands. All the tears he hadn't wept suddenly flooded from his eyes. Amara was running from the saloon. 'I'm sorry. Excuse me.' She put her hand on his shoulder. He turned towards her, his face wet with tears. She stroked his cheek. 'Don't cry or I'll cry too. I always do,' she whispered.

And so he kissed her. He couldn't stop himself. It was like being caught by an unseen current and they were both swept away on it. She had never been kissed before but she responded in a way that made her wonder for the rest of her life. It seemed entirely natural and familiar at the same time as being almost revolutionary. However, when they stopped she burst into tears and for half an hour she was inconsolable. She had been strictly brought up, was deeply religious. To betray her unknown husband was a cardinal sin. Yet she clung to Tom as she sobbed her heart out.

Outside, the lights of Alexandria slipped over the horizon in a long, thin glow. There was no moon.

There was nothing to say. They held on to each other and swayed gently as the ship ploughed on. Later, when she had cried herself to the point of exhaustion, they sat down and told each other everything and it all ended at a single point, the intractable fact. Amara was married.

They sat there all night and watched the flat pale edge of Alexandria slowly crystalise into an esplanade, palm trees, apartment buildings. Art Deco. Colonial. Off-white. Not the magical city of Alexander the Great. More like a down-at-heel French croisette.

Madame Kasta seemed to be a heavy sleeper, or if not, she turned a blind eye as Amara climbed up to her bunk, snoring merrily in her nightcap, lying on her back with her little paws in the air. Did a puffy eye open as two slender ankles passed by?

Tom got to the cabin as everyone was getting up.

'Hello, hello,' said the Morris brothers. 'Have you been kipping on a lifeboat with a lovely lady?' The lifeboats were the only places a segregated couple could meet, and at night they moaned and shuddered comically. A black market had blossomed around them, run, naturally, by the Italians, with concierges and watchmen on each deck. If you wanted some private time with your wife you had to book in advance. Lifeboat 4 on Deck 6 could be your only chance for intimacy on the whole six-week voyage.

Even Trelawny joined in the fun. 'Who is the mystery lady? Not that bearded hunchback you were dancing with?'

'Her daughter, more like,' said Ross.

'Now that's a bit of skirt I wouldn't mind having a look up.'

'We had you down for a nancy boy.'

Suddenly Tom was taken by a flush of male aggression. He moved towards Finn Morris, shoulders back, chest flexed. 'I had you down for being an illiterate cunt. And I was right.'

'Steady on.'

'No. You steady on. I have to sit around this cabin, day in, day out, listening to you lot banging on. Nothing's right. Nothing's good enough. You're like a broken fucking record. Now leave me in peace.' Up until then he had hardly spoken, and the room was stunned. In the ensuing silence Tom climbed onto his bunk, smiling to himself – what fools these mortals be. Including me – and fell into a deep sleep.

While he dreamt the ship arrived at Alexandria. Everyone was on deck to watch. Tug boats skimmed towards them from all directions. The *Oriana* was a clanking, groaning albatross, exhausted from her journey. They towed her past a crusaders' castle, bleached white, squat and square on its ramparts, into the harbour. The horn boomed across the sound and into Tom's dreams. At the dock, the passengers gaped and craned down at the seething mass, all men, their jellabas, their jackets, their magicians' hats and head dresses, their donkeys and carts. The English were warned of delays, should they wish to go ashore. They were not popular in Egypt. Threaded through the crowds, soldiers in pairs, armed, vigilant, waiting for something to happen. It was the second year of the Nasser regime and things were brewing up for a confrontation over Suez. In two years, the canal would be nationalised, the British expelled. For now, there was an uneasy peace and immigration officials were terse at the customs house.

Madame Kasta was not happy.

'But it's Alexandria. I will never be here again,' Amara reasoned.

'Look, child, I don't care what you do. You're young. I don't want you to waste away. Even now you look better. I don't want to deliver a drowned rat to my cousin. But neither can I present him with a fallen woman. Who will pay? Me!'

'And me.' Amara blushed. Women could tell when another had been kissed. There was something in the air, something in the scent of a woman who had just discovered love. 'Cousin Semina, I can assure you—'

'Don't assure me about anything the Lord may upbraid you with later in heaven. Remember, he sees everything. Look, I am on your side. I just want you to be careful. I don't like the idea of you disappearing with some Indian guru we don't even know. With a man we don't even know.'

'He is very kind.'

'No man is *very* kind. Unless they want something.'

Amara burst into tears and threw herself onto her bunk.

'Come on, child. Let's play cards. We can decide later.'

An odd quartet climbed into a carriage at the docks that evening. Krishnamurti appeared like a wraith from the first-class gangplank, pristine in linen, accompanied by his business manager, a small Indian gentleman named Rajagopal, also expensively suited, meticulously polite, with ringed eyes and fingers. They both seemed to speak all languages known to man and conversed in Arabic with the driver.

'I thought it might amuse you both,' Krishnamurti said as they settled themselves on one side of the carriage, 'to look around the town on the way to dinner. By the way, I can't travel backwards. Would you mind? Sorry.' The two occidentals clumsily changed places as they set off at a spirited trot towards the old town. The evening was warm. Neither Amara nor Tom had ever seen anything like Alexandria that night. The lights, the smell of burning charcoal, of lemon trees, the people, the chaos in the streets – it was all overpowering, particularly for Amara, who until last week had seen nothing of life beyond the small hillside village in which she had been born.

There was no sign of the ancient world. It had been buried long ago under the modern city, half Victorian, half decayed. But now even that was being effaced, engulfed by Nasser's plans for

Egypt. They drove through crumbling colonial streets called Washington and King, past a bedraggled Strand Palace Theatre, cables and signs and hoardings dragging it all down like poison ivy into the underworld, where the cisterns of Alexander's city hid in the dark. 'Plip plip plop,' laughed Krishnamurti, describing them. You could feel all this. There was a palpable energy in the streets, magnetic almost, pulling everyone along, whether they liked it or not. Egypt was on the move.

The carriage arrived at a Victorian circus of converging avenues. Amara had never seen so many people, so many cars, the drivers' hands pressed to their horns, the people weaving through the traffic, an ocean of faces craning, crazy eyes popping, hands reaching up. The Indians sat erect and unperturbed, while Amara held on to the side of the carriage, afraid of falling out. Soon the crowds melted away and they could hear the reassuring clop of hooves again as they drove into a genteel neighbourhood where the din of the city was merely an echo.

'I thought you might like to get a taste of downtown Alexandria, but I see it has unnerved you, madam.'

'I don't think I have ever seen so many people.'

'How does it feel?'

'It feels strange, being in a heathen country,' she said tightly.

Krishnamurti smiled. 'Do you think God doesn't come to this part of the world?' His voice was grand, colonial like the architecture.

'No.' Amara had a stubborn side.

'Perhaps you are right. Alexandria contained the greatest library in the known world. Right up until the fourth century. It was destroyed by Christians once they got their claws in here. Perhaps God left at that point. Threw in the towel.'

'What happened?' asked Amara. They were now trotting along a tree-lined street. The moon appeared, pale and patient, and the clouds turned pink. Lights flickered on in large white villas as the day fell away. Turtle doves called to each other from the tall pines. A large American car drove past, crammed with young men shouting and waving.

Krishnamurti looked up at the spectacular sky and sighed.

'Hypatia must have seen this moon, this smudge.' He had a melodious voice, mesmerising. 'She was the last librarian.'

'When was this? Before the war?' asked Amara.

Krishnamurti laughed and they all laughed with him. It was impossible not to. His energy was infectious. 'Yes. A long time before the war. In AD 452 a group of Christian thugs stripped her, dragged her through the streets and cut out her eyeballs. Later they burned the library and a thousand-year night fell over the world.'

'Christians would never do that.'

'Open your eyes, child,' said Krishnamurti kindly, taking her hand. 'Life is not as black and white as you think. Remember that in the days to come.'

Now there were more cars and a gentle traffic jam as they turned into some gates. Sophisticated diners were clambering from chauffeured cars in front of a large bungalow. Servants in white jackets and plum-coloured fezzes surged from a portico to greet them. Polite and silent, they never turned their backs but led the group up the marble steps sideways with arms gesturing.

'This is the Auberge des Pyramides,' said Rajagopal. 'The best place in town. We are meeting some associates here.'

Inside a large hall, fans made strange clicking sounds in the ceiling and Krishnamurti's elaborate combover took to the air. Dark furniture, chess board floors, faded portraits of stiff-looking ladies in silk dresses and hats – all rotted in the sea air. Staff stood to attention under pointed archways leading to coat checks and powder rooms and the gentlemen's conveniences. They were ushered into a large dining room. At the far end two ladies encrusted in jewels waved gloved arms.

Palms leant over the windows and candles flickered on tables of starched pink. Murmured conversation, knives and forks scratching against plates, a piano playing show tunes from Broadway, and yet it was distinctly Egyptian. A mirrored wall at the end gave the impression that the room went on for ever. Dinner went on for quite a long time, course after course, Egyptian specialities that the young lovers were encouraged to try. Conversation lurched from stilted French to Greek to English. Two men, husbands to the bejewelled ladies, arrived. After much bowing and kissing of hands they sat, eased into their chairs by expressionless servants. They were black-tie disciples of Krishnamurti and they all looked at him with bulbous eyes over their curled moustaches. They began to talk in Arabic. Some kind of business deal was being conducted and Krishnamurti occasionally waved as if a terrible smell was wafting in his direction. Tom took Amara's hand under the table. It didn't matter that they understood nothing. They were moored like two boats, their anchors clasped together under the pink linen sea.

There seemed to be some sort of problem and the master became vexed. Rajagopal touched his arm but he jerked it away. It appeared that Krishnamurti was giving a talk in Cairo. Spurred on by the success of a previous one a few months before, money had been introduced to the spiritual equation, like a cold front in tropical weather, and a kind of storm began to crackle. One of the men passed Krishnamurti – who they affectionately called Krishnaji – a bag that was clearly full of cash. He froze. It was a step too far and nobody moved for fear of a thunderclap from heaven. The ladies' earrings glittered dangerously in the candlelight while their smiles congealed. Smoker's teeth gleamed behind painted lips as they waited for a response.

'I never touch money,' snapped the master finally. 'Talk to Rajagopal. Later.'

'We have sold two thousand seats.'

'Is she coming?'

'We will see. In any case, she has asked to see you after the performance.'

Tom understood very little. Amara less. And yet the evening was bewitching. These people were like characters in a play. An Agatha Christie mystery. The women's hair was built up into incredible backcombed beehives. The conversation lurched from one subject to another, one language to another, while Krishnaji was the silent centre of attention. Always watching. Occasionally he said something funny. They were discussing a meditation weekend in Switzerland (of all places). 'I kept having awful thoughts,' one lady confessed. She sounded like a wood pigeon, with her thick accent.

'Oh,' moaned the other. 'I was determined not to think – and I didn't.'

'But that's just another thought, isn't it?' ventured Krishnaji.

'What is?'

'Being determined not to think.'

'C'est vrai?' They all laughed. 'Wrong again.' They took their spiritual failure in their stride and kept cooing. Amara and Tom caught each other's eye and nearly burst out laughing. Krishnaji winked.

'We have a great treat in store,' one of the women said to Tom. 'Tell your friend. We are going to listen to the Star of the East after dinner.'

'Wonderful.'

It was a large music hall built in the 1920s. Outside the main entrance, hundreds of people were trying their luck with a phalanx of uniformed guards. The Egyptian men of the party held tickets above their heads and elbowed the group through the crowd. Inside, the theatre was already packed to the rafters. Four tiers, a grand circle and stalls that stretched like a football pitch

under a gigantic chandelier. It shone a pale toothless light over
the audience, mostly men. People still streamed in. To add to
the mayhem, waiters in white jackets served drinks, squeezing
back and forth along the rows, holding trays of glasses above
their heads. The chaos seemed natural to everyone. The noise
of the crowd echoed round the large auditorium; the smell of
hair oil and body odour, of perfume and smoke, was intoxicating.
They found their seats and after some negotiation managed to
evict the indignant chancers squatting in them. This audience
was at a fever pitch of expectation. They were on a historical
wave and the singer – Umm Kulthum – was their star, shining
the way to a new dawn for Egypt that in fact would never come.

The lights jerkily dimmed and the curtain swept back to
reveal a large orchestra spread across the stage, mostly strings,
all played by men in evening dress. A small glum woman sat
on a chair in front of them, hands folded on her lap. She wore a
lime-green kaftan and her feet didn't touch the ground. Her hair
was jet black, pulled off her face and built into a similar halo to
the ladies at dinner. It must have been the mode. The orchestra
started, that discordant – to the occidental ear – tirade of violins
and cellos answering questions from the kanoon, up and down
strange scales, past oriental trills and glissandos. There were
bongos and a triangle, chimed every so often by a man with a
fantastic moustache and comic concentration. An accordionist
played a theme. It was answered in a fury by the violins – and
then she stood up. The audience became hysterical. It was
strange, because she was discreet, shy, buxom, unremarkable.
She sang quietly, with precision, her hands clasping awkwardly
at the song as it came out of her mouth. And yet she was utterly
fascinating. She held a scarf in one hand. Everyone felt that
Umm Kulthum was singing straight into their heart. Her song
was their struggle. Amara felt this – even though she didn't
understand the words. The flow of truth, of empathy, coming

from this unusual woman's mouth, the bond she had with the audience, was mesmerising. Krishnaji watched with eyes filled with tears and of course the Egyptian audience understood layer after layer that escaped foreign ears. She would repeat the same phrase – with a subtle variation each time – and it drove the audience wild. Again and again they burst into delighted laughter and applause. The concert lasted three and a half hours.

'What's she singing?' Tom whispered to Krishnaji.

'She is singing about her broken heart. How the man she loves has not come. How she is alone in the moonlight. About her dreams for the future.'

Later they were escorted down a labyrinth of passages to a dressing room where Umm Kulthum lay exhausted on a divan. Her face was grey and she could hardly move but she took Krishnaji's hands and kissed his wrists. She smiled politely at the others from afar. Her ladies formed a protective ring around her and only Krishnaji was allowed inside, and only for the briefest moment. She looked like a beached whale, drained. With a strange, polite firmness, they were moved in and moved out on an invisible wave, the diva waving hopelessly from her divan as Krishnaji left blowing kisses.

In the car back to the docks the party were in high spirits. They still had not talked about Tom's grandmother, Victoria.

'Can you remember her?' he asked Krishnamurti.

'Of course. She was there at a rather delicate moment of my life. I remember her quite distinctly. They all loved table-turning, that generation. She was keen to contact the dead. I remember that.'

'She had lost her entire family in the war.'

'Yes,' the master answered dreamily. 'That's how a lot of them arrived at Adyar. But really, she hadn't lost them. That was the problem. She kept them draped over her shoulders like winter furs. She never let them go. I said the dead are dead and the living are living. Then of course she died. She never really approved of me after the debacle of '23. She was there in Madras when I disengaged myself from the whole Theosophical circus. She said cruel things. She said it broke the heart of a certain lady.'

'Annie Besant,' said Tom, the name released suddenly from some inner chink in the brain, never uttered since early childhood. Krishnamurti looked sharply at him. 'Yes. She was a great disciple of Annie Besant. So was her mother, by the way. They went way back to Madame Blavatsky days. But she walked in the valley of death, so to speak. If you do that for too long, it's only a matter of time.'

'Were you there when she died?'

'No. I had taken the first train out of town. They had all come, you see. They thought I was the new messiah. But I wasn't. They wanted someone to follow. I couldn't be that person. She stayed in Adyar and died.'

The boat looked deserted in the pre-dawn. Everyone was asleep. The lights glittered on the decks. A few sailors were on watch. They said goodnight on the dock before retreating to their separate gangplanks, Krishnaji and Rajagopal to the first-class deck and Amara and Tom to the underworld.

'It was a wonderful evening. Thank you,' said Amara. She had tears in her eyes.

'We'll never forget it. Will we?' said Krishnaji, kissing her hand. He and Rajagopal were like two men from another century.

'We start for the canal tomorrow early, I believe. It's very dull. Let's play some cards or something. I am leaving the ship at Aden.'

*

The canal was – as predicted – dull. Flat desert on either side. Flat brown water on the canal. Occasionally another ship appeared on the horizon, small at first, growing bigger, suddenly huge, shimmering in the desert heat – it was suddenly hot. The boats greeted each other with great booms from their horns. People waved, if it was a liner. On the cargo ships the languid sailors ignored the emigrants. They went on with their day, that elegant seafaring ballet, throwing ropes, polishing wood, leaning and smoking, unimpressed to be on one of the great wonders of the world. In the evening the *Oriana* came into the Red Sea. Somewhere they could hear the call to prayer, coming and going on the breeze. That night the stars shone fiercely in the black sky. It felt biblical. One could easily imagine the archangel appearing from heaven. There was no light around the ship. It was as if they were ploughing through space. Tom and Amara sat up late, talking, falling silent, laughing, reaching for each other's hands. Sometimes at dawn there was a mist over the sea and then it felt as if they were sailing through the clouds. Apart from that the days were long. There was no wind and the temperatures rose steadily. The climate in the underwater cabins rose too. They became used to the smell of unwashed flesh.

Tempers frayed in the heat. Fights exploded out of nowhere. Amara and Tom were walking round the deck one afternoon. It took about eight minutes to make an entire tour. On the port side, a table of English were sitting next to a table of Italians, all talking among themselves, minding their own business. Drinks were being served. Laughter and knitting, singing and smoking. By the time they turned the corner and came by again a full-scale skirmish had erupted. Children screaming. Men throwing chairs at each other. One woman held a wig in her hand and her (now) bald sparring partner was trying to scratch her eyes out. Sailors rushed in and as usual Pat Hannaway was the eye of the storm. He was put in the ship's only prison cell and returned unbowed to the cabin two days later.

It was all enchanting to the improbable couple who fell deeper and deeper in love as the ship ploughed on. They didn't think of the end of the journey. They just lived for the day. Their love was chaste. Amara had made it clear – without words – that there would be no happy ending in a lifeboat. They hardly spoke of their feelings. They didn't need to. They spent a lot of time with Krishnamurti and Tom even introduced the master to Trelawny. It was not a successful meeting.

'My dear, I can't stand that kind of thing.'

'What kind of thing?'

'Oh, you know. Don't think and it will all go away.'

'He's not saying that.'

'Oh. Then what is he saying?'

Tom couldn't quite answer but he felt it. Love would not have blossomed between him and Amara without Krishnamurti. 'If anyone's a messiah, it's him. I remember my father saying that. I think he was right.'

One person who adored Krishnaji was Madame Kasta.

'What a gentleman. And can you hear? There is a rustling sound when he comes in.'

It was true. There was a strange breeze when he appeared, as if an air conditioner had suddenly been turned on. A fluttering in the air.

'I've said: it's going to end in tears,' she said to no one in particular when they were playing cards one afternoon.

'Everything ends in tears, though. Don't you think, Madame Kasta?' replied Krishnaji. He was wonderfully worldly.

'That's a rather gloomy prediction, sir.' Her plumes ruffled in umbrage before she went on. 'I thought you were in the business of saving souls.'

'I am not in business. Everyone must save their own soul. Gin.' He put his cards on the table.

'Oh.' Was all Madame Kasta could say.

The next day Krishnaji was leaving. They were to dock at Aden for a night. A farewell dinner in the town had been arranged by Rajagopal.

'I'm afraid it will be bully beef, probably. But at least we shall be able to visit Rimbaud's house.'

'Friend of yours?' asked Madame Kasta. She was learning to be sophisticated.

'A great friend. But dead before I was born. A poet. He wrote some extraordinary things when he was very young and then stopped. Came to Aden and simply disappeared. A wonderful story.'

'That's what we're doing,' said Amara.

'Not exactly,' quipped Madame Kasta. 'You have a husband waiting for you. Just in case you had forgotten.' A strained silence fell on the table. Tom shuffled and dealt.

Later, close to land, he and Amara were leaning over the side of the ship. Villages fell from the scrubby slopes into the sea, the last hovels built on stilts over the water. Brown water, brown land, brown hills barely visible in the brown sky. Coloured fishing boats bobbed about in the wake of the ship. Men and boys in turbans and loincloths stood and watched, still as statues. The mountains, no more than misty lines in the distance, crept closer, then towered over them. The tracks turned to streets, shacks turned to houses. A town rose, minarets and domes, flat roofs and water towers, a whole city contained in a crater and circled by mountains. They had arrived at Aden.

'Doesn't it feel strange to have seen all this?' Tom said. 'All this life floating by. Soon it will all be a memory. As if it had never happened.'

They were silent.

'But we will talk about it for ever,' Amara replied finally. 'We will say, "Do you remember when …"'

He said, 'Not to each other. We've never talked. Meaningfully.' He could feel her flinch beside him at the sudden change in direction.

'What can we say?'

'Well, a lot. For a start—'

'We know what happened. What will happen. What words are going to change things?'

'I want to plan for the future. Our future.'

'What plan can we make? Here we are. Sailing down the Red Sea. We have become great friends.'

'Great friends?'

'We've had something we never dreamt of. Can't we leave it at that?'

'I can't. No. I don't ever want to lose you.'

She turned to him and stroked his cheek with her hand. 'I will always be there somewhere. No one can take away what we've had. You've become a part of who I am, who I will always be. You've given me the strength to go on. I was completely broken when I got on this ship. Thanks to you – dear friend – I have been mended. But life has dealt us these cards. These are the facts. I have a husband. I am married to him. In a church. In God's presence.'

'Oh, come on.'

'Don't. That's all there is to it.' She leant her head on his shoulder for a moment. 'I'm going to have a rest before we dock.'

He watched her walk off down the deck. He would die rather than lose her.

Aden was dusty and hot. Mosquitoes with long legs hovered in swarms around the main square. Everyone laughed as Madame

Kasta walked into one such cloud. She waved her arms and ran off screaming down the hot street. Two soldiers in kilts guffawed. British soldiers everywhere, sprawled conspicuously in the bars, watching from the shadows of the arcades as the caravans arrived in the main square from Harar. Platoons marched through the midday sun, the barked orders of their sergeant majors, shrill and strangled like cockney peacocks in the white heat. The British had been in Aden for a hundred years but they still didn't fit in. Local men sat around in small groups in high-piled turbans and jackets over raggedy skirts and flip-flops, watching and waiting. Built over an extinct volcano, the mountains round the city provided almost Gothic ramparts to the town, jagged and crumbling. They seemed to be watching and waiting too.

The market was large, and almost deserted, under huge drapes on poles, punctured by slices of light, smelling of dung. Traders were packing up. A man from the Indian consulate met them on the dock and conducted them to a house behind the main street with no doors or windows. 'This was where Arthur Rimbaud lived. Before he moved to Harar.'

Krishnamurti seemed unconvinced. 'I never believe anything anyone tells me,' he whispered to Tom.

'You could step inside,' the man from the consulate said. 'This place was a hotel in 1871. Everything happened here.' He didn't sound particularly convinced. Huge weeds grew out of the broken floor. The beams had rotted and the house hung in a frozen fall. The upper floors gaped through holes in the ceiling. The staircase had collapsed and lay in a heap, and the sun shone through the broken roof in a dramatic shaft of light. One half expected Jesus to step out of the beam.

'Is there still something sacred?' Krishnamurti asked in a thin, high voice, looking up at some pigeons who were flapping around in the rafters.

'What do you mean?'

'Here. In this shell, this husk from which the butterfly formerly known as Rimbaud took wing. After all, here we are. We have come thousands of miles on this pilgrimage to be close to a person we love. But is there anything left? Have the bricks and mortar absorbed anything from him? Is there a trace?'

Tom looked around. The noise of the town, cars, voices, horns, horses blew through the house on the breeze. The pigeons murmured in the roof. A shutter swung on a rusty hinge with a rhythmic groan. The old mosaic floor, through which the weeds had grown, was the same one that Rimbaud must have stood on, stepped across. Somewhere under those rotting beams he must have sat in a room at this godforsaken desert outpost and wondered what had happened to his life. Was there a trace?

'It feels pretty sensational to be here.'

'But that's just you. *You* leaving home. *Your* feeling of wonder. Coming from Ireland and all that, it's obviously dramatic. But can you feel *him* now that he's gone? Does one feel God in a church?'

'Will I be able to feel you once we have parted?'

Krishnaji looked at him with affection. 'That depends on you. And where you're going.'

It felt like wartime at dinner in Krishnamurti's hotel. Soldiers sprawled at tables and a commanding officer with film-star looks who introduced himself as Mad Mitch made everyone laugh with his languid upper-class drawl.

Krishnaji was still taken up with Rimbaud. 'He wrote everything before he was twenty, you see. Then he turned his back on it all. Nobody had appreciated what he was saying. They couldn't understand it. They had no ears. Or eyes. None of those frauds.'

'Except for Verlaine,' corrected Tom.

'Yes, but at the time Verlaine was no use to anyone, drunk,

violent, wallowing in whatever-you-call-it, self-pity. So Rimbaud just packed up and left, disappeared. What was he thinking when he arrived here? Unknown. Unknowable. He became somebody else. It's a wonderful dream. To be able to do that.'

'You did it, in a way,' said Tom.

'But there was no escape. That's what I found out. From oneself. As long as there's a self, there is no escape. And that's why I was interested to come here. That hotel we saw earlier gave me a kind of clue. No doors or windows, just a shell open to the elements. The desert breeze blows everything away. I didn't feel him happy. Resolved. At peace. I felt a wall of disappointment.'

Mad Mitch appeared at their table. 'Not still talking about Vah-lane and Ram-bo? I should motor you up to Harar. You can still see his house there. Though for how much longer God alone knows. Were you a soldier?' he asked Tom. 'You look like one.'

'I was. Household Cavalry.'

'Do you know Bob Benton?'

'He was my commanding officer. What's going on here? Why the overbearing presence?'

'The Queen was here last week, on a whacking great liner. Turning off the lights before bedtime, if you ask me. Any minute now the whole thing will blow up.' More soldiers joined the table. They talked and laughed about the bloody Bedouin, the situation, while the visitors went into themselves, and the rest of dinner was sad. Conversation petered out. Travelling companions form strong sudden attachments. They randomly converge and form a kind of body, moving together, experiencing the voyage together, and they had all grown close. Now it was over it was difficult to know what to say. Krishnamurti was accustomed to silence (emotion wasn't a part of his vocabulary) but the others felt awkward.

'It was wonderful to meet you,' said Tom. His throat was tight with an inexplicable feeling. The last tenuous link to his past was drifting off on the tide. Krishnamurti bowed his head in acknowledgement but offered nothing in return.

Similarly, when they were alone together Amara asked, 'What do you think I should do?' Krishnamurti looked irritated for a moment but relented and sighed. It wasn't easy being the messiah. He took her hand. 'Amara. You're looking through the eyes of the past. Throw all that away. Who is this God you worship? I could give you two sticks and put them on the mantelpiece over there and we could worship them and have a lovely time. Pretty soon they would be performing miracles. Don't throw everything away on beliefs. Or that silly Christian thing of praying until you are blue in the face to get better at some later date. While you're praying, you're still bad! Just change NOW. No questions. No choices. Live NOW.'

She didn't really understand what he meant.

His goodbye was brisk. Rajagopal followed suit. Then he turned and went upstairs. They both felt wounded. Mad Mitch accompanied them back to the ship, driving at breakneck speed through the deserted town.

'Is it all worth it? For this?' he drawled, gesturing at the port as they got out of his jeep at the dock. 'The odd boat comes along. Last week it was the Queen. This week it's you. Send my regards to Australia.'

And he laughed. Got back in the jeep and drove off waving.

All this and more turned round and round in Tom's head as he tried to sleep that night.

'Question everything. Look closely. Find out for yourself what's wrong and fix it.' Krishnamurti had left a book he had written for Tom with this inscription on the first page. 'In memory of our voyage together.' He lay on his bunk, sleepless beneath the waves. He longed for Amara. He pictured her through the hundred metal walls, all those staircases between them, from deck to deck, she was a million nuts and bolts away. Their relationship had flourished in the hothouse climate of Krishnamurti. In his orbit, falling in love felt natural, easy. Neither he nor Amara asked questions. Would the feeling of ease last without him or would all the insurmountable obstacles suddenly emerge from the darkness like icebergs, crashing into them, sinking their ship?

That Amara was his one and only love – of that, he was certain. He worshipped her. He could see under her skin. And he knew she loved him. They fitted together. Their life on board ship was a kind of paradise. The real world was held at bay. But soon they would be at Sydney. What was going to happen?

A party atmosphere gripped the whole ship as they approached the equator. The sea turned to glass, without a breath of wind. One night the Scots threw a ceilidh in the third-class bar. There were two fiddlers, a banjo, and someone appeared with bagpipes. The captain turned the engines off and the ship drifted as the piper walked around the decks, playing. The wheezy lament sounded ghostly and for a moment everyone felt the vastness of the ocean around them and they were lost in it. The Scots all wept and held each other. Then the reeling began. The kilted Scots taught the other passengers the steps. Strip the Willow, the Gay Gordons, the eightsome, the foursome, even the sword dance. Tom excelled at all of them, which was lucky because Amara was beginning to get a lot of attention. She loved the dancing, was the life and soul of the party. She began to come out of herself. The fun-loving teenager she had been before her forced marriage froze her to the marrow. Now she was defrosting. Everyone asked her to dance, and Tom was riven with jealousy, until performing the sword dance 'like one of us Jocks' got him a standing ovation that someone working on the till of a supermarket in Adelaide thirty years later remembered 'as if it was yesterday'. Even so, watching her dance along a line of clapping, whooping Scots – weaving from one to another, spinning round, faster and faster, her face flushed, her eyes bright, her hair flying about – was painful. How could he hold on to her? Now all the men had their eyes on her. Luckily they were married and their suspicious wives sensibly kept them within earshot.

They hit the doldrums and a couple of Neapolitans sang on deck. A sad ballad about leaving home, seeing Santa Lucia for the last time,

'O passagiero, venite via, Santa Lucia. Santa Lucia.' A man sang and a ukulele strummed.

Quickly the Italians gathered round. Then people appeared from all over the ship. From that moment, there was music every evening. The English put on a variety night. An old piano teacher from Reading on a tuneless upright instrument (he was joining his daughter in Melbourne) accompanied a busty publican's wife who belted out hits from between the wars. 'Don't have any more Mrs Moore,' she sang and the crowd roared.

On the night they crossed the equator there was a party for Neptune. Sailors dressed up as mythical figures. The captain played Neptune in a Stone Age costume and sat on a throne in front of the first-class swimming pool. He ordered various passengers to be dunked in the water. Pat Hannaway was the first. Two costumed sailors took him by his armpits. He fought tooth and nail and nearly pulled a table into the pool with him. There was no love lost between him and the crew. Finally, they took hold of a leg and arm each and threw him in. He landed with a great belly flop and a crash of water. The crowd were thrilled. It was a pagan event and quickly spun out of control. Everyone chasing everyone else. People crashing into the water. The kids screamed. The couples kissed for good luck and everyone got drunk. The next morning nobody got up.

*

After one of these parties, they were walking under the full moon on the deck. Holding hands. They were an established couple by now and enjoyed being seen as such, on nodding terms with the whole boat. Even Madame Kasta seemed to be sympathetic, if not openly complicit.

One of the Italians sidled up to them. 'Eh. Psss. Tomandro. There's a boat free. You wann eet?'

Sudden tension. Tom was about to stuffily refuse when Amara said, 'Yes. Let's take it.'

She opened her bag and rummaged for the money. They both felt ashamed as the Italian led them to the second-class deck and decorously handed Amara up into the lifeboat. Tom clambered in after her.

In the boat they found themselves on a makeshift mattress that smelt of perfume and had a rude smear of lipstick at one end that conjured up a clear picture. All-fours-head-to-the-ground was the term at Sandhurst and Tom smiled. How far was he now from the parade ground and the Knightsbridge Barracks. Stretched over their heads was a fitted tarpaulin, open at one corner. The boat's only light was a lamp on the deck that lit the interior with an orange glow – or at least half of it; the other half was pitch black. Slowly things emerged from the grainy dark – ropes, an anchor, lifebelts and rings, all the accoutrements of shipwrecks. It was cosy and deep, and they sat there in shock for a moment, then began to laugh.

'Will our lives be saved?' he asked, looking around, touching the sides of the boat. 'It feels like being in the breast of a bird, flying away across the sea.'

'Can you believe it?' She moved instinctively into the darkness. Soon only her legs were left sticking out of the shadows.

'Not really.'

'Don't get any funny ideas, though.'

'I won't.'

'I just want to lie next to you. Come on.'

'I can't see you.'

'Yes you can.' She laughed again and her hands reached out from the dark. He sighed.

'What's wrong? Don't you want to? Come on, dearest.'

He crawled down the boat and stood like a dog on all fours, looking down. Close to her, he felt a sudden lurch as if some magnetic force had turned the boat upside down and he was about to fall out, 'I don't think I can. It's too . . . '

'Stop talking.' And she pulled him down. They lay next to each other and now he could hear her heart beating. It was strong and regular. It excited him, gave him courage, and he edged his body closer, over hers, fingers crawling ahead in search of her hand. She turned her face to his and the beauty of it in the half-light made him gasp. Looking at her now, the past drowned in her eyes. It was erased. There was only her and now. His lips reached for hers, but he had forgotten to breathe and had to break away.

'What's wrong?'

'Nothing. I forgot to breathe.'

'Try again.' This time the kiss was tentative, tender, long, growing in confidence, their two faces moving in and out of the shadows. They were both innocent, inexperienced but any doubts either may have had were thrown overboard and the lifeboat sailed on. After a while she lay her head on his shoulder and coiled her legs through his.

He said, 'I don't think I have ever been as happy. Lost on the ocean in a lifeboat with you. I wish it could never end.' She didn't reply at first.

'Every night I lie on my bunk and can't sleep. What will it be like? When we arrive at Sydney. I try not to think about it, and yet . . . '

'Amara.' He kissed her again. Less chaste. 'Amara. Tell him.

Tell him you made a mistake. That you can't be with him. That you love someone else.'

Silence again. 'I do love you. I hoped it would go away. But it hasn't.'

'So let's run away. Let's get a house. In Sydney. Have children.'

'Bastards.'

'So what? It's Australia. That's why we've come. To get away from all that rubbish.'

'You may have done. I did not. I can't change everything – just like that.'

'Why not?'

'Because I love God more than you.'

'That's ridiculous.'

'Why?'

'You can't measure love. It's childish. It's not at eighty per cent for one person and twenty for another, like bottles of liquor. There is no difference in love.'

Silence again. 'But I have been married in church. In God's sight.'

'So unmarry in God's sight.'

'I can't. You don't understand.'

'No, I don't. I understand that you're holding our happiness in your hands and you're prepared to crush it. Throw it away. And for what? For some beliefs. And an old man who doesn't care about you anyway, beyond your capacity for housework. Will you make him happy? Will he make you happy?'

'I will try.'

'But you won't be able to. He'll see that you don't love him. He'll smell it on you.'

'He will smell nothing. There is nothing to smell. You're shaking.'

'Of course I'm shaking. I feel utterly helpless. In two weeks' time I will never see you again. I can't accept that reality for the rest of my life. That kind of darkness.'

Their time was soon up. A drunk couple were waiting as they stepped from the boat. The woman winked at Amara and nudged her man in the ribs.

Tom looked back as the new pair clambered on board, all bottoms and elbows. The island of Java had appeared on the horizon. In a few hours they would arrive at Jakarta.

That day he stayed in bed.

'Coming for breakfast?' asked Trelawny.

'No thanks. I don't feel very well.' And he didn't. A nagging pain in his belly became more intense as the day wore on.

By afternoon Trelawny had called the ship's doctor. The usual suspects were there, playing cards and giving advice, the Italians, the Morris brothers. Even Pat Hannaway was concerned. They stood behind the doctor while he examined a groaning Tom, listening with his stethoscope, pressing waxy fingers into various parts of his abdomen. At one such probe, Tom yelped. The doctor took a thermometer from his bag and slipped it into Tom's mouth. 'Hmm,' he said. 'Stay here.'

He left and returned several minutes later with the captain.

'Look here, sir. I'm afraid you need to have your appendix removed. Fairly urgently. The good news is it couldn't be better timing. We've notified the British consulate. You're going straight to hospital. Don't say we don't look after you.'

'But how long will I be there?'

'A week, I should think. The SS *Cornwall* arrives in a few days. We'll get you on.'

'No. I can't.'

'I'm afraid you must. You have a short time before peritonitis sets in.'

'What does that mean?'

'It means you will die if we don't get the appendix out in the next couple of hours.'

From then on everything moved in a blur. The pain came and went in waves as his temperature rose and delirium set in. The smallest noise crashed like an express train screaming past.

'Find Amara.' Tom clutched at Trelawny's shirt as he was strapped onto a stretcher and carried up to the deck. He craned round at the sea of shimmering, wobbling faces to see if he could find her but there was no sign. Voices echoed, far away, suddenly close. As they clattered down the gangplank, he knew he was going to die.

A baby-faced officer in puttees met him on the dock and accompanied him in the ambulance. He held Tom's hand, which would have made him laugh. Today, his distress had no limits and he clutched the boy's fingers.

'You're in a bit of luck, I'd say. Judging by the sound of things.'

'Where am I going?'

'To the cottage hospital at Admhanaproor. It's the best we've got out here.'

They drove out of the city, the ambulance bell clanging, into the open country. Fruit and rubber plantations fell from the hills either side of the road. They sped through small villages leaving a dust cloud in their wake, past men in white, women in coloured sarongs. Tom saw it all from the window, but in the window was his own reflection, the ghostly shadow of a man lost in love, and anyway all he saw was Amara. He kept saying her name, as if, by pronouncing the sacred word, some miracle would occur. The ambulance turned into a military zone, a sentry box like a child's toy either side of a black and white barrier raised by a soldier who stood to attention and saluted. A bad omen, thought Tom. The last post.

The cottage hospital was deep in a grove of palms and

comprised four or five whitewashed bungalows. In the shadows of their verandahs, patients sat in wicker chairs. Nuns in white administered care. Some nurses, also in starched white, walked through the trees, bright like ghosts in the dappled light. There was a missionary feeling to the place. This was the last coherent thought Tom had as he drifted in and out of consciousness. Behind it all, woven into the fever, the pain, was Amara disappearing on the ship.

He was put onto a gurney and rushed straight into surgery. Men in white coats appeared over his head, leaning down, curious. More nuns. 'I'm a Catholic,' he whispered.

'Me too,' replied a nun, smiling. 'Now don't worry. I've seen all this before,' she said as she stripped, injected and shaved him. He had no idea where he was, who the people were around him. They came and went with the spasms of pain. Their tense faces told him nothing. A mask appeared and he struggled as it was held over his nose and mouth. With a hiss, the gas came and he tried to fight but eventually he fell into a black pit.

Krishnaji was there.

'I thought you were still in Aden.'

'I wanted to see you. To tell you myself.'

'Tell me what?'

'You have to let her go.'

Now he was back on the ship. The horn was booming; the noise of it bounced back and forth across the harbour. They were finally arriving at Sydney. In the middle of the sound was a liner covered in lights and fireworks exploded in the sky over it.

'What's going on?' someone said.

'It's the Queen. She's arrived.' A band played on the Queen's ship and the music wafted across the water. 'Can you see her?'

'There she is.'

'Look at her. Makes you want to turn back.'

'Not bloody likely. She can 'ave it, England.'

There was no turning back. Tom realised that now. As the jolly old *Oriana* groaned and docked, all the poms stood there, uncertain, suddenly shy. This was it.

'Bye-bye, Ron.'

'See ya, Betty.'

'Send us a postcard.'

'See you in Brisbane. If we ever get there, for the love of Mike.'

'Don't be scared,' someone said.

'Amara.' There she was, standing next to Madame Kasta. They both had small suitcases. They were wearing coats and hats.

'Amara.'

She looked at him sadly.

'Come with me,' he begged. He was weeping. 'Please come with me. You're everything. The only thing that matters.'

She shook her head sadly. 'I can't. Not right now. I love you but it's not our time.'

They stood there for a long moment, not daring to look at each other. Finally, she looked up and touched his cheek. 'Go on. Just walk down the gangplank and don't look back. Go on.'

'I can't,' he whispered.

'It has to be. Now go.'

He moved towards the gangplank, swept along on a wave of people, shadows really, flitting past. He looked back at Amara. She smiled. 'Remember. We'll talk about this for ever.' She laughed and disappeared into the crowd.

'No,' was all he whispered. No more strength.

I must do as she says. And he started down the gangplank into a blinding light.

*

The next afternoon a man from the British consulate arrived to inspect the body.

'Good-looking chap. Pity,' was all he said as the sheet was pulled back over Tom's face. 'What got him?'

'We got to him too late. Peritonitis.'

'We've talked to the *Oriana*. They left Java early this morning. No one seems to know much about him.'

'What shall we do with him?'

'The consul says we should bury him here in the English cemetery.'

'What a shame. No one he knows to say goodbye.'

'Well, find out if he has any people left and if they want him back. Usually they don't.'

Tom was discovering many new things. The soul stays close. For a while. It retains some type of earthly form, the carapace of life, dimming with every passing day but still casting a shadow – and while it remains in the realm of time, it can sometimes be seen, like the reflection of a face in a window. Sometimes it is trapped. Tom stayed with his body, still not sure what was happening, not sure he was even dead. The proverbial penny dropped at his own funeral. If you don't know you're dead then, you never will. The surroundings suddenly came into focus, as must happen when sight suddenly becomes available to a baby. He watched his mother and his aunt in the Irish rain, as the one (Iolanthe) pushed the other (Sylvia) in a wheelchair to the edge of the grave. Jim, the lawyer, stood nearby holding an umbrella. They scooped up soil in gloved hands and dropped it on the coffin which had been lowered by men he had known all his life into the earth of his fathers. Then he knew. The adventure was over. They almost saw him then, but they were wrapped up in their own grief. He whispered in their ears. 'I'm so sorry. I'm still here. I love you.' And they looked up into the sky and felt a cool breeze on their faces. A hawk surfed high above. 'There he is,' cried Sylvia. 'Fly away, darling.' And she blew a kiss.

The *Oriana* arrived at Sydney. The Queen *was* there in the harbour. Her ship in the dark was like a galaxy of stars, spangled with lights. Amara watched with Madame Kasta. Neither woman spoke. Finally, Madame Kasta went to the cabin to 'get some rest'. Tomorrow a new life was to begin. Alone, Amara considered throwing herself overboard, but she knew she would never do it. Suddenly fireworks began to explode overhead. Showers of coloured lights rained down. It had all been a dream. Tom was there beside her – but only just. He could feel himself going. He whispered in her ear. She looked round suddenly.

'Oh, Tom. Why were we so unlucky?'

'But we met. At least we met. That was already a piece of luck ... '

She half heard him, like a child hears its parents as it drifts off to sleep.

'We met under an unlucky star. But I promise you I will never forget.'

'Yes, you will. You must.' He felt himself moving away, dissolving, drifting, and he used all the force left in him to hold back. He stood by her bunk all night and the next morning he followed her onto the quay where her husband waited. 'I will always be in your heart,' he whispered. And she whispered back, 'I love you. Pray for me.'

Amara stood frozen for a moment, feeling some deep inner movement that her conscious mind couldn't fathom. Then she turned and looked at her new husband and smiled. He was quite nice. Old, chubby, well-dressed, neat. He had flowers. He smiled awkwardly, which she liked, and put out his hand, which she also liked. They introduced themselves and he led her to a car.

Madame Kasta followed. He politely helped them in, got into the driver's seat and drove off.

Trelawny watched all this from the ship. Everyone had left. He picked up his case and made his way down the gangplank. He was wearing a mackintosh and carried an umbrella. He floated through customs. He glanced back at the ship. The last vestige of Britain.

'Goodbye, Charlie.' He snorted. 'And good riddance. So this is Australia.' He looked furtively at the handsome customs official. 'I think it'll do very nicely.'

THE END OF TIME

SHORT STORY OF MY LIFE
Adaptations.

The journey from performer to writer is a well-trodden goat path, an up-hill, down-dale struggle from which we thespians have reaped varying degrees of success, but which at the very least gives us a much-needed sense of purpose during the long winter afternoons of the soul when the phone doesn't ring.

Adaptations are a good place to start.

I am of course green with envy at the wonderful successes of actor/writers such as Emma Thompson reading the box office receipts of the novel she had adapted of *Sense and Sensibility* to Jane Austen at her grave. I took a picnic to Noël Coward's tomb earlier this year to explain why my series about him, commissioned by Warner Bros., had failed to get any 'traction'. I have often sat beside that grave over the years. I had a lot to explain. In the rage of youth, I fucked up his play *The Vortex* most nights with my insane antics. I would never have been forgiven had he been alive. Dead, he is more pliable, and we have shared many happy afternoons on that dramatic, deserted hillside where the fireflies come out at dusk and glow around the grave like sprites and fairies.

The human fairies are long gone, all dead, the last clipped echo is almost lost on the breeze and Coward may be dying finally too. It is only a matter of time before the alumni of RADA add him to the list of playwrights they are uncomfortable performing. As it is, I was told by the lady from Warner Bros. that everything had changed since the BLM movement and that my approach to the Coward story was out of synch with the times.

You win some, you lose some.

Out of the blue, I was asked by two charming producers to make a series out of Proust's mammoth seven-volume novel. Though thrilled and amazed at being considered for the job, I wasn't initially enthusiastic. Apart from the obvious misgivings – would I ever be able to scale such a sheer peak? – I wondered if a series of Proust would, could ever get commissioned in today's climate crisis.

The narrative moves at a glacial pace, hardly punctuated for cliffhangers and commercial breaks. There is also the difficult Albertine story which is endless but considered sacred. Proust goes to great brilliant lengths to dissect other people's dishonesties but his own are shoddily patched together into this unconvincing love affair, claimed by the authorities to be sublime. Albertine quite simply behaves like a boy and the hundreds of pages devoted to the narrator's jealous manoeuvres conjure up a petty queen enthralled by a footman rather than an asthmatic buck in love with a lesbian. None of it makes sense to the modern reader. Yes, Albertine is sleeping with women but she's actually a bloke!

In the play that I am currently rehearsing (*A Voyage Round My Father* by John Mortimer), the father, my character, says 'There's a lot of damned dull stuff in old Proust.' And I heartily concur. On the other hand, reading the books again I was swept away, amazed all over again at their brilliance.

Amazed to have got through them for one thing, amazed at how eventually they take hold of you like a tide and sweep you off and drown you into a kind of trance until suddenly it's over.

In one sense these books were the cornerstone of my own career as my first job out of drama school was as an extra in a legendary production of Proust at the Glasgow Citizens Theatre called *A Waste of Time*. Adapted by Robert David MacDonald and directed and designed by Philip Prowse, my whole creative life – such as it has been – was born out of this production. It was the most exciting thing I have ever taken part in. The show lasted four hours. I was the Duc de Châtellerault, covered in make-up, every night at 7 p.m., scowling in the background. Later, on the night bus crossing the Gorbals to my digs on Glasgow's Southside, I literally tingled with happiness. I was part of a brilliant company, living in a wonderful alien city, splashing through the puddles under the orange street lights, disappearing into the thick Scottish mist.

(By the way, in their version Albertine was shadowed by a muscular skinhead in a singlet.)

I made a classic mistake with the charming producers. Unsure that I would be able to deliver a decent pilot I decided not to strike a deal until I knew I could pull the job off. I re-read the books and with some help from the aforementioned Philip Prowse came up with the script. I worked Proust's real life into Marcel's and, luckily, I could leave the problem of Albertine for later, if indeed later would ever happen.

I rang up one of the charming producers with the good news.

'Oh,' he said carefully. 'Well. I'd love to hear your ideas.'

'Ideas? No, I've written a script. I've written it.'

It transpired that he had changed his mind and no longer wanted to do the series.

Showbiz is remorseless – like nature. One's skin thickens. One's original features disappear under the hide – which accounts for why all old actors over-act, because when the skin is young, thin and tight one can express everything with the twitch of an eye – Pacino in the original *Godfather* is a perfect example – while later on that eye is squinting out from curtains of marbleised flesh and one's reaction to a simple line like 'Cup of tea, love?' can be to look like *The Scream* by Munch.

I have worked on a handful of adaptations. Only one wound still suppurates. One adaptation. I longed from the age of fifty to make a TV series of *Travels with My Aunt* by Graham Greene. It is my book for all time. Every character is a legend. Aunt Augusta, Mr Visconti, Wordsworth (wonderful knackers), Tooley and Henry Pulling, to name but a few.

Istanbul, Chelsea, Asunción, the *Orient Express*, the River Plate, *Travels with My Aunt* is an epic travelogue and the greatest coming of old age story ever told. Again and again, I have begged for the rights. But no. Each time I enquire of the hard-headed agent I get the same rebuff, while she distributes Greene's work with abandon for interesting re-interpretations (I'm being polite) like *Brighton Rock*.

Well, I have at least written a version of *Swann's Way*. And while it may never make it to the screen, it now has a flickering existence in this book.

SCRIPT TITLE

Written by

Name of First Writer

Based on, If Any

Address

Phone Number

THE END OF TIME

PART ONE

1. BLACK SCREEN

> MARCEL (V.O.)
>
> Sometimes in the dead of night, or listening
> to the noises from the street at dawn, I found
> that the idea of death had taken up permanent
> residence within me – in the way that love
> sometimes does. I felt like a dying soldier,
> desperate – but unable to summon the force –
> to write his last testament, to express his life
> in words before it was snuffed out.
>
> And my task was longer than his, my
> words had to reach more than a single person.
> But how?
>
> By day, all I could hope for was to try to
> sleep. If I could work, it would only be at night.
> But still I couldn't begin. Empty pages lay
>
> (MORE)

MARCEL (V.O.) (CONT'D)

across my bed, like unmarked gravestones –
my thoughts would not take seed – and the
names of the dead remained unwritten.

I was still waiting for that event, that
apparition, that click in the head, where time
would suddenly stand still and everything
would appear as one – the past, the present,
even the future – as it must seem from the
eye of the swirling universe, and the words
would suddenly pour from pen to page and the
edifice I had dreamt of building would finally
be achieved. Would it be a church where little
by little a group of faithful would discover
some sort of truth or harmony, or perhaps
even a grand general scheme, or would it
remain, like a druidic monument on a rocky
isle, forever unfrequented, I could not tell. But
time was running out. I had to begin.

Noises of traffic on a rainy street. Footsteps.

2. EXT. AVENUE KLEBER DUSK 1918

More cars than carriages splash through puddles on the
shining cobbles. People pass by. Chatter, suddenly close.
A wet blue dusk is folding into an autumn night. It's Paris.
1918. Various views. On one side the white towers of the
Sacré-Coeur hang over a patchwork quilt of rooftops and
chimneystacks. On the other the rusticated corner of a
modern apartment building. On its fourth floor a solitary
lit window.

3. EXT. WINDOW AVENUE KLEBER DUSK

A metal balcony. Dead flowers. A glow from behind heavy drapes.

4. INT. BEDROOM DUSK

The sound of the traffic sharply cuts away to a static silence as we move around a small cork-lined room, past complex medical paraphernalia, cylinders of oxygen, enamel basins, syringes and phials, a cumbersome breathing apparatus – bellows, mask, coils of tubes – to a bed. A MAN lies on it, apparently dead, just a head and shoulders tucked into crisp linen sheets.

A door opens. It is FRANÇOISE, a housekeeper. She carries more paraphernalia on a tray.

The corpse speaks.

> MARCEL
> What time is it?

> FRANÇOISE
> Time for you to do your business.

> MARCEL
> Not tonight.

> FRANÇOISE
> Yes. Tonight. You don't want to be
> embarrassed later in front of that lot.

She puts her things on a table and strips the sheets off the bed. The man is skeletal under a sweat-drenched nightshirt.

FRANÇOISE (CONT'D)
Mind you, these days what are they? Not the
real thing any more. Now. Over we go.

She expertly flips the man onto his front while at the same time pulling up the nightshirt to reveal a pair of bony legs leading to an even bonier bottom. She leans over to the table and takes a big rubber bulb with a nozzle. Without waiting to see what she does with it we move on up the body to find the face of the man buried almost in the pillow. It turns to the side.

The man is MARCEL PROUST. An owl's face with an untrimmed moustache. Accompanied by some strange off-screen gurgles his face visibly relaxes.

MARCEL
(dreamy)
Did you know that the Princesse de Conti had
an enema before every reception at Versailles?
She said it kept her cool.

FRANÇOISE
No I did not.

MARCEL
Oh. It's in Saint-Simon. You should read it. It's
quite marvellous.

FRANÇOISE

I've got better things to do with my time,
like looking after you. Now. What are you
wearing? You shouldn't be going out anyway
in your state. What is it? Grand tenue? I don't
think. It makes me laugh to think that piece
of muck that was Madame Verdurin is now
the Princesse de Guermantes. What a joke. It
makes my blood boil. Do you remember that
time . . .

MARCEL

No. I don't. I don't remember anything. I
couldn't even write today. I'm a blank.

FRANÇOISE
(grimly watching her work)
It's a shame they don't make one of these for
the brain. You're blocked up all over if you ask
me. I'd give anything to see all the shit coming
out of your ears! Hah. Five years stuck in this
room to write a book and not a bloody word.

MARCEL

I haven't found the right title.

5. EXT. AVENUE KLEBER DUSK

Marcel emerges from the building in evening dress and
a fur-lined overcoat. He holds on to Françoise and moves
with difficulty towards a car door held open by a good-
looking chauffeur. AGOSTINELLI. They lower him into

the back seat. Françoise hands him two sticks. The door is
carefully shut.

Agostinelli leaps round to the driver's side and gets into
the car.

Françoise stands alone as the car moves off towards the
Étoile.

6. INT. CAR DUSK

Marcel watches glumly as Paris slides past. Agostinelli drives.
No expression on his handsome face. Finally . . .

>   MARCEL
> So. Was it as much fun as you thought it was
> going to be?

>   AGOSTINELLI
> What?

>   MARCEL
> Whatever it was you said you were going to be
> doing.

>   AGOSTINELLI
> No. No. They let me down. Typical.

>   MARCEL
> They don't seem to be very reliable, your
> friends.

AGOSTINELLI
Well, they're not really friends.

MARCEL
If they're not friends then why are you
seeing them?

Agostinelli clenches his jaw. Says nothing. Instead he nearly
runs over a pair of YOUNG SHOP GIRLS out for the
evening.

AGOSTINELLI
Fucking tarts. Disgusting.

MARCEL
I thought you liked that kind of thing.

AGOSTINELLI
Certainly not!

SILENCE for a moment. Both faces inscrutable. Agostinelli
watching the street. Marcel watching Agostinelli's neck.

MARCEL
I've been thinking about spring. I want to just
drive. Don't you?

AGOSTINELLI
(not really)
Well, I'd need to know where you want to go.

MARCEL
I thought I'd made that rather clear.

>   AGOSTINELLI
> Nothing you ever say or do makes anything
> clear.

>   MARCEL
>   (happy at last)
> L'histoire de ma vie.

7. EXT. HOTEL DE GUERMANTES DUSK

The car turns from the street through an elaborate arch
into a large courtyard. Flambeaux gutter in sconces against
the walls of a palace – the Hotel de Guermantes, the home
of the Guermantes family since the fourteenth century.
GOOD-LOOKING FOOTMEN sit on the steps and
grudgingly stub out their cigarettes as the car comes to a
halt. They get to their feet and watch as Marcel struggles up
the steps, a strange crustacean, all sticks and stiff legs, until
a MAJOR-DOMO bounds from the front door to help. The
footmen slink off.

Times have changed.

8. INT. GUERMANTES VESTIBULE DUSK

A huge double staircase. Marble walls. A larger-than-life
bronze of a Guermantes on a horse. Marcel breathes with
difficulty as he considers the long climb. Can he make it?
The major-domo takes his coat. A sudden shriek from the top
of the stairs.

CHARLUS (V.O.)
Marcel. Is that you?

Marcel looks up to see the BARON DE CHARLUS – a
seventy-five-year-old stick insect in evening dress. Dyed
black hair, a weightlifter's curled moustache, long thin legs
and a pot belly. He is accompanied by a pale YOUNG MAN
and comes clattering down the stairs towards Marcel into a
gigantic and harrowing close-up.

CHARLUS
Don't go in. Everyone's dead. Hannibal de
Bréauté, Antoine de Mouchy, Adalbert de
Montmorency, dead! Charles Swann, dead.
Boson de Talleyrand, dead. They're all dead.
Only you survive. Typical.
(to the major-domo)
Get me my coat.
(to Marcel)
You don't look well. Perhaps you have the
Spanish flu? Old Mother Verdurin got it.
Unfortunately, she recovered. Not only did
she recover but she is now my cousin. Can
you believe it? Sitting upstairs in my sainted
mother's drawing room – at this precise
moment – giving one of her filthy musical
soirees.

The major-domo returns with his coat. Charlus puts on a top
hat and gloves. Marcel stares.

> CHARLUS (CONT'D)
> There is no God. We should see each other. But
> perhaps not. There is so little to say these days.
> From next spring I shall speak only in tongues.
>> (to the young man)
> And what are you waiting for? Find the car, for
> God's sake.

And he's gone. Pushing the boy before him.

Marcel looks doubtfully at the stairs. A CONTRALTO
begins to sing somewhere far away. It is 'Le Spectre de la
Rose' by Berlioz.

9. INT. ENFILADE OF ROOMS NIGHT

Marcel appears over the horizon, from the staircase, and
moves slowly through an ivory and gilt salon. A few guests,
bored by the concert, turn as he passes. Their attention
unnerves him. He leans against a table to catch his breath,
gulping for air. His vision blurs. He rummages in a pocket
for a phial which, with shaking hands, he breaks into a
handkerchief. He covers his nose with the handkerchief and
breathes in deeply.

A beautiful YOUNG GIRL sees him and comes over.

> MLLE DE SAINT-LOUP
> Are you all right?

Marcel looks up. She shimmers. He stares at her for a long
moment as his breathing returns to normal.

> MARCEL
> (finally)
> You remind me of someone.

> MLLE DE SAINT-LOUP
> (laughing)
> Everyone says that. My mother, probably.

> MARCEL
> Your mother?

> MLLE DE SAINT-LOUP
> My mother. The Marquise de Saint-Loup.
> Look! She's over there.

She points into the drawing room where the concert is taking place. On the end of a row of chairs sits a RED-HEADED LADY, an older version of the young girl. A group of men stand round her. She turns, looks through them directly at Marcel.

10. FLASHBACK – TANSONVILLE DAY

A little BOY spies through a hedge on a little red-headed GIRL standing in a garden. The little girl turns and looks back.

11. INT. ENFILADE OF ROOMS NIGHT 1918

The red-headed lady gets up. The men stand back and bow while she walks towards Marcel. She kisses him on both cheeks.

GILBERTE

Marcel! We probably shouldn't. This wretched
flu. But they say only the young can get it.
Did you hear that? I see you've spotted my
daughter. But you haven't seen my mother.
We're all here, you see.

MARCEL

Madame Swann is here.

GILBERTE

Look. Over there.

A tiny OLD LADY, skin and bones, sits talking to a younger
woman, her nurse. Marcel is shocked.

GILBERTE (CONT'D)

You were so in love with her. Do you
remember?

MARCEL

I was in love with you.

GILBERTE

Nonsense. I threw myself at your head several
times and you always dodged.

MLLE DE SAINT-LOUP

Maman!

GILBERTE

Well, you did! What are you doing here? We all
thought you were dead.

MARCEL

Some invitations are irresistible, even for us
ghosts. The new princesse seems to be finding
her feet.

GILBERTE

They're big enough, God knows. All those
years at war with my mother and now she's my
aunt so they have to be friends. It's funny how
everything turns out.

The contralto warbles to a climax in the song. Polite applause.

MARCEL

Her position may have changed but her
repertoire has not! The same old songs. Any
minute now we'll have the Vinteuil sonata.

They laugh.

GILBERTE

When I married Saint-Loup they all said it was
the end of the Faubourg. And yet here we are.
    Electric-lit ghouls in the forbidden city, a
Jewish marquise, a haberdasher's daughter
posing as a princesse, and an old courtesan
kept alive by paraffin injections.
    Goodbye, my dear. I'm leaving. You'd
better hurry or you'll miss the Vinteuil. Come,
daughter.

MLLE DE SAINT-LOUP

Goodbye, monsieur.

> MARCEL
> (kissing the young girl's hand)
> Your father was a wonderful man. I miss him
> every day.

The girl inclines her head. Marcel bows.

> MARCEL (CONT'D)
> (to Gilberte)
> And so was yours!

They laugh.

12. INT. DRAWING ROOM NIGHT

He arrives in a large domed room where the concert is being
held. A hundred people sit in rows of gilt chairs. All eyes
are fixed on a QUINTET OF MUSICIANS and a BUSTY
FEMALE SINGER. In the first row – directly in front
of the singer – sits a very old lady with the waxy face and
large hanging lips of a deep-sea fish – the PRINCESSE DE
GUERMANTES (the former Madame Verdurin), hands
clasped over her bosom, enraptured by the music. Marcel
moves round to the back of the room. She turns to say
something to the person behind her and sees him. Her face
freezes.

The song ends. The Princesse gets up to congratulate the
singer.

PRINCESSE

And now the real reason that we are all
gathered together is of course to worship at the
altar of our deity – Vinteuil.

The blue-blooded GUERMANTES FAMILY, to which
she is the latest addition, sit en masse in the front row. The
Princesse's husband, the PRINCE DE GUERMANTES,
looks sheepishly at the patriarch – his cousin the DUC
DE GUERMANTES – who glares at the Princesse. Her
bohemian banter is falling on deaf ears, but she gushes on
regardless.

PRINCESSE (CONT'D)

My life changed, not necessarily for the better,
but a transformation was achieved when I
encountered for the first time the sonata we
are about to hear.
Vinteuil may be physically dead but each
note is a call from the other side where his soul
still vibrates with ours.

The Duc clears his throat deliberately.

DUC DE GUERMANTES

Is this a concert or a bloody séance?

PRINCESSE

Enough words. We are here for music.

DUC DE GUERMANTES

Oh Christ.

The Princesse billows down into her seat. Everyone waits for her to settle. A frozen moment of concentrated silence as the musicians are poised to begin. Only Marcel moves. This music changed his life too and not necessarily for the better.

Gasping for breath he makes for a concealed door in a large mirror and disappears. As the door swings shut we see the reflected musicians begin.

13. INT. BALLROOM NIGHT

A huge empty room the size of a football pitch with wall-to-ceiling windows at one end, draped and electric-lit. At the other, THREE FOOTMEN are setting up a buffet. Another concealed door opens and Marcel appears. They bow but continue with their work. He nods and hobbles across the room, a weaving silhouette against the light of the huge windows, coming finally to a halt and slowly falling to the floor.

The three footmen rush towards him and pick him up.

> MARCEL
> Let me just sit down for a moment.

> FOOTMAN
> You'll be more comfortable in the library.

> MARCEL
> No. I'm perfectly all right. I shall just get my breath back and be on my way.

Reluctantly, they lower him onto a chair in the corner.

FOOTMAN
Can we get you something?

MARCEL
How kind. Perhaps some tea.

The three boys turn.

MARCEL (CONT'D)
Wait. Do you have . . .

They stop.

MARCEL (CONT'D)
Lime blossom?

FOOTMAN
Yes, sir.

They move off. Marcel has another thought.

MARCEL
And . . . And . . .

They stop again, turn.

FOOTMAN
Monsieur?

MARCEL
A little something. To eat.

FOOTMAN
Monsieur.

One of the boys retrieves his sticks from the middle of the
room and brings them over.

FOOTMAN (CONT'D)
Here we are, sir.

MARCEL
Thank you.

FOOTMAN
Should we fetch somebody, sir?

MARCEL
No. No. Thank you. There is nobody. They're
all listening to the music.

A few bars waft through the walls. Also a kind of tinnitus like
a faraway shriek.

CLOSE on Marcel. He rubs his ear.

MARCEL (CONT'D)
The Vinteuil.

The two other footmen are back with a tea tray and a small
table which they place beside Marcel. One of them pours tea
into a cup. There is a napkin and a plate of cakes.

MARCEL (CONT'D)
Thank you. Thank you.

The footmen retreat to the buffet table at the other end of the room.

The tinnitus gets stronger.

Marcel reaches for the napkin. It is starched and crinkles in his hand. The sound reminds him of something. He freezes for a moment, searching the back of his mind – can't find it – then dabs at his perspiring face.

> MARCEL (CONT'D)
> Ahh! A madeleine.

CLOSE-UP – His shaking fingers take a cake and he is about to dip it into the cup of tea when another hand, sensibly ringed, comes into the frame. The tinnitus stops abruptly and like a radio finding a wave . . .

> GRANDMOTHER (V.O.)
> Don't hurry so, my sweet child. Break it first
> and let it absorb the vapour of the tea.

For a moment an OLD LADY is sitting at the table. She crumbles the madeleine into the tea.

> MARCEL
> Grandmamma!

> GRANDMOTHER
> Like this. Now breathe. Just breathe. So
> excitable. Such imagination.

She stirs the madeleine into the tea and offers a spoonful of
the mixture to Marcel. He closes his eyes.

BLACK OUT. The sound of a deep sigh.

> FOOTMAN (V.O.)
> Monsieur.

14. DREAM SEQUENCE INT. BALLROOM NIGHT

The room is crammed with people. A lot of noise. Marcel
wakes.

> FOOTMAN
> Monsieur. It is time to get up.

> MARCEL
> Yes. Maybe.

He gets up, takes his sticks and moves with purpose through
the room. An underwater feeling. The noise and the tinnitus
are almost deafening.

Ancient faces, jewelled and gloved, tail-coated and toothless,
loom towards him, their faces melting as he passes, becoming
fuller, gaining teeth, hair, colour – the years falling away, in
fact. Time is going backwards. The blue-blooded crowd is
like a shoal of glittering fish, surging and bending against an
invisible current dragging them into the past. Marcel ploughs
through it towards a patch of blinding light, the surface,
maybe, or a door. It is a door. Into a garden.

Disoriented and breathless, but illuminated, he pushes
through the throng towards it . . .

15. FLASHBACK EXT. COMBRAY DAY

. . . and stumbles out into the open air. A magic moment of
complete stillness. And colour. The sound of birdsong, a
church bell. Gravel under his feet. We are in the garden of
a large house on the edge of the village of Combray. Forty
years earlier. A table is laid for dinner under a chestnut tree.

Crunch, crunch, crunch, coming closer. THREE
FORMIDABLE WOMEN in black sit round a table having
tea, all looking at a SICKLY LITTLE BOY who stands in
front of them.

The little boy turns and sees Marcel. They regard one
another for a long moment. Marcel gasps and reaches out but
the little boy just stares, then turns back to the women.

And the story begins.

He is LITTLE MARCEL and his GRANDMOTHER holds
a teaspoon. His GREAT-AUNTS FLORA and CELINE
watch disapprovingly.

> MADAME AMADEE
> Come on, darling.

He climbs on to his grandmother's knee and cuddles up to
her, eyes closed, while she feeds him from the teaspoon.

MADAME AMADEE (CONT'D)

Some lovely lime blossom tea and a madeleine.
Good for the nerves. It gives us the courage to
go upstairs to bed.

GREAT-AUNT CELINE

Oh really! Stairs are stairs. We don't need
courage to climb them.

The great-aunts snort with derision and look over at the men,
MARCEL'S FATHER and GRANDFATHER, who are
sitting on wicker chairs in the shade, reading the papers.

MARCEL

(lowered voice so the men don't hear)
But I hate my room. I want to stay down here
with Mamma and you.

GRANDMOTHER

But now you have that wonderful magic
lantern – you can play with that if you can't
sleep.

MARCEL

(trying to keep calm)
But I want to be down here. I have to be near
Mamma.

GREAT-AUNT FLORA

Marcel. You know perfectly well that Monsieur
Swann is coming for dinner.

MARCEL
Does that mean Mamma won't be coming to
say goodnight again?

He wants to cry but he knows he can't. This a strict
household. Françoise, the young housekeeper, comes in with
a tray.

FRANÇOISE
Not with Monsieur Swann here.
    (to the ladies)
He sent over a case of wine. Something
very nice.

GREAT-AUNT CELINE
And so he should. He dines with us practically
every night.

GRANDFATHER
Except when he is dining with the Duc de
Broglie. Look at this! 'Charles Swann is one
of the most regular attendants at Sunday
luncheon' it says here. Good old Swann! I long
to ask about him about old Broglie, the father.

GREAT-AUNT CELINE
Ask Swann? A stockbroker? Why?

GRANDFATHER
Why? Well, because the old duke was very
close to Louis Philippe. Why can't I?

GREAT-AUNT CELINE

I see no reason to ask questions about people
we don't know.

(changing the subject)

Just think, Flora, I met a young Swedish
governess today who told me some most
interesting things about the co-operative
movement in Scandinavia.

GRANDFATHER

(under his breath)

I see no reason to ask questions about co-
operative movements we don't know.

GREAT-AUNT CELINE

(ignoring him)

We must have her here to dine one evening.

GREAT-AUNT FLORA

To be sure! But I haven't wasted my time
either. I met such a clever old gentleman at
Monsieur Vinteuil's yesterday, who knows the
actor Maubant quite well ...

The two sisters shriek with excitement while the grandfather
looks at them, exasperated. His son winks sympathetically.
His wife sighs. Marcel observes, wrapped in his
grandmother's arms.

MARCEL

(whispering)

Swann. Stockbroker. Swann. Stockbroker.

16. INT./EXT. HOTEL DE GUERMANTES HALL NIGHT 1918

More arms around Old Marcel who is being more or less carried down the stairs by two footmen. A third one helps him into his coat, his scarf, his hat. They take him outside where Agostinelli stands by the car.

CLOSE on Marcel's face as he is lowered into the back seat. A victorious glitter in his eyes. The apparition has occurred. As the car turns out of the courtyard he looks round at the receding house through the rear window.

>   MARCEL
>   (laughing)
>   Swann.

17. FLASHBACK EXT. COUNTRY LANE COMBRAY EVENING

A door in a wall on the edge of some woods opens and CHARLES SWANN appears. A good-looking man of fifty. He closes the door carefully and sets off down the lane. It is one of those enchanted evenings from childhood in the fields above Combray. Cows and trees throw long shadows across the grass. The windows of a farmhouse are gold in the setting sun.

Pigeons call to each other in the woods. The clip-clop of a horse somewhere in the village. Swann carries a basket of peaches. He wears a pale linen suit and a straw hat.

MARCEL (V.O.)

Our utter ignorance of the brilliant social life
which Swann led was, of course, due in part to
his own reserve and discretion.

Swann stops and talks to a GIRL herding a family of goats up
the lane. He fancies her.

MARCEL (V.O.) (CONT'D)

But also to the fact that middle-class people
in those days took what was almost a Hindu
view of society, which they held to consist of
sharply defined castes.

The girl laughs at something Swann says. He bows and
walks on.

MARCEL (V.O.) (CONT'D)

In my aunts' opinion Swann belonged in
none of them. Not because he was a Jew,
but because he had married a woman they
considered little better than a common
whore. In fact, they thought him fortunate
to be invited with such regularity to dine
with us. None of us suspected, like a family
of innkeepers who have in their midst a
celebrated highwayman without knowing it,
that Swann was one of the most distinguished
members of the Jockey Club and a particular
friend of the Comte de Paris and the Prince of
Wales.

Swann turns from the lane into a sloping field of poppies. At the bottom, another wall, another gate and the village beyond, built into the hill, rooftops, chimney pots and a church steeple.

18. EXT. GARDEN COMBRAY EVENING

Little Marcel watches his family with a strange intensity. He has large round eyes, a pale face and thin, worried lips. As usual, the family are discussing Swann. Despite being a servant, Françoise throws in her opinions with abandon.

> FRANÇOISE
> Don't you remember that time he came to see us after dinner and his coachman said that he had been dining with a princess?

Snorts of derision.

> GREAT-AUNT FLORA
> A nice sort of princess.

> GREAT-AUNT CELINE
> A gypsy princess, probably.

> GRANDMOTHER
> Celine!

> GRANDFATHER
> Well, there's his name in the *Figaro* all the same.

GREAT-AUNT FLORA
I should hate to have my name printed like
that and I shouldn't feel at all flattered if
anyone spoke to me about it.

MARCEL'S MOTHER comes out of the house.

MOTHER
(to her husband)
Well, I wish you would ask about his daughter.
Just a word. Ask him how she is.

Squawks of indignation from the great-aunts.

FATHER
No. No. NO! You have the most absurd ideas.
It would be utterly ridiculous.

With his mother's arrival Marcel is suddenly taut. The moment
is coming when he will have to go upstairs. He fixes her with
a desperate glare but she ignores him and goes back inside the
house.

MARCEL
Maman!

The two men look at him sternly.

GRANDFATHER
This little man looks tired. He should go to
bed. We're dining late tonight.

FATHER
Yes. Yes. Off you go. Run along.

MARCEL
I need to say goodnight to Maman.

FATHER
No. No, leave your mother alone. You've
already said goodnight, that's enough.

MARCEL
We haven't.

FATHER
These exhibitions are absurd. Now go on
upstairs.

19. EXT. FIELDS COMBRAY EVENING

Swann strides up to the gate at the bottom of the field.

20. EXT. GARDEN COMBRAY EVENING

The tinkle of a bell somewhere in the garden. Grandmother
rises, puts out her hand for Marcel, neatly avoiding his
planned outburst of grief.

GRANDMOTHER
Come along, little one. That will be Monsieur
Swann. I'll take you to the stairs on my way to
meet him.

They go into the house. The bell rings again.

> GREAT-AUNT CELINE
>
> Goodness me. The bell. Who on earth can
> it be?

> GRANDFATHER
>
> You know perfectly well who it is. Now see
> that you thank him for the wine.

> GREAT-AUNT FLORA
>
> We can't rub his nose in our gratitude. He
> doesn't want everyone to know that he more or
> less pays for a seat at our table!

> GRANDFATHER
> (whispering)
>
> Flora!

> GREAT-AUNT FLORA
>
> Well, I'm sorry. I shall express myself
> with discretion and tact. Now don't start
> whispering. How would you like to come
> into a house and find everyone muttering to
> themselves?

21. INT. HALLWAY COMBRAY HOUSE EVENING

A sturdy oak staircase climbs the three floors of the house.
Grandmother pats Marcel on the bottom and sends him up
before going through the hall and out the back door.

The child climbs extremely slowly, a dark face, pulling himself up by the banister with his hands, one step at a time. He stops at a window and sees his mother and grandmother walking through the garden with Swann. They come in.

> MOTHER
> Do tell me about your daughter. Is she feeling any better?

Before Swann has time to answer.

> FATHER (V.O.)
> Ah there he is! Come along, Charles, we're in the garden.

> MOTHER
> Let's talk later. Only a mother can really understand these things. I'm sure that hers would agree with me.

Marcel listens, torn between misery and fascination. Grandmother, disapproving of the conversation, gently but firmly pushes Mother and Swann into the garden. Marcel leans his head on the banister with a heartfelt sigh and tries to get a better look into the garden.

He watches Swann greeting the great-aunts. Françoise passes.

> FRANÇOISE
> Up to bed. I'll be there shortly.

22. INT. MARCEL'S ROOM NIGHT

A large romantic room with a canopied bed and a smaller iron
one in the corner. A fireplace, an armoire, a washstand and a
desk all appear from the gloom, cumbersome and polished, as
Marcel lights a lamp. An operatic feeling. The sound of the
dinner party can be heard through the window. Distraught,
he watches from behind the curtains.

The table below glows with candlelight. Françoise helps the
ladies into their chairs. Grandmother at one end. Grandfather
at the other.

Marcel's mother sits down, gravely beautiful, and glances up.
Marcel ducks behind the curtain. Swann sits next to her.

> MARCEL
> I have to see Mamma. I have to.

He sits down at the desk and takes a sheet of notepaper and a
pencil. He writes laboriously, mouthing the words.

> MARCEL (CONT'D)
> Mamma, please come and see me. I have
> something to tell you.

He studies the letter, crumples it up and starts again.
Françoise comes in with a jug of hot water.

> FRANÇOISE
> Come along, young sir. Time for bed.

MARCEL

Françoise, will you give Mamma this note? I
promised her I would write.

FRANÇOISE
(suspicious)
Whatever for? Don't dawdle. Get into your
nightshirt and I might take it to her.

He hands her the note, which she studies for a long moment
as he quickly undresses, watching her all the time.

FRANÇOISE (CONT'D)
Have you washed your face? I'll try to slip
it to her between the courses. But I'm not
promising.

Marcel runs to her and hugs her, sobbing.

MARCEL
Thank you. Thank you.

FRANÇOISE
Now, now. What's all this? Too much
excitement, if you ask me. If you go on like
this you'll be packed off to a seminary or
something.

Marcel stops dead in his tracks.

FRANÇOISE (CONT'D)
We don't want that, do we? So stop snivelling
and get into bed, young man. I'll see what I
can do.

Marcel jumps into the small iron bed. The springs creak.
Françoise tucks him in, sits down beside him and strokes his
forehead. She quite likes him, despite everything.

FRANÇOISE (CONT'D)
I don't know what's got into you this summer.
Always crying for your poor mamma. Why are
you so unhappy?

We drift off across the room as she talks, past the canopied
bed, the old armoire and out the window, under the stars and
the full moon to the party below.

23. INT. MARCEL'S CAR PARIS NIGHT 1918

Agostinelli is talking. Marcel doesn't listen. His face is grave,
but alive in a new way.

24. INT. MARCEL'S BEDROOM COMBRAY NIGHT

Marcel runs to the window and watches as Françoise appears
below on the verandah and whispers something to Mother
and discreetly passes her the note. She reads it. Whispers
back. Françoise leaves.

Marcel races back to his bed.

25. INT. MARCEL'S CAR PARIS NIGHT 1918

> MARCEL
> (whispering)
> There is no answer.

> AGOSTINELLI
> What?

26. INT. MARCEL'S BEDROOM COMBRAY NIGHT

Françoise stands at the door, a silhouette against the corridor light.

> FRANÇOISE
> There is no answer.

She closes the door. Marcel lies in bed without moving. Eyes wide open.

TIME RELEASE SHOT. The evening passes while Marcel doesn't move a muscle. Moonlight creeps across the room.

CROSS CUT with the next scene, only Marcel's lips move, mimicking the grown-ups in the garden.

27. EXT. GARDEN COMBRAY NIGHT

Grandfather and Swann are discussing Louis Philippe.

> GRANDFATHER
> Do you think they got along?

> SWANN
> I think he found them very congenial
> neighbours.

> GREAT-AUNT FLORA
> (interrupting with a diabolical intensity)
> The King was not the only person who found
> his neighbours very nice.

> SWANN
> I'm sorry?

> GREAT-AUNT CELINE
> (also to Swann)
> Yes, indeed. Some people are very lucky,
> aren't they, dear Monsieur Swann, to have such
> congenial neighbours?

The sisters exchange a victorious wink. Swann and
Grandfather are bewildered.

28. INT. MARCEL'S BEDROOM COMBRAY NIGHT

Marcel still motionless.

The conversation at the dinner below crescendos and falters. Voices suddenly clear, laughter and goodbyes. Then the bell at the garden gate.

> GREAT-AUNT FLORA (V.O.)
> I can't get over the change in Monsieur Swann.
> He is quite antiquated.

> GREAT-AUNT CELINE (V.O.)
> I shouldn't wonder. I fancy he has a lot of
> trouble with that wretched wife of his who
> lives in plain sight with you know who.

> GREAT-AUNT FLORA (V.O.)
> I certainly do, sister. A certain Monsieur de
> Charlus, as all Combray knows. It's the talk of
> the town.

29. INT. MARCEL'S BEDROOM NIGHT 1918

We are back in the cork-lined bedroom. Françoise undresses Marcel, who sits on the bed. He stares into space as she puts a nightshirt over his head.

> MOTHER (V.O.)
> I thought he looked much happier. I think
> myself that in his heart of hearts he no longer
> loves that woman.

> GRANDFATHER (V.O.)
> Of course he doesn't. He wrote me a letter
> about it, years ago.

30. EXT. GARDEN COMBRAY NIGHT

CLOSE-UP Grandfather

> GRANDFATHER
> By the way, you two – you never thanked him
> for the wine.

The great-aunts shriek.

> GREAT-AUNT FLORA
> What? Never thanked him? I think, between
> you and me, I put it to him quite neatly.

> GREAT-AUNT CELINE
> Yes you managed it very well. You didn't
> embarrass him!

> GREAT-AUNT FLORA
> Well, you did it very prettily too.

> GREAT-AUNT CELINE
> Yes, I was rather proud of my remark about
> 'nice neighbours'.

They laugh like geese.

31. INT. MARCEL'S BEDROOM COMBRAY NIGHT

Marcel hears the laughter from his room.

> GRANDFATHER (V.O.)
>
> You call that thanking him? You can be quite
> sure he never noticed it.

> GREAT-AUNT FLORA (V.O.)
>
> Come, come. Swann isn't a fool. I'm sure he
> understood. You didn't expect me to tell him
> the number of bottles, or to guess what he
> paid for them?

> MOTHER (V.O.)
>
> I'm going upstairs. Goodnight, everyone.

Marcel leaps from his bed.

32. INT. STAIRCASE COMBRAY NIGHT

The staircase is dark. Mother climbs slowly, thoughtful,
caught in the moonbeams. Boards creak with each step. And
something else. She looks up and sees Marcel standing on
the second-floor landing. He runs down the stairs and throws
himself on her. Before she can speak they both hear Father
coming through the hall on his way up, the light of his candle
throwing an ominous shadow up the staircase wall.

> MOTHER
>
> Off you go, quick! Do you want your father to
> see you waiting here like an idiot?

> MARCEL
> (desperate)
> Come and say goodnight.

A battle of wills. Father starts up the stairs.

> MOTHER
> Go back to your room.

Marcel doesn't move.

> MOTHER (CONT'D)
> All right. I will come!

Too late. Father has appeared.

> FATHER
> What's going on here?

Marcel is frozen with fear. Mother too.

> MOTHER
> He couldn't sleep. He's upset. He wants me to
> go with him to say goodnight.

Father looks at Marcel, clearly in a terrible state. Fury, astonishment, and then boredom.

> FATHER
> (finally)
> Go with him, then.

> MOTHER
> Yes, but we don't want him to get into bad
> habits . . .

FATHER

Habits? What habits? You can see the child
is unhappy. I should hope we aren't gaolers.
You'll end up making him ill. There are two
beds in there. Get Françoise to make the big
one up for you and stay with him for the rest of
the night.

Anyway, I'm off to bed. I'm not such a
nervous wreck as the rest of you.

The three of them stand there for a moment in a strange
stand-off.

MARCEL (V.O.)

Many years have passed since that night.

33. INT. MARCEL'S BEDROOM PARIS NIGHT 1918

He is sitting in bed. Paper and pen are on a tray with legs. A
pot of coffee and a cup.

MARCEL (V.O.)

The wall of the staircase up which I had
watched the light of my father's candle
gradually climb was long-ago demolished.

34. INT. STAIRCASE COMBRAY NIGHT

Father goes into his room and shuts the door. Marcel is
amazed. So is his mother. She takes him up the stairs and
into his room on the next floor.

                    MARCEL (V.O.)
And in myself too many things have perished
which I thought would last for ever ...

35. INT. MARCEL'S BEDROOM COMBRAY NIGHT

Inside the room Marcel breaks down completely, holding on
to his mother for dear life.

                    MARCEL (V.O.)
And new ones have arisen, giving birth to new
sorrows and new joys which in those days I
could not have foreseen, just as now the old
ones are hard to understand.

Mother undoes Marcel's arms from around her waist and
carries him to the bed, where she lays him down and tucks
him in. He is still inconsolable and finally she begins to weep
as well.

Françoise bustles in with blankets.

                    FRANÇOISE
Goodness me, Madame, what a din. But what
on earth is the young master crying for?

                    MOTHER
          (stroking her son's head)
I don't think he knows himself, Françoise. It's
his nerves.

>   MARCEL (V.O.)
> But lately I've been able to hear, if I listen
> carefully, the sound of those cries which I had
> the strength to control in my father's presence,
> but which I could no longer hold back when I
> found myself alone with Mamma.

36. INT. MARCEL'S ROOM PARIS 1918 NIGHT

Marcel writes.

>   MARCEL
> In reality their echo has never ceased. It is only
> because life is now growing more and more
> quiet around me that I hear them anew ...

He smiles.

37. INT. MARCEL'S BEDROOM COMBRAY NIGHT

The child sleeps in the arms of his mother.

>   MARCEL (V.O.)
> Like church bells which are so effectively
> drowned during the day by the noises of the
> street, until they suddenly ring out through
> the silent evening air.

The church bell in the village strikes the hour.

END OF PART ONE

PART TWO

38. INT. MARCEL'S BEDROOM COMBRAY DAY

Sunshine leaks through the shutters. A cock crows. Marcel wakes. His mother sleeps beside him. He watches her for a moment and then gets out of bed, careful not to wake her.

39. INT. STAIRCASE DAY

Marcel closes the bedroom door and runs screaming with sheer joy down the staircase.

40. EXT. HOUSE COMBRAY DAY

The shuttered house in the sleepy village. Marcel's screams break through the silence.

41. INT. GREAT-AUNT CELINE'S ROOM

Great-Aunt Celine snores in a bed cap. The screams and footsteps don't wake her.

42. INT. GREAT-AUNT FLORA'S ROOM

However, Great-Aunt Flora wakes with a start. She can tell who is making the noise and clucks disapprovingly before turning over and going back to sleep.

43. EXT. COURTYARD DAY

Marcel tumbles out into the sunshine, screaming, and charges into the open door of the kitchen, which is on one side of the large back yard.

44. INT. KITCHEN COMBRAY DAY

A whitewashed barn dominated by a large fireplace and ovens. A sturdy central table at which a PRETTY KITCHEN MAID with flushed cheeks stands cutting a pile of asparagus. She is heavily pregnant. Marcel looks around to check that no one else is in the room and then creeps towards her, hands out liked a pantomime villain. It's a secret game they have played all summer. She turns and screams, and he lays his head on her belly.

> MARCEL
> Sshhh!

Eyes closed, he listens for signs of life and hears a heartbeat. The pretty girl looks down at him with a mixture of affection and fear, pushing him suddenly away as Françoise enters.

FRANÇOISE

Stop loitering, girl. I never saw such a one for
wasting time as you. Where's that asparagus?

KITCHEN MAID

It's making me feel sick. I can't cut it. Look –
it's made my hands swell.

Marcel backs off, observes with interest the cruel side of
Françoise as she loads up a tray – plates, cups, cutlery, coffee.

FRANÇOISE
(snorting)

It's not the asparagus that's making you sick,
you silly girl. It's your slatternly ways, in the
name of Our Lady! And what are you doing
here, young man?

Take this coffee up to your Aunt Leonie if
you want to do something useful. The doctor
is with her so be very quiet. She's had a bad
night.

Marcel lifts the heavy tray carefully.

FRANÇOISE (CONT'D)

And mind you don't spill anything.

45. INT. BEDROOM COMBRAY DAY

Grandmother watches from her window as Marcel carries the
tray across the courtyard to another door which leads to Aunt
Leonie's part of the house. She sighs.

46. INT. MARCEL'S ROOM PARIS NIGHT 1918

Old Marcel lies in bed staring at the ceiling. Turns towards the camera.

> MARCEL
> The house and the surrounding farms
> belonged to Aunt Leonie.

47. INT. AUNT LEONIE'S ROOMS DAY

Marcel opens the door to a darkened room and creeps inside, closing it quietly behind him. It creaks. He freezes. In a room beyond AUNT LEONIE sits up in bed on lace cushions in a lace hat under a thick pink eiderdown. She is being examined by DR PERCEPIED, a fat jolly country doctor with bushy sideburns. There is a window by the bed commanding a bird's-eye view of the town, the high street, the church and a sort of square around it.

> MARCEL (V.O.)
> Since her husband's death, Leonie gradually
> declined to leave ... first Combray, then her
> house in Combray, then her bedroom, and
> finally her bed, and now lay in a perpetual state
> of vague grief, ill health, paranoia and piety.

Marcel lingers in the darkness.

> DR PERCEPIED
> Well, that's a very strong pulse.

LEONIE
(glacial)
How very peculiar. I feel as though I may faint
dead away at any moment.

DR PERCEPIED
I don't think you will.

Leonie grunts with indignation and waves the doctor away.
He packs up his bag. Marcel takes his cue and comes in with
the tray.

LEONIE
Ahh, Marcel. What's this? Coffee? Is Françoise
trying to kill me?
        Coffee so soon after my pepsin. It could
be fatal. I ask you! Goodbye, Doctor. If I am
dead before lunch I daresay you will be very
surprised.

DR PERCEPIED
Very. Good day, Madame. Well, look who's
here. Good morning, Marcel.

MARCEL
Bonjour, Dr Percepied.

The doctor leaves. Leonie looks out the window.

LEONIE
Hand me my drops, Marcel. I am simply too
weak to sit up. Quickly. I say, isn't that
(MORE)

LEONIE (CONT'D)
Monsieur Legrandin and his sister leaving
church early?

In the street below a tall, thin man walks with a woman into
the boulangerie. Leonie reaches for the bell rope and tugs it
several times. A bell rings far off in the depths of the house.

LEONIE (CONT'D)
Look. They're off to buy a cake or something.
How odd. Leaving Mass before the elevation.
God is gracious up to a point but when you
have made as spectacular a marriage as
Monsieur Legrandin's sister . . .

Marcel puts the tray on the table and brings the drops over
to the bed from a chest of drawers covered with bottles of
medication and presided over by a statue of the Virgin.

LEONIE (CONT'D)
Thank you, mon trésor. What I mean is you
don't become a marquise all on your own. Not
if your brother is an engineer. God lifts us,
Marcel. We don't. Remember that.

Marcel watches solemnly. Françoise bustles in.

LEONIE (CONT'D)
Ah, Françoise. There you are. Close my
curtains, please. I have a blinding headache.
Then go down and ask Theodore why
Monsieur Legrandin left church. Is it his colic
again?

A carriage draws up outside the house, flowers fixed to the horses' harnesses. Leonie gasps and sinks into her bonnet.

> LEONIE (CONT'D)
> Wait a minute. Who is going to see Cousin
> Adolphe at this hour?

> FRANÇOISE
> (sneering)
> One of his actresses, I expect. If you know
> what I mean.

At the word actress Marcel's eyes bulge. Everyone leans towards the window just as an OLD MAN and two YOUNG WOMEN appear round the corner and look up from the street. Eye contact all round!

> LEONIE
> Ugh! There is Monsieur Vinteuil with his
> daughter. Looking straight up. Not coming
> here, I hope. I see Mademoiselle Vinteuil's
> 'friend' is back.

They all draw back comically and Françoise closes the curtains. Leonie reaches for her Bible and rosary. Marcel inches his way out of the room.

> LEONIE (CONT'D)
> (to Françoise)
> Hurry up, girl. Today's view is too bothersome.
> Really, I shall swoon. In nomine padre filii e
> spiritus sancti. Phew. What a day.

48. INT. PASSAGE COMBRAY DAY

Marcel closes the door behind him and runs down the stairs. This time a silent scream of ecstasy.

49. EXT. STREET COMBRAY

Out in the street he inches his way around the corner under his aunt's window and then runs all the way to the next-door house. The smart carriage festooned with flowers waits outside. A liveried COACHMAN stands by the horses' heads.

Marcel tears into the house and up the stairs.

50. INT. UNCLE ADOLPHE'S ROOMS DAY

A lady's voice can be heard laughing from behind a half-closed door. A chubby VALET runs across the hall and tries to stop Marcel from entering. Too late.

51. INT. UNCLE ADOLPHE'S BEDROOM DAY

Marcel bursts in to find UNCLE ADOLPHE, a military bachelor in his late fifties, sitting on a chair, legs akimbo, in a shirt and waistcoat, a cigar clenched between his teeth under a substantial moustache. He is glaring at a heavily made-up LADY in pearls and pink satin who sits on a sofa and is still laughing.

They both turn in shock. Marcel runs to kiss his uncle.

ADOLPHE
(embarrassed)
My nephew.

Is all he offers by way of introduction. A pause.

LADY
(badly disguised provincial accent)
How like his mamma he is.

ADOLPHE
But you've never seen her.

LADY
What haven't I seen?

ADOLPHE
(testy)
My niece. You've never met my niece.

LADY
I beg your pardon, my dear, but I passed her
countless times on the stairs last year in Paris
when you were so ill.

Uncle Adolphe rises, clearly embarrassed.

ADOLPHE
What nonsense. Have a cigarette.

Marcel hardly dares to look at the lady, so just stares at his
great-uncle.

                    LADY
No thank you. I've become used to the ones
the Grand Duke sends me.
          (she giggles. Adolphe snorts)
I told him you were jealous.

She extracts an elaborately engraved cigarette case from her
bag, studying Marcel coquettishly. He stares back. She winks
and he goes red. More giggles. She waits for Adolphe to light
her cigarette. Marcel nearly faints. A woman smoking!

                    LADY (CONT'D)
But of course I know this
     young man's father. I met him at your house.
          (overly sincere)
He was so good, so exquisite to me.

                    MARCEL
(quivering) Are you an actress?

                    LADY
          (giggles)
Not quite, no.

                    ADOLPHE
Come now.

                    MARCEL
What play are you in?

                    ADOLPHE
It's time you were running along.

LADY

It's a comedy. Called Life.

ADOLPHE

For God's sake.

MARCEL

(grown-up)

I'll look out for it.

ADOLPHE

Now off you go.

The lady holds out her hand and Marcel, in a moment of insane panache, takes it in his and kisses it, turning purple at the same time.

Adolphe is amazed. The lady laughs.

LADY

Look how gallant he is. Quite the ladies' man.
Just like his uncle. Won't you come for tea
with me one day?

MARCEL

Oh yes, I should . . .

ADOLPHE

Certainly not. He's very busy, winning all the
prizes at school. A veritable Balzac, aren't you?

MARCEL

No.

Adolphe leads Marcel from the room.

> ### LADY (V.O.)
> He's an artist. But I adore artists, they're the
> only ones who understand women. Adieu,
> mon cher!

Giggles and sighs.

52. INT. ADOLPHE'S HALL DAY

Marcel jumps up and covers Adolphe in kisses.

> ### ADOLPHE
> Now, now, calm down, young man. Listen
> here, Marcel. Don't mention our little party,
> will you?
>   Not to anyone. They wouldn't like it over
> there.

> ### MARCEL
> (more kisses)
> Of course not. Never. Ever.

More kisses and he runs from the house.

The sound of a church congregation singing a hymn. Ave,
ave, ave Maria.

53. EXT. CHURCH COMBRAY DAY

Bells ring as the faithful flood from the church.

Marcel, hand in hand with his grandmother, surrounded by his family, is still elated from his meeting with the lady in pink.

They pass MONSIEUR LEGRANDIN, who is fawning at the CHATELAINE of a nearby château.

> FATHER
> (offering his hand)
> Good morning, Legrandin. Fine day.

Legrandin pretends not to hear, instead darting off to give orders to the chatelaine's COACHMAN.

Father is put out.

54. EXT. COMBRAY BRIDGE EVENING

The family are on the old bridge over the Vivonne river. Monet moment. Marcel is jabbering to himself.

> GRANDFATHER
> I'm sure you're imagining it.

> FATHER
> He just walked straight past me. I should feel sorry if we had vexed him.

Marcel is definitely over-excited. His cheeks are flushed, his breathing slightly strangled.

GRANDMOTHER
What are you muttering about, young man?

MARCEL
I can't talk to you now. I'm having tea with an actress friend.

GRANDMOTHER
Oh. Which actress is that?

MARCEL
Mmm. She has a secret name. You can't say it out loud.

GRANDMOTHER
Well, give me a clue. What play is she in?

MARCEL
(grandly)
It's a comedy called Life.

FATHER
Stop talking nonsense, Marcel.

MARCEL
It's not nonsense. I'm going for tea with her when I get back to Paris.

FATHER
(to his wife)
You see: you and your mother are indulging
him too much. Already he was a fantasist. Now
he's going mad.

MARCEL
(over-excited)
I am not. She's beautiful. All in pink. She says
she met you once and you were exquisite. And
then she invited me for tea.

FATHER
And where did you meet this goddess?

MARCEL
At Uncle Adolphe's. Everyone stops.

GRANDFATHER
What is this?

MARCEL
(suddenly uncertain)
What?

GRANDFATHER
What actress did you meet with Uncle
Adolphe?

MARCEL
Oh. She didn't say her name. We had tea in his
bedroom. It was such fun. I kissed her hand,
and she said I was a real gentleman. Just like
(MORE)

> MARCEL (CONT'D)
Uncle Adolphe. She was beautiful, Mamma. I
kissed my first actress!

> FATHER
Enough.

> MARCEL
But I did.

> FATHER
> (shouting)
Enough!

Marcel stares at his father, frozen. His breathing becomes
more and more strangled. His cheeks burn. Tears pour from
his eyes.

> MOTHER
Look what you've done.

Marcel has an asthma attack. The men clearly think its
staged. The women fuss over him. He is carried home.

55. EXT. COURTYARD DAY

Marcel lurks in the shadows while Françoise chases a chicken
around the yard. Raised voices can be heard from Uncle
Adolphe's open window.

As the argument reaches a climax Françoise catches the bird
and chops off its head.

MOTHER (V.O.)
Marcel! Marcel!

Mother comes into the courtyard.

MOTHER
Marcel, why don't you go to Theodore's and
collect my cake? I forgot it earlier.

56. EXT. STREET DAY

Marcel walks along the street with the cake in a box. An open
carriage swings round the corner. Uncle Adolphe sits behind
his COACHMAN, sees Marcel and waves.

Marcel, embarrassed, looks the other way.

MARCEL (V.O.)
I was gripped by such pain, such remorse at
what I had done that it seemed insufficient
to simply raise my hat or wave my hand
as though I owed him nothing by way of
explanation. And so I turned my head away.
My uncle thought that in doing this I was
following my family's orders and he did
not forgive them. He died many years later
without any of us ever seeing him again.

The carriage drives off into the distance.

The sing-song voice of the village PRIEST incanting the
Hail Mary in Latin. The congregation joins in.

57. EXT. CHURCH COMBRAY DAY

A group of TEENAGE BOYS tear around the square playing
some rough version of tag. Dust billows around them. From
inside the church the drone of prayer can be heard.

58. INT. CHURCH COMBRAY DAY

It is the Month of Mary. A large statue of the Virgin
shimmers and bends over banks of candles and flowers. The
altar is festooned with hawthorn. The CONGREGATION is
on its knees saying the rosary. Beads in all shapes and sizes
coiled around hands of all shapes and sizes. The faithful of
Combray sound like a swarm of bees and can be just as lethal.

The CURÉ, tall and withered, stands beside the statue all in
white.

Marcel sits between his mother and grandmother, observing
the congregation.

Various people we have seen or are about to see.

MONSIEUR VINTEUIL the old piano teacher sits with his
very butch daughter and her 'friend'.

Dr Percepied watches MLLE VINTEUIL and her
'FRIEND'. Whispers something to his wife. She looks at
Mlle Vinteuil and smirks.

Monsieur Legrandin the engineer mouths the sacred words while eyeing the same chatelaine and a group of gentry with barely disguised hunger.

THEODORE the boulanger sits proudly with his brood, a wife and four children.

The whole village is there, in fact, watching and waiting for something to happen. And then it does.

The curé raises his arms to address the congregation and in the dramatic pause before he launches into another decade of the rosary screams can be heard from the teenage boys outside, followed by a clearly articulated profanity.

The curé presses on but it is too much for Monsieur Vinteuil and he leaves the church.

59. EXT. CHURCH COMBRAY DUSK

The boys have fallen into a kind of scrum, shouting and laughing. Monsieur Vinteuil storms across the square towards them. He looks deranged, hair all over the place, purple-faced, spittle shooting from his screaming mouth.

> MARCEL (V.O.)
> The Month of Mary that year had a special
> significance for Vinteuil, the man who – in
> happier times – had taught my grandmother
> and her sisters to play the piano.

He grabs one boy by the collar. The others run, laughing.

60. INT. CHURCH DUSK

Silence in the church as Monsieur Vinteuil's voice rings
through the nave from outside.

> VINTEUIL (V.O.)
> Are you laughing at me, you bloody deviant?
> By God, I'll crack your heads together if I get
> my hands on you.

Various reactions. Mlle Vinteuil looks at her 'friend'. Marcel's
family pretend not to hear.

Dr and Madame Percepied are revolted. Legrandin prays to
the Virgin for a title.

The Virgin stares blankly down.

> MARCEL (V.O.)
> The old man, recently widowed, railed
> constantly against the modern world, against
> inverts and degenerates, seeing new infections
> around every corner.

61. EXT. CHURCH COMBRAY DUSK

The congregation pour from the church. More bells. Families
gossip in the evening light, throwing long shadows across
the square. They all avoid Monsieur Vinteuil, who scans
the horizon for marauding boys. He sees Marcel and his
grandmother and waves.

                              VINTEUIL
              There seems to be a deplorable fashion for
              slovenliness in the young these days, wouldn't
              you say, Madame Amadee? Ahh. Here they
              are, those naughty girls.

The naughty girls in question, Mlle Vinteuil and her 'friend',
appear round the corner of the square in a small barouche
pulled by a pony at breakneck speed, laughing, narrowly
missing a family walking home from church.

                            MARCEL (V.O.)
              He didn't know what the whole of Combray
              had been aware of for some time. That the
              disease had struck much closer to home than
              the back streets of the village to which he had
              appointed himself the moral guardian.

Vinteuil climbs aboard. The barouche groans and sinks with
the added weight as he squeezes in next to the two women.
Mlle Vinteuil cracks the whip and off they trot, a comic
silhouette against the setting sun.

62. INT. MARCEL'S BEDROOM PARIS NIGHT 1918

Marcel lies in bed. Begins to laugh silently. Tears pour down
his cheeks. Is he laughing or crying?

63. EXT. STREET COMBRAY DAY

More laughter from inside an open window as Monsieur Vinteuil is walking along the street. He hears his own name and stops dead in his tracks.

>   MARCEL (V.O.)
> He discovered that the exact nature of his
> daughter's relationship with her friend had
> been a subject of debate and ridicule for
> some time.

64. INT. DR PERCEPIED'S HOUSE DAY

Dr Percepied is holding forth to a group including the curé and several other MEN from the village. They are all crying with laughter at the doctor's impersonation of Vinteuil. Only the curé remains nonplussed.

>   DR PERCEPIED
> Vinteuil says she would have made a
> remarkable musician. She has artistic fingers!

>   CURÉ
> Who?

>   DR PERCEPIED
> Mlle Vinteuil's friend!

>   CURÉ
> Well now!

> ### DR PERCEPIED
> Well now, indeed. It seems that they are making a lot of music together.

Huge laugh.

> ### DR PERCEPIED (CONT'D)
> It's true. Old Vinteuil told me just yesterday. After all, the girl certainly has a right to enjoy playing her instrument.

More laughter.

65. EXT. STREET COMBRAY DAY

Monsieur Vinteuil listens with a blank look on his face.

> ### DR PERCEPIED (V.O.)
> 'It's not for me to go against a child's "artistic vocation"',' said Vinteuil.

> ### CURÉ (V.O.)
> Does he play music with his daughter's friend as well? I think that's very nice. Why are you all laughing?

66. INT. DR PERCEPIED'S HOUSE DAY

Big nasty close-up of Percepied waggling his tongue suggestively. Screams of laughter.

DR PERCEPIED

Heaven help us. There's a lot of music going
on over there if you get my meaning. Filthy
women! The other day I met old Vinteuil near
the cemetery. He was ready to drop.

Standing ovation.

67. EXT. CEMETERY DAY

Vinteuil stands by his wife's grave.

MARCEL (V.O.)

Now Vinteuil spent whole days at his wife's
grave and when he thought about his daughter
and himself from the point of view of society,
from the point of view of their reputation,
he knew that they had arrived at the lowest
depths and there was no way back. And so his
manner acquired a new humility.

68. EXT. STREET COMBRAY DAY

The family are talking with Swann and Vinteuil appears
around the corner. Too late to turn back. An awkward
moment. Swann offers his hand to Vinteuil.

MARCEL (V.O.)

To such an extent that one day he talked at
great length to Swann, with whom for a long
time he had barely been on speaking terms.

SWANN

Please send your daughter over to play with
Gilberte at Tansonville. And do come yourself.

MARCEL (V.O.)

It was an invitation, which two years earlier
would have incensed Monsieur Vinteuil, but
which now filled him with so much gratitude
that he felt obliged to refrain from the
indiscretion of accepting.

Swann tips his hat and leaves.

VINTEUIL

What a charming man. But what a pity he
should have made such a deplorable marriage.

The great-aunts chime in. A lively discussion ensues on the
unsuitability of Swann's marriage.

69. INT. MARCEL'S BEDROOM PARIS NIGHT 1918

Marcel writes.

MARCEL

Monsieur Vinteuil did not send his daughter to
visit Swann, an omission which Swann was the
first to regret, because he had been meaning
for a long time to ask him about someone
of the same name, a relation of his, Swann
supposed, that he had known in his youth.

Screams of pain.

70. INT. STAIRCASE COMBRAY NIGHT

The kitchen maid is having her baby. Mother appears on
the stairs, shouting for Françoise. Marcel watches from the
shadows of the third-floor landing.

Doors open and the great-aunts peep out but quickly
withdraw.

71. INT. KITCHEN MAID'S ROOM NIGHT

Dr Percepied delivers a dead baby to the screaming, sweating
kitchen maid. Madame Amadee and Mother watch. Françoise
is the grudging midwife. All in their nightdresses, holding
candles. It's like a strange nativity.

72. INT. KITCHEN DAY

A few days later. Early morning. Françoise is working. The
kitchen maid returns.

> FRANÇOISE
> Well I never. That's quite some time you've
> had your feet up, my girl. We thought you'd
> gone away on holiday. Good. You're just in
> time. They're walking to Méséglise today.
> Taking a picnic. You can get going on that
> asparagus.

The kitchen maid goes to her station and weeps. Françoise watches with a vicious chuckle.

73. EXT. COMBRAY STREET DAY

Marcel, his parents, grandparents and great-aunts leave by the front door of the house.

74. INT. AUNT LEONIE'S ROOM DAY

> LEONIE
> There, Françoise, didn't I tell you They're going the Méséglise way.

> FRANÇOISE
> No. I told you.

75. EXT. STREET COMBRAY

The procession continues, via the postbox where Father deposits some letters.

Via the boulangerie. Marcel runs in. Theodore stands behind the counter. A package exchanges hands.

Past the GUNSMITH, who waves as the group passes by, out of the village.

76. EXT. ROAD OUTSIDE COMBRAY

The family arrive at the white fence of Swann's estate. Lilac trees in full bloom wave in the breeze. Past a Gothic lodge.

> GRANDFATHER
> Didn't Swann tell us yesterday that the wife
> and daughter were in Rouen? We might
> cut across the park, since the ladies are not
> at home.

They turn into the park. The house, large and gabled, peeks over trees at the end of a long avenue. The park slopes down on one side towards a lake.

Marcel lags behind. Flowers of all sorts, forget-me-nots, periwinkles, nasturtiums, all seen through his childish eyes, bright, vibrant, quivering, glittering with dew. They seem to pulse with life. He freezes in front of a closed rose, eyes like saucers.

> MOTHER
> Come on, Marcel.

He comes to and runs after the family.

77. EXT. SWANN'S ESTATE DAY

They walk through some woods. Marcel looks up. A lone bird calls out. The high branches wave against the clear sky. The soft noise of the breeze. Otherwise, silence. Marcel is entranced.

They take a path that runs along a hedge. The family are
ahead again. Through the hedge can be glimpsed some
formal gardens, a gravel path bordered with flowers, a hose
and a sprinkler making a rainbow of water.

Marcel is looking through the hedge when suddenly he hears
footsteps on the gravel path inside.

A PRETTY YOUNG GIRL of ten is running towards him.
She has red hair and a white dress. She sees him looking
through the hedge and stops. Looks right back.

Like two animals they just stare, neither moving a muscle.

Finally, she smiles. He does not. This must be the girl he has
heard so much about, the product of the scandalous marriage.

LADY'S VOICE
Gilberte! Gilberte. Come here.

In the distance the diabolical mother appears. Marcel gasps.
She is also in white, her face veiled like a ghost. She is
accompanied by a MAN, a stick insect with a pot belly. It's
Monsieur de Charlus, her lover.

The girl looks towards her mother and then back at Marcel,
giggles and shrugs before running off.

Far away now, the mother takes her daughter's hand and
the three of them walk away towards the house. The girl
looks back.

A hand on Marcel's shoulder snaps him out of his trance.

FATHER
Come along, Marcel. Stop spying.

The family move on. The grandmother reaches for Marcel's hand. He takes it.

GRANDFATHER
Poor Swann, what a life they are leading him – sending him away so that she can be alone with her Charlus. I could tell it was him. I recognised him at once.

Marcel is in a dream. Looks back. And whispers.

MARCEL
I love you.

LATER they are sheltering from a summer downpour under the trees in a wood.

MARCEL (V.O.)
We called it Swann's Way. From Combray to Tansonville, to the woods at Rousinville, the church at St-André-des-Champs to Vinteuil's house at Montjouvin. We hid from the rain among the trees ...

78. EXT. ST-ANDRÉ-DES-CHAMPS

Another walk. Another downpour. Now the whole family shelters under the porch of a church. Marcel points out the angels to his grandmother.

> MARCEL (V.O.)
> Or under the grave faces of the carved saints
> above the porch of the church.

> MARCEL
> Grandmamma. That one looks like Françoise!

Everyone laughs. And they melt away in the rain leaving only
MARCEL, older now. Fifteen.

> MARCEL (V.O.)
> And later on I formed the habit of going out
> by myself on such rainy days when my parents
> abandoned the idea of a walk, during that
> summer when we came to settle my Aunt
> Leonie's estate; she had died at last.

79. INT. AUNT LEONIE'S ROOM EVENING

The whole family are gathered around Leonie's bed.
Françoise wipes her mistress's face with a damp cloth.

> MARCEL
> Causing by her death no great grief, except
> to one person. During the long fortnight of
> her last illness Françoise never left her for an
> instant and did not leave the body until it was
> actually in the ground. When my aunt was too
> ill for Françoise to lift her unaided she would
> send for Theodore rather than one of the
> kitchen maids, who might get into my aunt's
> good books.

Theodore and Françoise carefully lift Leonie up on the pillows.

> LEONIE
>
> Theodore. Is that you? I saw Madame Amiel today with that dog. What is its name?

> THEODORE
>
> Balthazar, Madame.

> LEONIE
>
> Balthazar. That's it. One of the Magi. Caspar. Melchior. Balthazar.

She swoons.

> MARCEL (V.O.)
>
> And when they bent down together to raise her head from the pillow they had the same naive and zealous expressions . . .

80. EXT. GRAVEYARD DAY

The whole family around the grave.

> MARCEL (V.O.)
>
> . . . as the little angels in the porch under which we sheltered, who thronged, with tapers in their hands, about the swooning Virgin.

Earth is thrown on the coffin by the curé. Françoise is stone-faced.

81. EXT. ST-ANDRÉ-DES-CHAMPS DAY

Marcel – aged fifteen – stands alone under the porch. Looking up.

> MARCEL (V.O.)
> And it seemed to me that those carved faces, naked and grey as trees in winter, were simply storing up life and waiting to flower again, in countless country faces, reverent and cunning like Françoise and Theodore, glowing with the ruddy brilliance of ripe apples.

The rain stops and he goes on with his walk. Across rolling cornfields towards a house built into the side of a hill.

> MARCEL (V.O.)
> It was the last summer for Vinteuil as well. In those final years he had given up hope of copying out the whole of his later work, the modest pieces, we imagined, of an old piano teacher.
> Now they would have to remain unknown for ever. No one mourned his death. Least of all the daughter whose reputation had so smeared his own.

Marcel lies down by some bushes on the hill overlooking Montjouvin, the Vinteuil house. A great view through an open window straight into the salon.

82. INT. VINTEUIL SALON DAY

Framed by the window, Mlle Vinteuil – in deep mourning –
is talking to her 'friend'. She holds a framed photograph of
her father.

> FRIEND
> I'm sick of seeing you wearing black.

> MLLE VINTEUIL
> Then undress me.

> FRIEND
> What are you doing with that horrible picture?

> MLLE VINTEUIL
> It's not so horrible. It's my daddy. He wants to
> do something to you.

She spits on the photograph.

> FRIEND
> What can he do, my girl? He's dead.
> Thank God.

> MLLE VINTEUIL
> He wants to lick your bum.

They laugh.

> FRIEND
> Go on then. I don't mind if he does.

83. EXT. VINTEUIL HOUSE DAY

Marcel gasps.

84. INT. VINTEUIL SALON DAY

The friend turns round and bends over. Squeaking, Mlle Vinteuil rubs the photograph up and down her rump.

> MLLE VINTEUIL
> Mmmm. Yummy.

> FRIEND
> Oh. Go on, Monsieur Vinteuil. Go on. Get
> your tongue in there. Yes.

Giggling and panting, they both get worked up and put the photograph down on the table and kiss.

> FRIEND (CONT'D)
> Do you like the way we kiss, Daddy?

CLOSE-UP of the photograph. On one side the friend's breast appears. On the other Mlle Vinteuil's mouth. Mlle Vinteuil chews her friend's nipple while old Vinteuil observes.

85. INT. HALL COMBRAY HOUSE DAY

Marcel runs upstairs. The family can be heard talking on the verandah.

MOTHER (V.O.)
Marcel?

86. INT. ATTIC ROOM DAY

The voices of the family in the garden. The coo of a pigeon
in the gables. Apples stacked in boxes on the floor. An open
window with tendrils of plumbago snaking into the room.

Marcel takes down his trousers and masturbates. Strangled
breathing. Orgasm. Sperm drips down a leaf on the window.
Marcel laughs but also has an asthmatic attack.

87. INT. MARCEL'S BEDROOM PARIS
NIGHT 1918

Marcel stares into space. Suddenly he reaches for the bell
rope and pulls. A bell rings far away.

88. EXT. PARIS STREET NIGHT 1918

A carriage stops outside a house in a run-down district north
of Pigalle. Marcel gets out.

He rings a bell. A small window opens in the door. And
closes. Then the door opens and Marcel goes inside.

89. INT. BROTHEL PARIS NIGHT 1918

A run-down suite of rooms, low lit, armchairs and sofas. Boys in various stages of undress circulate, offering themselves to a clientele of men who drink and smoke – some in evening dress, some in trousers and shirts, some in dressing gowns.

A JOLLY BARMAN wearing make-up presides behind a bar.

JUPIEN the brothel-keeper makes a fuss of Marcel, taking his coat etc.

> JUPIEN
> Well, well. What a nice surprise. How have we been keeping? It's been a while, hasn't it? Everything is prepared. Unfortunately, the archangel Gabriel isn't here any more, but there's a new boy who knows the ropes. Sit down for a moment while I go and get things ready.

Marcel sits and Jupien disappears behind a curtain. A cockroach makes its way across the floor. Marcel watches it, at the same time listening to the whispered conversation behind the curtain.

90. INT. OTHER SIDE OF THE CURTAIN NIGHT

Jupien is whispering and waving a hat pin at a ROUGH-LOOKING YOUTH.

> BOY
> What the fuck?

JUPIEN

It's quite simple, dear. At the moment before
he does his business ... you just ...

He makes a stabbing gesture with the hat pin. The boy looks
bemused.

BOY

Why?

JUPIEN

(pushing him out of the room)
Why? Darling, I didn't advertise for a
philosopher. Just get on with it, please. Or
get out.

He draws the curtain and comes back into the room, all
smiles, stepping on the cockroach as he passes. Marcel
winces.

JUPIEN (CONT'D)

Come, Monsieur.

91. INT. PASSAGE NIGHT

Jupien leads Marcel down one of those passages from bad
dreams. Doors on either side. There are various sounds
related to sex: moans, whippings, screams. He unlocks a door
and makes a theatrical gesture.

JUPIEN

It's not the Ritz, I always say. But it'll do.

92. INT. ROOM BROTHEL PARIS NIGHT

Alone in the dismal room Marcel – fully clothed – sits on the bed. Luxuriating in the sounds of sex. Smiles. The door opens. The boy comes in. He has a cage with a rat inside. He places it on the table near the bed. Marcel looks at the rat with a horrified intensity. The rat looks back, twitching its nose. Marcel gasps. The boy produces the hat pin. Puts that on the table too, strips and leans forward to touch Marcel.

> MARCEL
> Don't touch me.

The boy watches as Marcel begins to masturbate inside his trousers. As he approaches a climax the boy uncertainly opens the cage and the rat scampers out. It tears round the small room. Marcel, terrified, climbs onto the bed, screaming and coming at the same time. The boy tries to stab the rat with the hat pin but fails.

93. INT. PASSAGE NIGHT

Jupien has been listening at the door. Now he bursts in.

94. INT. ROOM NIGHT

> JUPIEN
> What are you doing? You're supposed to kill it
> in the cage.

The rat leaps out of the room and disappears down the passage.

> JUPIEN (CONT'D)
> Well don't just stand there.

The boy takes the cage and leaves.

Marcel, on the verge of an asthma attack, searches in his pocket for a vial, which he breaks into a handkerchief and inhales.

> JUPIEN (CONT'D)
> He's just started. I AM sorry.

Finally, Marcel looks up. His breathing has returned to normal.

> MARCEL
> That was the best yet.

He starts to laugh.

THE END

Huge thanks to Antonia, Clare and the two Zoes for their patience and support, and to Andrew and Luke my agents.